PRAISE FOR *ALWAYS GREENER*
BOOK ONE OF THE GENERAL BUZZ SERIES

★ ★ ★ ★ ★

"A stinging science fiction satire…
hilarious and horrifying."

—*Foreword Reviews*

"A cultured, witty, and very British attack
on vapid reality TV values."

—*Kirkus Reviews*

"An absolute joy to read. As clever as it is hilarious,
as profound as it is captivating."

—James Dashner,
author of *The Maze Runner*

Explore more of THE GENERAL BUZZ universe:
LawlessAuthor.com

For more great science fiction and fantasy novels:
UproarBooks.com

Publisher's Note:
If you enjoy this novel, please leave a positive rating and/or review on Goodreads, Amazon, or other similar websites to let other readers know. Reviews work! Support your favorite authors.

BOOK TWO OF THE GENERAL BUZZ

THE RUDE EYE OF REBELLION

J.R.H. LAWLESS

1419 PLYMOUTH DRIVE, NASHVILLE, TN 37027

THE RUDE EYE OF REBELLION

Copyright © 2021 by J.R.H. Lawless.
All rights reserved.

Published by Uproar Books, LLC.

Reproduction of this book in whole or in part, electronically or mechanically, is prohibited without written consent, except brief quotations as part of news articles or reviews. For information address: Uproar Books, 1419 Plymouth Drive, Nashville, TN 37027.

All persons, places, and events in this book are fictitious. Any resemblance to persons living or dead is coincidental.

Edited by Rick Lewis.

Cover illustration by Khristian M. Collins.

ISBN 978-1-949671-10-0

First paperback edition.

For O, R, and N

*"Il n'y a rien de mieux qu'un
rêve pour créer le futur"*
—Victor Hugo

***Unthread the rude eye of rebellion
And welcome home again discarded faith.***

William Shakespeare
The Life and Death of King John
Act V, Scene IV

1

"I do hope I haven't kept you waiting. Have you ordered yet?"

As he spoke, Ed's head bobbed a little in the tailored micro-gravity, like an olive in a martini, unaware of the impending toothpick.

Giving his tie one last nervous tug, he took his seat at the restaurant table across from the formidable Ms. Heath, who looked every bit as pointed as the aforementioned toothpick in her exquisitely tailored emerald green pantsuit.

Mars above, that woman weighed next to nothing on Earth. Up here, the mere act of a sneeze might provide enough propulsion to send her pinging around the room like a pierced balloon.

The thought of the new Red Corporation board chair's spindly body flapping wildly behind her head as she rocketed about the restaurant added a touch of genuine pleasure to his hello smile.

Ms. Heath, on the other hand, did not seem at all amused by his arrival.

"Just a dopamine cocktail," she answered, punctuating with a wave of her manicured hand. "I don't really *eat* anymore, as such. Most of us Paradise Mars long-timers don't, of course."

Ed felt his face burn even redder than it already was with so much blood pooling up there in the restaurant's low gravity. He lifted his eyes and pretended to be absorbed by the restaurant's famous full-ceiling viewing window—with its unparalleled and incredibly-expensive-to-maintain panorama of the surface of Mars above—until he had the embarrassment at his *faux pas* back under control.

"Oh, don't worry," carried on Ms. Heath, lifting her sparkling drink for a sip. "You'll understand soon enough, once you've had a chance to settle in. I know it's your first time here, but you'll be one of us soon, after all."

The RedCorp chairwoman said the words almost as an afterthought, but they were music to Ed's ears. They encompassed everything he'd toiled to achieve over his three decades as a Corporate commissar, watching over the various entertainment products that kept Red Corp's advertisement dollars flowing and the consumer masses in their place: quiet and content behind their lenses.

Paradise Mars was the end-goal at the top of the global corporate ladder: a life of luxury, free from stress, in the hollowed-out shell that used to be the Martian moon Phobos. A place where laws were didn't exist and gravity was just another commodity, to be consumed or ignored at will.

At long last, Ed the Editor was home.

Now, he just needed to hang on until they let him relocate here permanently.

Ms. Heath chuckled, setting her glass back down. "As long as you have everything in order back down on Earth, that is. Are we certain everything is under control with *The Grass is Greener?*"

Ed was tempted to respond with one of his usual condescending laughs but stopped himself. One did not joke with Ms. Heath—especially when it came to the Red's flagship reality show. Her personal involvement in selecting, and controlling, the show's host had been among the achievements that had catapulted her to this lofty new position in the Corporation and in the Solar System.

"Yes, yes, of course," he answered, with a little cough. "I made sure everything was in place for the show to keep on ticking over. Most of the actual work is automated now, and the algorithms have very precise instructions on how to run everything with minimal input from us at RedCorp HQ. Everything is in ship-shape for the grand launch of our third season. And our Mr. Argyle is still there on the ground, alongside the residual human staff," he added, in dismissive tones. "With AI that good, even Argyle can't muck things up. And we still need a human figurehead to host the show, after all."

Ed punctuated his little monologue with a nervous laugh, but Ms. Heath didn't seem to want to take the hint he was done and that she could let him off the hook. She simply sat in silence, peering at him over steepled fingers. Damn the woman, that was supposed to be *his* trick to make underlings uncomfortable.

In the tense silence, all of the sounds in the restaurant[1] seemed to amplify. The live chamber orchestra down in the trenches were like the bad news that seemed to plague Red Corp's infotainment feeds lately: best heard from afar, not seen up close and personal. Still, they were giving an admirable rendition of *Mars, Bringer of War*, considering they had to play at an unnaturally low volume—low enough not to hinder the conversations, but just loud enough to cover the retching sounds from the newer arrivals who were busy living it up like Roman senators in the tailored gravity. Eat, retch, repeat. Here on Paradise Mars, they would never have to feel the weight of the rich food, but they still needed to have waiters close to hand with the shiny, platinum-plated "convenience receptacles," known to the rest of humanity as "buckets," prepared for that exact purpose.

Live human waiters, as well—such extravagance. Not because of the cost of the people, of course. People came incredibly cheap. But the cost of transporting them here, of providing them with food, water, and air to breathe, must have been colossal. Such conspicuous waste.

---

[1] A word that didn't exist until the late 18th century, when a man opened a shop near the Louvre and started selling meat consommé designed to "restore" the customers' strength—alongside actual meals, which broke caterers guild law and led to a lawsuit he somehow won. Every restaurant in existence today—and, indeed, until the End of the Universe—owes its title to a litigious 18th century Parisian.

Ed loved the sight of it—almost as much as he loved the word "conspicuous."

With the conversation at the modern corporate equivalent of a Mexican standoff, Ed feigned nonchalance by allowing his eyes to drift slowly about the room to the closest waiter—a perfectly nondescript gentleperson of indeterminate age in a generic black suit jacket and with unremarkable brown hair parted on the left. Such precision blandness was exactly what restaurants had been striving for in their wait staff since the Proto-Indo-European word for "fine" had first been married to the Proto-Indo-European word for "dining," allowing one entrepreneurial stone age hunter to charge more for three slivers of undercooked mastodon than the less-savvy gatherer down the street was charging for an entire winter's supply of yarrow seeds.

Yes, there they were—the platonic ideal of waiteriness. And Paradise Mars had achieved it, of course. What was Paradise Mars if not the culmination of countless generations of social stratification? And Ed was not about to be out-stratified by a toothpick in a business suit, no matter the gravity[1] of the situation.

"Very well, then," Ms. Heath said at last, breaking the silence around the table. "And Mr. Argyle himself is still… contained? No relapse into the disruptive nonsense we had to stamp out during the first season?"

"Oh, absolutely," Ed replied, perhaps a bit too forcibly. "Nothing more than the expected level of discontent at his level of employment, and we have the standard surveillance and management measures in place to provide him with the necessary illusions and opportunity to vent."

Ms. Heath took a long sip from her chemical cocktail of a drink, the sort that would be both illegal and most likely lethal anywhere that didn't have the blissful lawlessness and expensive replacement

---

[1] *Gravity* was considered a purely physical phenomenon all the way back through the Latin *gravis* to the PIE root *gwere*. It took the French to expand the definition to include philosophic weightiness in the 13th century.

organs that Paradise Mars could offer. "Let's hope you're right. Wouldn't want to have to pull Argyle off the show mid-season for a bit of resocialisation down in the lower levels here, now would we?"

Ed laughed obligingly, but the not-so-subtle reminder that Paradise Mars was just as much Hell as it was Heaven, depending on your performance, was not lost on him.

"You can count on it," he said, dabbing at his forehead with an unbelievably soft nano-material napkin. "I've even got him doing double duty as PR damage control for the little incident down at the Space Elevator construction site, so that's synergy and extra savings right there."

Ms. Heath finally smiled at that, and lifted her glass in salute. Sensing the lull in the conversation, their waiter appeared next to the table with impeccable timing. Was it the same gentleperson Ed had been examining earlier or another of their indistinguishable colleagues in servitude? He couldn't be absolutely certain one way or the other. Paradise Mars was *that* good.

"Is sir ready to order?"

Ed's stomach clenched in queasy protest. All those G-force shifts—between the standard ride in the Lightway shuttle, the zero-G and tumble of docking, and all of the gradient gravities here on spinning Paradise Mars—had taken a toll. And the tense conversation certainly wasn't helping any.

On the other side of the restaurant, a patron let out a loud *hurk* and bellowed for a waiter and their "receptacle."

His clenching stomach heaved in sympathy.

"I'll have what she's having," Ed the Editor replied, pointing at his boss's zero-calorie, zero-nutrition, and quite possibly zero-taste cocktail, with his best attempt at a genuine smile.

Ms. Heath's own smile turned into an outright grin. "Look at you. It's like you belong here already."

2

The young woman's corpse lay twisted and broken in the shadow of the budding Space Elevator. Liam Argyle refused to let a wave of dizziness and nausea do so much as redden his cheeks. Three glasses of scotch on the way to Ecuador hadn't made him spew. He'd be damned if he let them come back for round two here on the ground. Besides, the cameras were live. He couldn't afford to lose face in front of his audience.

"There it is," he carried on, putting the burnt-out Quito suburbs around him out of mind and following the camera's eye up toward to the base of the Space Elevator, a tower already so impossibly tall it made the human mind quail[1]. "Has it already been over a year since we were last here, GiGalos? That first season finale was a beauty. A moment none of us are going to forget anytime soon. But just wait until you see what *The Grass is Greener* has in store for you this season."

His cameraperson—a new guy, but that was another sore point he refused to think about right now—signalled for him to carry on walking with a curt hand gesture. Flashing a smile at the viewers, Liam turned and started walking down the devastated streets,

---

[1] In 14th century English, "to have a morbid craving," from the PIE root meaning "to pierce." Both are highly appropriate here.

resolutely ignoring the rubble and the personal effects abandoned left and right by the fleeing residents of the barrio[1].

"Our teams will be scouring the four corners of the Earth to find the very best candidates, the most down-and-out, the greatest victims of modern society to submit to you, our discerning viewer. This year again, and perhaps more than ever, it will be up to you to vote and decide who has it bad, who has it worse, and where…" Liam made the traditional pause for effect, but didn't really feel as if his heart were in it today, for some reason. "…the grass is greener."

Liam faltered for a second as a message from the show's Editor and Corporate minder, the presciently named Ed, popped up unbidden in a corner of his overlay: *Enough showboating, Argyle. Get to the bit about the Elevator riots. RedCorp needs our version of the story out there right NOW!*

Damnit. The Editor knew better than to risk throwing Liam off his game by sending messages when he was live on feed, with over four billion viewers around the Red-connected world watching what was, supposedly, a preview of the upcoming season of the world's most popular reality show competition. The viewers might be in the dark about the abrupt turn he was about to make, but Liam knew exactly where he was going without the Editor's invasive backseat driving.

"I just wish we were back at the Elevator today for better reasons. But the truth is that we're here to speak with the brave victims of the Space Elevator riots. To show them all our support in these trying times. These poor women, men, and enbies came here from all over the world, leaving their families behind to provide the expert work and skills needed to make this wonder of human ingenuity into a reality," he said, lifting a grey suit-clad arm up to the monster towering above him, almost in supplication. "The very symbol of everything modern Corporate humanity has achieved."

---

[1] From the Arabic *barriya*, meaning "open country," turned into the dense city districts of Spanish-speaking America through the magic of Al-Andalus.

Liam lowered his arm, then turned back to face the camera, a calculated scowl on his normally pale but currently orange-stage-makeup-lathered features. "They came here, sacrificing so much, only to be targeted by cowardly protests and attacks from misguided locals. People who can't see how lucky they are, how honoured they should feel, to have the gateway to the stars, the key to humanity's future, right on their own doorstep."

Shaking his head in exaggerated sadness, he resumed his slow march toward Elevator Plaza, treading carefully around the more dangerous bits of bombed cement and twisted rebar littering the road.

"It is my pleasure and my solemn duty, as host and producer of this show, to start this third season by interviewing one of these brave workers. So they can tell us first-hand what they've suffered. How they've been delayed in their important work for all humanity. And how things are, hopefully, better and back on schedule, now that we at RedCorp, in accord with the other members of the Corporate Council, have completed the urban pacification operations that were so urgently required to restore the peace."

Liam swallowed, his throat like sandpaper. Might just be the smoke and grit in the air, but those last few words really didn't want to come out. Was he coming down with a flu? If he did, it'd be Corporate's fault[1], yet again. Sending him off to the damn Andes without any notice, to run damage control for their latest PR mess.

Luckily, that's when the little feed status light in his AR display went from green to amber, signalling an advertisement break. Liam stopped, breathed a sigh of relief, and stretched. Craning his jug-eared head as far back as he could without falling over, he tried to make out the tip of the main Elevator shaft, its nanocarbon end lost somewhere in the Ecuadorian mists far above.

However little he believed the rest of the PR crap they were

---

[1] Originally from the Latin *fallere*, "to deceive."

forcing him to spout, he was at least genuine when he spoke about the Space Elevator representing hope for all humankind. He truly could not wait for it to be completed. Maybe out there, somewhere beyond the pull and drag of the planet's gravity well, humanity would have a real chance to evolve. To improve.

Because they were all sure as hell doomed down here on Earth.

"It was horrible," moaned the Elevator construction crew supervisor, a wiry Japanese salarywoman in full-body drone piloting gear, goggles and all, who spoke in halting but very precise English. "We tolerated the protests. Every day, the locals gathered outside the operations centre. We had become used to them. We came here to do a job. Operate the construction drones and build the Elevator. Not to be popular."

Liam nodded thoughtfully so they'd have something from him to cut to when they put together the highlight[I] reel. "You're a very brave woman, Ms Megumi. So when did things change? When did the protesters turn violent?"

At his words, the technician shuddered in her black, high-precision haptic[II] suit. Liam had to repress a grin. Nothing like a bit of drama to make an interview more entertaining.

"Last Wednesday," she replied once she'd composed herself. "One of the drones laying down the west-side cable tether got a jam. No way to disengage the strand at a distance. Or to break off the strand, of course," she added, as if she'd suddenly remembered she was talking to toddlers who needed to be told fire was hot. "Our diamond nanocarbon does not break. It makes the Elevator possible."

Liam jumped in, to get the interview back on the track his

[I] "The brightest part of a subject" in early Enlightenment painting.

[II] "Touchy," in Greek. Same origin as the "Apse" at end of a cathedral. Insert obligatory Catholic priest joke here.

minders at RedCorp HQ had so carefully and clearly laid out. "And, speaking for our viewers all around the world, allow me to say how grateful we all are for your technical expertise, Ms Megumi. The Space Elevator could not be in more competent hands. But please, tell us more about the start of the violence that delayed your so-very-important work."

Megumi adjusted her goggles. "It happened when we were boarding the emergency crawler. We were quite tightly packed in as we waited for it to commence the ascent[1]." She paused, as if for breath. "I suppose I should be thankful the job was so small it needed a full human crew, and not just me with the drones. If there hadn't been so many bodies between me and the blast, I would not be here today to speak to you about it."

Trusting the cameraperson behind him to pick up the little tear escaping from the edge of the construction worker's goggles, Liam leant forward and nodded in support and encouragement.

"The security people told me, after everything was finished, that they hit us with one of a dozen wild, improvised mortar shots. Natural gas canisters launched from bits of vehicles and food printers." She lowered her head, and Liam had to lean in even farther to pick up her voice. "All I knew was the explosion, the crush of bodies. The heat and the roar. I thought I was paralysed. For a moment, I think I was. With the shock."

Without warning, the distraught labourer snapped her head back up again. Liam reeled back under the intensity of her glare, even through the obscuring goggles.

"But when I was able to move my arms and legs again, they were stuck. My co-workers were piled on top of me, broken and still sizzling from the blast. It was like being trapped in an oven. Roasting meat and all."

Liam really wished Megumi would look down again. Or at least

---

[1] In the 15th century, this meant "to mount for copulation." But then again, what hasn't meant that, at some point or another?

look away. It was hard enough to stick to his carefully planned list of facial reactions without the victim staring him straight in the face while telling her story.

"The ground security team pulled me out just in time. I was barely clear of the charred bodies when the crowd of protesters roared. It sounded just like another explosion. And then they surged past the barriers, over the remaining security people, and into Elevator Plaza."

Just like everyone else in the Red-connected world, Liam had seen the satellite footage over and over again for the past week. From that height, the rioting crowd looked inhuman. More like a swarm[1] of insects than a group of people.

Liam had enough experience with Corporate media manipulation to know this effect was entirely intentional.

"And what did you discover afterward?" Liam prompted.

"Nothing as bad as we feared. The damage was only superficial. It takes more than a bunch of wild locals to damage the nanocarbon of the Elevator itself," she added, a sneer breaking through her grief for the first time in the interview.

"But what about the locals themselves?" Liam asked, his big mouth running away with him again before his brain could do its job and shut him up.

"Nothing the clean-up crews couldn't handle in a couple of hours," the construction worker replied, with a dismissive wave of her hand. "I cannot believe how ungrateful those people are."

Or were.

This time, Liam managed to keep his thoughts to himself.

"The fools," the technician added with a shake of her head. "If they had just waited calmly, they could have sold their homes for a fortune once the Elevator is operational. Now, I hear the bosses have all the leverage they need for the local government to requisition and sell off the land for peanuts."

---

[1] From the PIE root meaning "to buzz." But also, "to whisper."

Liam jumped in his seat as a loud WHARP of alarm fired off from his speaker implant, against the bone below his left ear. In case he'd missed it, a flashing red priority notice lit up the display in his AR implants. *END THIS NOW!*

"Well, that's all the time we have for today," he said in a rush, jumping in to cut off his guest, who clearly had a lot more to say on the subject. "But thank you so much for your testimony, Ms Megumi. The world owes you a debt of gratitude. And now, a word from our sponsors!"

"That's a wrap, Mr Argyle." The wiry Nollywood-trained cameraperson—Job Akintola, Liam reminded himself with a surreptitious[1] glance at the AR identity tag floating behind the shorter man's head—leaned against his tripod and wiped his brow. "I just got the green light from Corporate on the content we uploaded. They've got everything they need, so we can pack up and get the hell out of here."

The man smiled, and that smile stabbed at Liam like a knife made of solid guilt. His old cameraperson, the shaggy giant Carpentiere, used to grin at him the exact same way at the end of a long day out in the field, interviewing contestants. But Liam wasn't ever going to see the friendly Canadian's face again. He'd made sure of that.

Damn, he needed a stiff drink or ten. But Elevator Plaza was still a construction site and not a working spaceport. He had no intention of hanging around a few decades for the overpriced departure lounge bars to open. And he'd already polished off the meagre supplies the Editor had stocked on their private jet. All that was left was water and RedCorp's toxic energy drink, Sinner-G.

Ed the Editor might think he was a big deal when it came to pointing out where this word or the other really came from. But as

---

[1] "Stolen" or "snatched" (*rapere* in Latin), plus "from under" (*sub*), demonstrating how discretion has always been about having friends in low places.

far as Liam concerned, the little man had no idea what *living* meant, and that was the only word that mattered.

Just thinking about the jet reminded Liam of where it had to land, in the middle of a closed-off motorway nearly two kilometres away. On the other side of the rubble, the abandoned knickknacks, and the burnt-out slum houses. On the other side of that poor girl's body, and the dozens like it that Liam had nearly succeeded in ignoring during the long walk to the Plaza. Nearly.

It was all still there, down the deserted, smoky road that waited, like a hungry maw[I], at the south side of the Plaza. He couldn't face that walk again. Not without the cameras rolling to keep him focused on the job at hand, on what was important.

"We don't have to walk all the way back to the shuttle, do we?" Liam said. "Surely, there must be some way we can get RedCorp to come pick us up here at the Plaza."

Akintola raised an eyebrow. "What's wrong? Mr Big-Shot Host is afraid of a little bit of exercise? Is the air up here too thin for you?"

"It's not that," replied Liam, a red flush burning his clean-shaven cheeks. "It's just—"

The cameraperson interrupted him with a burst of booming laughter so deep it seemed like it couldn't possibly be coming from his small frame. Liam simply stood there, baffled, and wondering whether he'd ever actually seen someone double over laughing before.

"You are too easy!" Akintola said at last, straightening up to catch his breath. "I'm just teasing[II] you. But it's your own fault, really. If you'd bothered to read the field schedule, you'd know the jet is long gone."

"Gone?" repeated Liam, eyes open wide and jug-ears spread even

---

[I] From the Old English *maga*, meaning "stomach." I'd make a political joke, but there's no beating the meaning of "trump" in the U.K. (don't hesitate to look it up if you don't know it already). Or the first meaning of "to trump," which is, of course, "to deceive, to cheat" (*tromper* in French).

[II] "To pluck, to pull apart"

wider, not entirely unlike a surprised horned owl. "You mean 'gone' gone? How the hell are we supposed to get back to London?"

Akintola smirked. "You didn't think they'd leave a private jet just sitting around all day waiting for us, didn't you? Those things cost a fortune. But look behind you, Mr Argyle. That's our ride home right there. Best ride in the world."

Confused, Liam spun around and looked through the rubble-strewn Elevator Plaza. Then he stopped and looked up. And up. And up some more.

"Please tell me you're joking again."

"Not this time. RedCorp has booked us a one-way ticket back to London on the Elevator suborbital express[1]. A quick trip around the accelerator, straight out the top, and less than an hour later our capsule touches down in Old Blighty. Been looking forward to it for months. It'll be the trip of a lifetime."

That was precisely what Liam was worried about. He knew these capsules. One of his all-time best shows was when he'd put the urn with the ashes of *The Grass is Greener*'s first season winner, the young medical experimentee Usnavi, into one of them. Just before launching it and him on their merry way to Paradise Mars. The grand prize—a life of lazy luxury in paradise—wasted on a little pile of carbon soot in a pretty vase.

The idea of climbing into one of those capsules was terrifying, and the suborbital ones were even worse. They weren't just sleek, metal coffins, like the space-going ones. They had landing rockets strapped on, as well.

"Are you sure it isn't too late to get that jet to come back?" he said in a whimper, head craned back so far he could nearly see the roofs of the buildings behind him. "I can walk two kilometres with my eyes shut if I have to."

---

[1] From the Latin "to squeeze out," which became "to speak clearly," then "specifically, on purpose." Hence the "express train" that goes directly to a specific station.

He'd rather play hopscotch with the corpses and debris than get locked into a metal bullet and fired up the Elevator launch tube.

"Chin up, old man," said the cameraperson, laughing again and patting him on the back. "Time flies, and so shall we."

3

Lemmeoutlemmeoutlemmeout—

"This isn't so bad after all, eh, Mr Argyle?" The cocky camera operator lounged against the deep padding of the wraparound acceleration couch, his equipment safely stowed away in the cargo space below. "Feel that gentle acceleration. It's so smooth, you'd almost think we aren't moving at all."

He was right, damn him. And that was a big part of what was driving Liam around the bend. Feeling enclosed in a buzzing metal sphere, going nowhere, was bad enough. But that was just what his senses were telling him. His mind knew better, knew that he was zipping through miles upon miles of railgun tunnels winding underneath the mountains surrounding Quito.

Whatever his body had to say, the normal-feeling gravity was a complete illusion, the result of the capsule's gentle acceleration to launch velocity. His brain knew the truth, as he was thrust head-first, at ever more insane speeds, through the railgun launch tube warren.

And the worst was still to come. He'd seen launches before. He knew the blast that came when the accelerated capsule left the vacuum of the tube and hit the rarefied air up at the business end of the Elevator base tower. After that, everything was said and done. Thrown like a steel marble across the world, without any control, to trust in the computers and the landing jets to bring you back down intact.

Why people thought this was a desirable experience was more alien to him than the microbes they'd found on Mars.

On the couch beside him, Akintola somehow took Liam's queasy silence as an invitation to talk some more. "Haven't you ever wanted to go to space, Mr Argyle? What a story to tell, eh?"

"No, Mr Akintola," Liam said at last, trying to keep the peppercorn yeast-slice sandwich he'd had for lunch in his stomach. Looked like he'd have to say something to shut the man up. "Why would I want to go to space? Is there anywhere less natural for people to be? Anywhere more uncomfortable, more hostile to our survival?"

"There's always Cleveland."

Liam rolled his eyes. The only more obvious joke would have been—

"Or my mother-in-law's house," added Akintola, clearly happy for the conversation. "And I hear the bigshots up on Paradise Mars are mighty comfortable living in space. A lot more than everybody else down here, that's for sure. Isn't that what you Corporate types all fight for, anyway? Working yourself to the bone, doing whatever you need to climb that ladder, so that one day you can hop in a capsule, and ZOOM!"

He illustrated by bouncing a fist off his other open hand with a loud clap that echoed through the humming cabin. Liam really wished he hadn't.

"Straight off to luxury retirement floating around Mars, with no gravity to pull at your bones and no pesky laws to stop your fun!"

"Not really my speed," said Liam, not bothering to add that it also wasn't his paygrade. He was nowhere near the top of the Corporate ladder, where the ultimate reward of dispatch to Paradise Mars started becoming at least conceivable. But damned if he was going to confess that to his annoying camera technician. "My pleasures are more down-to-Earth. And I'll remind you that you're just as much a Red Corp employee, a 'Corporate type,' as I am. Whatever that means."

The man had the gall to chuckle at this. "Red Corp today, SyneDeal or Triumph Global tomorrow. I'm a free agent, me. Cheaper for them, and that way, I can choose when to move on to the next gig. No Corporation is ever going to make me do something I don't want to, just to make a cred."

"I bet that's nice," grumbled Liam. He turned away from Akintola and flicked on his lenses' entertainment suite with a quick, angry swipe of a hand.

Whether it was the deliberate discourtesy or something in Liam's voice, the cameraperson took the hint and finally left Liam alone to come to terms with being stuck underground in a speeding capsule.

Soon, however, that was one problem Liam no longer had to deal with. With little more than a ping of warning in his AR display, the whole world suddenly shifted and spun around him.

"Better buckle in!" shouted the technician over the increasing whine coming from all around them, as he strapped his own over-the-shoulder harness into place across his chest. Liam barely had time to shake himself out of his augmented reverie and click his straps into place before the whine turned into a sharp explosion of sound, followed by nothing at all.

Gravity seemed to have decided to follow sound out the door, because not only was everything suddenly silent, but Liam also had to fight back an urge to retch as the enclosed cabin was plunged into weightlessness. If he hadn't managed to get those straps on in time, Liam would be free-floating right now.

A click to his left broke the silence, and Liam turned to watch Job Akintola squirm out of his straps and push off, floating into centre of the cabin like a space butterfly pushing out of its cosmic cocoon.

Liam didn't quite see the point. There wasn't enough room to move around or do any of the fun weightless acrobatics people always talk about for their first time in zero-G. But Akintola didn't seem interested in doing flips. He floated straight up to the bulkhead opposite Liam, braced both hands against it, and simply floated there, peering in rapt fascination at the tacky red upholstered metal.

"It's a shame you're so scared of space travel," the cameraperson said after a minute of quizzical observation by his cabinmate, "because you're missing one hell of a show out there. A real one, too, not like what we do."

"I'm not—" Liam started to say in protest, before cutting himself off. He didn't have anything to prove to a lowly technician. And his legitimate fears had been about the acceleration and launch, which were clearly now past.

There was also the landing ahead, of course. But he had no more control over that than he did over flash floods in Croydon back when he was a weather announcer. So he might as well unbuckle for now, during the relatively safe period between the two bits of madness. He could get his own feel for weightlessness, and have a look at whatever external display Akintola found so damn fascinating. No reason not to, right? Right.

Having talked himself into a corner, Liam swallowed, took a deep breath of air out of unhelpful instinct, and unfastened his harness.

Without the straps pushing down against his chest, his suit-clad bottom gradually stopped pressing against the plush cushion of the seat, leaving it behind with more trepidation than a swimming child refusing to release their parent's hand. He flailed slightly in the sudden freedom from any grounding contact, feeling lost and absurd in a sort of invisible hammock.

Luckily, Akintola completely ignored his embarrassing antics and left him plenty of time to get his bearings, rotate, and, with a cautious kick against the padded floor, glide over to the bulkhead.

"What's so fascinating over here, then?" Liam asked, trying to sound as if his heart weren't racing faster than a lightsail probe as he stared at the mottled red paisley wall pattern.

Akintola turned to face Liam, grinning and bobbing slightly in the air. He tapped a rough-skinned finger against his temple. "You need to turn on the shuttle's local feed," he said, before leaving Liam to his own devices and turning back, wide-eyed, to the capsule wall ahead.

Grumbling, Liam twitched his fingers through an AR menu that, for the first time in his life, he could meet on equal, free-floating terms. He soon found the local broadcast icon and flicked it on with a quick index stab in the cool cabin air.

Instantly, the kitsch[1] bulkhead decoration faded away before his eyes. Instead, he saw a gulf of cloud swirling around weird wavy brown spikes, bathed in the golden light of an early sunset sky. It took Liam a second or two to reconcile his body's perceptions with the scale of the vista in front of him and realise he was looking down at the Andes.

Vertigo gripped him, and his own personal world swayed, even though the capsule itself was supremely stable and calm. If he hadn't been floating free, the realisation of what he was looking at, where he was, and where he was headed, would have knocked him on his bespoke-suited arse.

Below, the peaks of the Andes stretched out from beneath the cloud cover to the horizon. They seemed to reach out toward the escaping capsule like jagged fingers, stretching to catch a flyball. But they were doomed to fail, and shrank visibly, second by second, as Liam and Akintola soared ever farther from the Elevator launch rail, to whatever fate awaited them at the unthinkable landing, far ahead.

Desperate for an excuse to focus on anything other than that landing, Liam pressed his hands against the reassuring solidity of the now invisible bulkhead and leaned forward to look beneath the sharp edge of the capsule floor.

"Holy shit," he heard a voice say. It was probably his, but he was beyond caring.

---

[1] From the German dialectal "to smear"—which is precisely what Liam hoped wouldn't happen to both the shuttle and himself, all across wherever they crashed.

The world beneath his floating body was a monstrous sprawl of human footprint, scarring the land and winding in uncontrolled veins between the hills and through the valleys.

His cabinmate laughed in mid-air next to him. "Now you're talking. This is the real stuff, right here. Too legit to Quito."

Liam groaned deep inside but couldn't be bothered to open a browser and search up whatever silly reference the man was making. This view was amazing. Unlike anything he'd ever seen in his life. Quito below was already nothing more than a splotch of humanity, falling ever farther away. The budding Elevator, which had seemed so impossibly huge, was already long gone behind them, and the whole central urban area of Quito along with it. What was left, so far out, were the tendrils of cheap tenements and industrial buildings servicing all the new cargo pipelines. Companies from around the world were already racing to stake their claim on servicing the Elevator, running cargo up and down the Andes the same way the Elevator would pump it up and down from Space.

Outside the alarmingly thin metal of the bulkhead, the world kept getting smaller and smaller. Ahead, a new glimmer appeared in the distance as evening raced to meet the capsule. The night lights of the other Andean sprawls—a huge one straight ahead that could only be Bogotá, and another to the far left that must be Medellín.

The cities were luminous sea stars from this height—small, fragile things, even though Liam's rational mind knew there were, between them, at least twenty million people like him living down there. And at least ten million of them would be religious followers of *The Grass is Greener*—hell, at this very moment, there were probably a million or two of them watching the highlight reel from what they'd recorded today.

Liam lifted his head to the darkening sky, where the first evening stars twinkled oddly in the rarefied atmosphere. What was it all worth, at the end of the day? The viewers, the contestants. The eternal doctoring, the lies, all in the name of entertainment and

RedCorp's bottom line. Would anything change if some engineer had left in one zero too many when programming the launch and this capsule just kept going up, forever? If Liam and Akintola sped off into empty space toward nothing but void?

Would anyone even miss the two of them?

Maybe Akintola, Liam had to admit, with a little self-deprecating[1] chuckle. Up here, there was no point in lying to himself anymore.

At least Akintola had a family that would, presumably, mourn him. A wife and two daughters back in Lagos, if the info in his mandatory AR ID tag was up to date.

What did Liam have? A job title as Host and Supervising Producer of the biggest show on the Red, sure. But with the Editor and Corporate commanding his every move, that was worth less than the lens pixels it took to spell out the words. If you took all his real power and influence at the show and added two slices of bread, you'd have a very bland sandwich. Just like the ones they served at Tantamount Mews, the Docklands warehouse that served as the show's offices and set.

Any fool who could smile for a camera could fill his designer shoes as host. In fact, that's specifically why they'd chosen him—a nobody weatherman at the time—for the job, instead of bringing in a big, established name. They needed someone whom they could mould. Whom they could control. Who owed everything he was to them, and who had no choice but to follow orders.

Liam had hidden from these truths for so long and had only come to recognise them slowly, like an oyster adding coat after coat on top of an irritating grain of self-awareness. And like an oyster, he'd had to develop the hardest of shells to shield himself from the harsh reality around him. From all the contestants' morbid lives, packaged up into bite-sized morsels of artificially produced, chemical-laden, nutrient-free mental sustenance for the starving masses to devour in the name of entertainment.

---

[1] "To pray for removal or deliverance from yourself"

And more often than not, with Liam himself handling the carving knife. Or at least holding them still on the chopping block.

Liam had long since given up trying to care—ever since his first trip to the Quito Space Elevator, in fact, at the end of the show's first season. Caring was too painful, and it didn't do a lick of good. The Corporate system was the worst thing in the world—except for all the other systems. There was nothing to gain from fighting it and everything to lose, for Liam at least. He liked his newfound social status, the new house, the parties, and the creature comforts. Endless bottles of creature comforts.

But those barely twinkling, twilight stars. That blue-black bruise of a sky, stretching off to an honest-to-Mars curve, along the distant ocean horizon.

There was no shielding yourself from those. So, for the first time in forever, Liam didn't bother trying.

The memory of that young woman's body, twisted, broken, and lifeless amid the rubble of what used to be her neighbourhood, her home, bobbed to Liam's eyes, more clearly than any AR projection and more sickening than any half-digested meal trying to make a break for it.

That wasn't just some picture on the RedCorp newsfeed, damnit. *She* wasn't, Liam rectified[1]. She was a person. Had been a person. A young woman with a family. With parents. A partner somewhere, if that was her thing. Maybe even children. A home in the suburbs of Quito, and all her life ahead of her.

And then RedCorp had decided that keeping the peace around the Elevator, and buying up all the surrounding land for a song—or a crappy corporate jingle, more like—was worth more than the PR cost of sending in their private security troops to make the problem with the locals disappear.

---

[1] From the Latin *rectus*, meaning "right," and not the Latin *rectum*, which is what Liam felt like.

That was bad enough. But as the capsule rose higher and higher, racing toward that curving horizon, Liam shuddered and admitted to himself that it was far, far from the worst part of the terrible day's events.

No, the worst part was that there would never be any PR trouble. There would be no cost for RedCorp, no repercussions for murder or the displacement of a whole barrio that only wanted a say in what was happening on its doorstep.

And they had Liam himself to thank. That was the job he'd been sent to do, and damned if he hadn't done it to the full satisfaction of his middle-management masters in their Corporate towers in London, New York, and Shanghai, just as they had come to expect from their faithful, smiling puppet, Liam Argyle.

Liam clenched his eyes shut, trying to hold back the odd rush of moisture he felt there, and thumped his fist against the invisible bulkhead. The bang of flesh against metal rang though the eerily silent capsule.

"You okay, man?" said Akintola, surprised out of his own once-in-a-lifetime suborbital transit reverie.

Eyes still firmly shut, Liam took all of the frustration and resentment welling up inside him and pushed it out through his mouth in a primal roar. In the air next to him, Akintola scrambled away out of panicked reflex. Clearly, the technician was nearly as surprised as Liam was himself.

Liam turned his head the other way, and only then, out of sight, did he open his watering eyes. "Sorry about that," he croaked, clearing his throat with a cough. "Just remembered I forgot to turn the food printer off before leaving home."

"Sure, man." Akintola let out a nervous chuckle, still floating as far away from Liam as he could in the confined capsule. "No problem. You can turn off all the fancy appliances you want when we land back in Old Blighty."

Liam rolled his charcoal grey eyes at the man's gall. Patronising him, his boss, so blatantly. That took serious balls. But the view from outside the still-rising capsule caught Liam's eye again and gave his brain a fresh squeeze, chasing all thoughts of bosses and Corporations from his mind.

They were even higher now, and the world below was a dark, wavy penumbral mess. Cloud, mountain, and ocean melded into a single mass, and Liam could no longer tell the difference between them. Not because of the rapidly falling night, no. But because, at this unnatural height, the human brain couldn't relate to the scale anymore. It needed human signs, and out here, at the edge of the ocean, they'd long since left the Andean sprawls and the country-sized swaths of clear-cut Amazon rainforest behind. Everything else was lost in coastal cloud and smog.

In contrast, the curved bow of the horizon was a crisp line where the mottled dark blue of the Earth gave way to the absolute black of space. Liam floated, staring at it, his mind emptying once again.

Space. That was space, right there, and the capsule was still racing up into it. That sharp cut in reality made everything down on Earth seem so petty. And if there was one thing Liam's job hosting *The Grass is Greener* was good for, it was knowing just how small and petty life down on Earth could get. That was his lot in life, his own cross to bear.

He'd been careful not to take anywhere near as much of a personal interest in his contestants last season. That sort of shell, that armour of professional distance, helped a bit. Made it easier not to take it too personally when his forensic corpse farmer from Lebanon had a work stress-induced aneurism and became one of her own strange crops. Or when his Australian rare animal "reproduction specialist" tried to make the show a little too interesting and ended up providing a bull shark he'd just manually collected a sperm sample from, for "conservation purposes," with a post-orgasmic snack.

And those had just been the most memorable live tragedies last year, the ones with the best ratings. He'd survived, and he'd convinced himself that if the show, and his role in it, wasn't getting any better, any less revolting[1] with time, then at least it became easier to put up with.

But his role when the cameras weren't watching him, his work as Supervising Producer for the show, certainly hadn't become any better.

Liam floated there in the silent capsule, gazing out at pinpoint stars that no longer twinkled and deep, textured, naked space, trying to convince himself that none of what happened to Carpentiere was really his fault.

He hadn't meant for the shaggy Canadian giant to lose his daughter. He'd done everything he could to help his long-time camera techie. The closest thing to a friend he had on the bare-bones team running *The Grass is Greener* out of Tantamount Mews. He'd tried get him as much time off as the needs of the feed could possibly allow. And it wasn't his fault if the little girl hadn't gotten any better. These things just happened, didn't they?

And hadn't it been unfair of the man to blame him, Liam, for losing the chance to be there when his daughter had asked for him? For being stuck running the feed when the doctors called him to let him know she had... passed on?

That sort of thing happened; it wasn't anyone's actual fault. Certainly not *his*.

But if that were truly so, then why did he feel like such a prick about it? Was there anything he could have done differently? If he'd found some way for Carpentiere to get more time at his daughter's side, would it have made any sort of meaningful difference, in the end?

It might have made Carpentiere feel better about it, said a scathing little voice deep inside Liam. It might have stopped him from sucking down a can of nanopaint and setting it to replicate uncontrollably.

There's no proof that's why Carpentiere did himself in, Liam

---

[1] "To overturn, overthrow"—both the stomach and the sense of social justice.

replied to himself. The clean-up crew didn't find any note, so we have no idea why he did it. And we never will.

The starscape view through the AR-censored bulkhead took a severe dip downward, and Liam and Akintola both took a sharp breath, as one. All of a sudden, the ride seemed anything but peaceful. No more pinpoint stars or beautiful horizon. Now all they could look at was the roiling, deadly dark of the open Atlantic Ocean, with two halos of light, one off to the far left and one closer, directly ahead.

That'd be Europe, Liam realised with a shudder. The entire continent, reduced to a glow at the edge of view. But it was coming up fast, and the little capsule was heading toward it in full-on nosedive.

With an obsequious little "ping," the urgent notice to strap back into the acceleration seating appeared in his heads-up display. Along with the scrolling local AR notice, "Thirty seconds to landing rocket ignition."

Liam spun in the air to face Akintola. "When they say 'rocket,' do you think they mean…"

The two shared a look, each searching for reassurance on the face of the other. Then, failing that, they both scrambled to push off from the still-invisible bulkhead and doggy paddle through the air. They grabbed their straps and worked their way back into the plush wraparound couch.

Outside the capsule, the lights of the European sprawls were now directly ahead—or, more accurately, below. Off to the right, Paris, Munich, and the Benelux were a continuous band of humanity, burning the midnight batteries. There was the briefest of gaps, and then a huge, blazing target straight ahead: the London sprawl, spread across the entire southeast of bonny England, from Milton Keynes to Dover.

And dead ahead, nestled inside its double ring roads like a particularly smug dartboard: London itself.

Liam wished terms like "dead ahead" would stop popping into

mind at times like this. But then he remembered to be careful what he wished for, and chose to focus simply on the dread of the incoming landing.

He was no rocket scientist, but the ground seemed to be zooming up far faster than something that large—and that solid—had any right to. They hadn't even started slowing down yet. He certainly wasn't looking forward to explosions going off on their fragile little metal dart... but shouldn't the landing rockets have fired by now? Had something gone wrong?

Or, just maybe, had he outlived his usefulness to RedCorp, so that they'd decided to get rid of him with as little fuss and as much publicity as possible? He'd heard stories...

The air-breathing rockets strapped to the sides of the capsule chose that moment to begin firing, thrusting the passengers deep into the acceleration couch padding. The crushing G-forces were far harsher than anything they'd experienced during the long, smooth rail-assisted launch.

Straight in front of them on the still-active AR screen, London was getting closer and closer, the general mass of urban sprawl resolving into individual blocks, individual buildings even. The constant streams of automated vehicles were like so many vital arteries of the necrotic body that was the city.

They were slowing down, as the pressure against Liam's skull and spine attested. But it was too little, too late! There was no way they were going to slow down in time to land properly. They were almost there!

"Whoo!" cheered Akintola, lifting his arms as high as he dared under the G-forces. The man was mad. Sure, the city was a beautiful sight from up here, a web of lights and humanity, with the Thames and the more famous monuments just resolving into full view. Not bad as final sights went—but that wasn't enough to reconcile Liam with the "final" bit.

They zoomed down the last few hundred meters, still going far,

far too fast to land safely. Liam started closing his eyes for impact—but no, damnit. If he were going to die here, he was going to do it with both eyes open.

And so, he saw the traffic lights playing off the glass and metal skyscrapers, including the glass nubs along the outside of RedCorp's European HQ, the Tulip. He saw the crowds of night workers and tourists swarm across Oxford Street in the brief lull the automated vehicles left for pedestrians. In the final second, he even caught a fleeting glimpse of a few upturned faces, watching the spectacle of a VIP arriving via suborbital capsule, like a particularly expensive meteorite.

Then there was nothing but black beneath them, and they plunged into it. The capsule rocked and spun, and the G-forces got even worse—but it wasn't exactly the crushing impact Liam had been dreading. And he was even more confused when the pressure eased up and spun gently. The whole capsule seemed to bob around the two of them.

With an unmistakable splash, the view at the front cleared up, a veil of water streaming off to reveal the bright, starless city night sky.

"Whew, what a ride," his cabinmate said, stretching his arms and legs in the once-again normal gravity. "But they always say the bit after splashdown is the longest part of a suborbital trip. And the most boring." He shook his head, with a little half-grin on his face. "It's funny, really. You travel thousands of kilometres in a single hour, but it takes nearly that long again for the landing basin drones to taxi you to disembark."

Liam listened in silence, his head ping-ponging between relief he wasn't dead, regret he didn't bother to read up about how suborbital travel works before launch, and a rising sense that something was off about what just happened.

"Wait a minute," he said at last, turning to face Akintola, who was the only person there to ask. "When we were coming in, London was in the window in front of us, but the G-forces were pushing us back into the seat. That doesn't make any sense. With the rockets firing to slow us down, we should have been pushed toward the ground. Not away from it."

Akintola chuckled and waved an arm through the air, encompassing the whole sphere of the cabin. "Man, this thing has cameras all over the surface. All that matters is that we got to see. One hell of a show, too; I'm just glad we didn't miss it. Who cares if they used the bulkhead up front to show what was really behind us?"

"I care," grumbled Liam, before his reeling brain could catch the words and stop them from passing his lips. But it was the truth. Liam felt betrayed. Even the beauty of the trip, the cosmic truth that had opened up windows he'd long since boarded-up inside the suburban privacy of his mind, was just another lie. Augmented Reality smoke and mirrors. Just like the show. Just like him.

In the couch next to Liam, Akintola stared at him in silence, then shook his head. "You know, I don't usually say this, and don't take it the wrong way. But maybe you need to talk to a professional, man."

"Yeah," replied Liam, deep in disgusted thought. He knew just the professional, too. That's where he'd get the medicine he needed.

4

"You sure you don't want to take it a bit slower?" asked Sabine, the usual nightshift bartender at the Jenkin's Ear on Sundays. "Sure, there's only a couple of hours before sunrise, but that doesn't mean you have to cram a whole night's worth of drinking in before then."

In a world where your average Jude got their chemical fix of choice—alcohol or otherwise—from Bargain Binge vending machines or, on special occasion, drone deliveries, the human bartender at the Jenkin's Ear was a nice touch. With her rough yet form-fitting country garb, she looked like she'd just come in from a romp in the fields, and was as much a part of the décor of the expensive Southwark pub as the antique mahogany counter, the green gas lamps, and the genuinely pungent pre-public-smoking-ban booth cushions. That sort of atmosphere didn't come cheap, and in the dead hours of the night, the Ear was nearly empty.

But it was just what Liam needed to wash the bad taste of the trip from his mind's palate. There was no doubt about it—he was rattled. Hell, he was maraca-ed. He was so nervous he'd started imagining the black car behind his on the way to the pub was some goon sent by HQ to punish his wavering faith.

He'd earned this drink, damnit. And all the next ones, too.

"Is that a challenge?" Liam replied to the bartender, only slurring his words the tiniest bit. With a grin, he pounded back his tall, chilled glass of gin and tonic, laid it carefully back down onto the wet bar top, and waved for another refill.

What was that, now? Four, or five? Eh, it didn't matter. Who was counting?

"You keep going like that," said the burly bartender, answering Liam's rhetorical question, "and I'll have to start giving you short measures. Nothing personal, it's bar policy. Just thought you should know."

Liam muttered under his breath. But it was hard to stay angry at a friendly face like that, especially when said face sat atop an arm currently pouring him another drink.

"Just keep 'em coming. I've earned these. I swear, sometimes I feel like I passed a deal with the devil. And didn't even get the special effects," he added, with a dark little chuckle.

Behind the bar counter, Sabine screwed the top back onto the London Gin, her straw-coloured ponytail swaying. "Sounds like you've got a story there, chum. Anything you want to talk about?"

Even with the juniper spirits dancing through his neural pathways, Liam knew he probably shouldn't be complaining about work in public. But this wasn't the first time he'd come to the Jenkin's Ear during the dead hours of the night to vent.

It wasn't as if he had anybody else to talk to. Not his mother, since he'd lost her last year to an undetected superbug, just three weeks after she'd moved into the shiny new house he'd bought her—with privacy guaranteed, all the way to the medical sensor-free bathrooms. That was what Corporate privilege got you—septicaemia, and an only child who didn't know how to mourn.

With the show's second season in full swing, he hadn't had time to mourn anyway, which was a blessing, really. At least the recording of the cremation ceremony was tastefully edited—and you could pause it to go to the bathroom as well, which was a plus.

He certainly couldn't talk things over with his so-called friends, either. Kyla was the only one who bothered to keep in touch at all these days, and even that was only for birthdays and Christmas. The old complicity[1] they'd shared since their days together at Birkbeck was long gone.

Plus, a physical bartender pretty much qualified as a therapist, didn't they? If the old vids were anything to go by, it was practically part of the job description. Liam wasn't sure how well that excuse would hold up if his bosses at RedCorp found out about his little nocturnal venting sessions, but what they didn't know couldn't hurt them. Or, more importantly, him.

"I just came back from a... a business trip, you could say."

"Cool. Overseas?" replied the country gentlebartender, with well trained tones of interest.

Liam sipped at his soothing glass this time, instead of swigging it, and repressed a little shudder as he remembered the splashdown. "Very much overseas. Twice, in fact. I had to go do damage control for something my company did over there."

Sabine turned to pop the bottle back onto the old-style presentation shelves behind the bar. "Something bad?" she asked, facing away from Liam.

"Yeah, pretty bad. Pretty bad." Liam smiled and clenched his teeth, trying to keep his emotions in check.

"Is that the devil deal you were talking about, then?" said Sabine, turning back to Liam, a calculated, professional smile on her rugged face.

Not trusting his own throat, Liam simply nodded.

"And did it work?" the bartender added, after a pause.

Liam blinked in surprise.

"Worked? What do you mean?"

"The damage control."

Liam nodded again, with an exhausted sigh.

---

[1] "Being an accomplice, a partner in wrongdoing," from the Latin for "folded, woven together."

"Yes, I suppose. They'd have sent me a great big glaring alarm if there was any issue. And it's never failed before."

"Refresh my memory," said Sabine, leaning forward against the bar top. "What was it again, last time you were in here? One of your people having an accident?"

"Worse than that. It was a long-time colleague, and it was suicide. I mean," Liam was quick to add, defensively, "it didn't happen at work or anything, and there was nothing to say it was our fault, as such."

The bartender lifted an eyebrow. "Then why beat yourself up about it?"

"I don't really want to talk about it, actually," said Liam, gazing down.

"Sorry," the rugged-looking Sabine rushed to say, pulling away and moving on down the bar to do one of the mysterious things below the counter that seem to keep bartenders so busy. "I didn't mean to pry. You're welcome to keep your story close to your own chest."

Liam let out a disgraceful snort into his lifted glass. "Yeah, some story," he replied, as he dropped it back down on the mahogany bar top. "A real page-turner."

The woman gave him a shrug. "Everyone's got a story, chum. They're all a person's really got, when you get right down to it."

"The only story here right now is the mystery of this empty glass," said Liam, with a nervous chuckle. "And that's a tragedy."

Still, as much as he wanted to laugh it off, there was something in what the bartender was saying. Maybe it was just the bottle's worth of pure alcohol in his veins, but as Sabine smiled and poured him another, quite likely short-measured, G&T, it struck Liam that the woman was right. Stories were all that mattered, in the end.

That's what *The Grass is Greener* was all about, after all. Showing the world the real lives of poor sobs and spinning them into narratives, ones the viewers were eager to lap up and make real, if only so they could feel better about themselves. About their own sorry, but not quite *that* sorry, lot in Corporate life.

Stories had power.

Liam took a swig of liquid courage and mustered his refreshingly daring thoughts as he watched Sabine go about her work behind the bar.

Hell, what was a Corporation, what was his own RedCorp, anyway, if not a story? The fiction that laws could create bodyless giants wielding godlike powers, dissociated and distinct from the physical people giving them life?

Stories were more powerful than people, he realised, and a thrilling shiver ran down his spine. Stories shaped how people saw reality, and each other. They were the single greatest weapon in the Corporate world-state's arsenal, the only one they needed, really. And Liam's show was their delivery system.

"Pour you another?" said Sabine, breaking Liam's train of thought. She already had the London Gin uncorked above his somehow empty glass, and the sharp juniper tickled his nostrils.

Surprising even himself, Liam shook his head, both to refuse and to clear it. "I'm good for now, thanks," he said, trying to hold onto the gossamer ideas arriving from long-suppressed parts of his brain. They sounded wrong, but they felt so very right.

"Suit yourself," replied the bartender, with a shrug of her tweed-clad shoulders. "You know where to find me."

Liam nodded without looking. What was it about stories, again?

Stories were powerful, yes. Look at the magic trick he'd just pulled off in Quito. He'd taken the massacre and forcible evacuation of thousands of people by armed Corporate paramilitaries and turned it into brave peacekeepers defending humanity's future and prosperity.

Mars almighty, why the hell had he refused that drink?

But the persistent little thrill coursing up and down his spine suggested that maybe there was something else his body craved[1] even more than blessed, numbing alcohol. Maybe there was an even

---

[1] "To implore, to demand by right"

better way to fight off the terrifying thought of what he'd become, how violently the world he helped create and maintain every day clashed with his so-called principles, and, more than anything else, how little he or anyone else could do to change that world for the better.

So what if people couldn't change the world for the better. Maybe, just maybe, stories could.

Closing his eyes, Liam pushed through the throbbing alcohol haze and focused on this new excitement deep within him. And he smiled. A beatific, almost child-like smile that lit up his pale, balding, jug-eared face.

Because he now knew what that thrill of excitement was. He had a name for it. It was the feeling of purpose.

If stories could change the world, all he had to do was make sure people heard the stories the world needed them to hear. Not the fake, so-called reality drama the show doctored and peddled. Real stories, with real people, to make folks wake up and realise things don't have to be this way. Not if we all remember that change is possible.

The rejected candidate file would be full of material. All of those real, honest, tragic stories that the Editor set up to be filtered out of the application system. Not engaging enough, he'd said. Too real, and too telling about the true misery that kept the cogs of the Corporate world-state spinning.

But the Editor had buggered off to his cushy new upper management job at that ugly, deformed phallus of a Canary Wharf skyscraper, the Tulip. He'd been all too happy to leave Liam behind to nominally run operations in the dingy warehouse studio in Deptford that still housed *The Grass is Greener*'s production team and set. And after spending the last year wallowing in drink and despondency, the last thing anyone would expect would be for Liam to suddenly regrow a conscience. To try to use his position to actually do some good for the world at large, and not just for RedCorp's ever-voracious bottom line.

Grinning from ear to ear, Liam signalled for his car to come pick him up with a quick flick in his AR display. The readout said twenty minutes to arrival, since the expensive car was still parked in the monstrous garage of his house in Richmond. It would need a while to hit the rich man's superconductor thoroughfare and zip straight into the heart of London to pick him up. But that was still a damn sight faster and more efficient than when cars still had people driving them, and a lot cheaper than paying for parking in the City. Plus, it gave him time for a last drink, to celebrate his new resolve.

"One more for the road, Sabine," he said, grin still plastered across his face. "And maybe something special, this time," he added, interrupting the bartender as she went straight for the bottle of gin again. "Something with some zing. Do you have anything aged, like an Armagnac?"

Liam remembered the name from one of the innumerable parties he'd attended over the past two years, when a single sip had driven him past drunk and out the other side into a strange sort of sobriety.

Sabine clearly knew it as well, since her eyebrows shot up to her pulled-back hairline. "You got something to celebrate? Because I've got a hundred-year-old Lacquy Bas-Armagnac down here that'll give you all the kick you could hope for. If you don't mind a taster setting you back three-hundred credits."

Liam started salivating just at the name on the label. With a nod, he gave Sabine the go-ahead, and watched as she opened some sort of protected area beneath the counter and ceremoniously lifted out a tall bottle of rich, golden spirits, cradled in both hands.

Speechless seconds later, Liam lifted the tall, tulip-bulb glass to his nose and breathed in the overpowering aromas of pear, liquorice, and oak. Even more so than the first time, when he'd just drunk it without knowing what it was, the mere scent of the liqueur chased the fog out of his mind, leaving him both clear-minded and amazed. How could so many complex sensations be blended into what was little more than a mouthful of fluid?

Then, closing his eyes, he took a sip, and everything around him—bar, show, overriding bosses, and revolutionary thoughts alike—faded from mind in the wave of blended flavours, ranging from crème brûlée, through walnuts and apricots, all the way to a mineral, flinty taste that invaded his senses and set up permanent residence.

Why did he waste his time with insipid G&Ts, anyway? That was just a smooth way to get drunk. This… Now this was drinking.

The complexity, the mingling of scents and flavours to produce a powerful whole; Liam couldn't think of a more promising start to his campaign to get the real human stories out there. To use his position to make a change for the better.

When his car arrived, Liam tipped the bartender and left. The taste stayed with him all the way home.

5

Liam's resolve did not dissolve[1] after morning had come. But getting the truth out there, the stories people needed to hear, turned out to be a good deal more complicated than his ethanol-addled brain had imagined.

The half-formed idea etched in drunken brilliance across the folds of his cortex during the previous night's revelries had been deceptively simple. He'd simply dig into the rejected application pile, find all the best, most damning stories about the true consequences of the Corporate world, and use the show to get them in front of people's eyes.

However, true to the rest of Liam's experience, things that seemed simple with five or six G&Ts in his bloodstream often proved to be damnably complicated in the morning. Getting access to the old applications was the easy part—all that took was an hour or so of frustrated struggling with the Mews's data archive system. The service had clearly been designed in the technological dark ages, using keys and commands that the shiny, gaming spec interface in Liam's "Supervising Producer" office didn't even have on its AR keyboard.

Liam suspected that retrieving data after they'd been thrown into the digital oubliettes had not been high on the list of priorities when

---

[1] Through some twist of time and minds, these two words have the same origin: to loosen or untie a problem is to "solve" it, which is to say, to settle it, to determine its outcome.

RedCorp designed its archive[1] system. And yet, finally extracting the rejected application files from the misnamed folder they'd somehow ended up buried in was only the start of Liam's worries.

He closed his office door, snuck past the Banksy prints on the otherwise bare wall to his far-too-comfy chair, and opened up the file with the glee of a child scarfing down a whole pack of cookies that used to be out of reach.

The applications were good. Within seconds, he already had more real-life tragedies than he could possibly fit into a year's worth of new segments.

Whole families starving in Colombia even after they'd sold themselves, young and old, into Corporate slavery, just so they could get so-called subsistence support; homeless folk harvested off the streets of Strasbourg for Corporate exec body mods and faced with threats from the privatised police forces when they tried to complain; child cyber-soldiers in Saudi Arabia executed for hacking at the age of twelve. Precisely the sort of people his employers wanted swept into the crematorium and never spoken of again. But the applications being so good, so devastating for the Corporate world's carefully and expensively maintained image as benefactors of an unruly mankind, was only salt in the fresh wounds of Liam's conscience.

The jug-eared host soon realised there was absolutely no way he could ever get these stories out through the show. Not with a regular, above-board new segment, at least. And it wasn't just the content; now that he looked into it, he discovered he had no authority to change the show's structure at all, as far as the software was concerned. The format was sewn up tighter than a Revenue Corp accountant's sphincter, and was shielded behind more levels of security and firewalls than Liam could fathom[II]. Any attempt to meddle with it

---

[1] "The origin, the first place." Today, ironically, archives are the last and final resting place of all the data of our lives.

[II] A *fathom* is the length of the outstretched arm; hence, "to fathom" means "to grasp, embrace."

would send alarms up the Corporate chain. Probably even past the Editor and up to his own boss, Ms Preston, the show's original mastermind, now enjoying her rewards for its unprecedented success—a life of pampered luxury and easy-going telepresence work from Paradise Mars.

Hell, the system was so locked down, the only way to get material like this broadcast directly would be to brute force your way onto the distribution servers in Barry's cubbyhole and input it directly into the feed. And however resolved Liam was to scratch this strange new moral itch and tell himself he was actually doing some good in the world, he wasn't quite so desperate as to throw away his freedom—and worse yet, his career—with that sort of smash-and-grab assault on the technician's domain.

No, there must be some other way to get the stories of the Corporate world's real victims out in front of everyone's eyes. There must be. But damned if Liam could see how.

It was therefore grumbling and disheveled, and with a throbbing hangover to boot, that Liam swung open the door to Tantamount Mews's so-called "Conference Room." He grunted an ungracious "Good morning" to the team packed into what was, every other day of the week, the warehouse's second largest closet. A couple of the show's five-person team smiled in reply, but the rest didn't even bother—not that Liam was in any position to complain, showing up ten minutes late to the show's mandatory Monday morning "team coordination session."

"Sorry I'm late, gang," Liam said, squeezing in to take his flimsy seat at the head of the tiny conference table, if you could call a pile of cleaning solvent boxes with a white tarp thrown over it a conference table, which they did. That was also company-mandatory "team building" terminology, just like the AR sign on the door. "I had some business to deal with."

"Oh," fretted Mary Artworthy, the Mews's long-suffering agency worker, who got stuck with all the cleaning, maintenance, and general factotum work without which the show would crash and burn—probably literally—within a matter of hours. "Did we leave another mess in the restroom, Mr Argyle? It's just that I have to sort those out before they set, you see, or else I'll never get the bile smell out of the tile grouting."

Liam coughed, feeling his ears go red and wishing the woman would pause for breath every now and again while speaking. Where did she learn to speak, anyway? Christie's auction house floor?

"No, Mary, and I'm sure I have no idea what you're talking about. Now, we do have an agenda to get through here, people, so if there's no objection, the first and only item is—"

An indignant intake of air interrupted him from the opposite end of the table. Liam looked up from his AR notes, straight into a trademark glare from his head field team coordinator, Norma Lee. This one simmered with even more barely contained violence than usual and was about ten times more intimidating than Ms Lee's tiny stature should allow.

"Excuse me," she said, and there could be no doubt the words were spoken as an order, "but that's yeastshit, Liam. Some of us here think that Corporate trying to buy our bodies is a little bit more important than stupid agenda items. Right, Mary?"

The woman in the soiled blue overalls sank into her own rickety seat a little and glanced between Ms Lee and Liam before giving a nervous nod.

"Right," she added, in a near squeak.

"You've got to do something about this, Liam," charged on Liam's nominal second-in-command at the Mews, a position even more laughable than Liam's own status as "Supervising Producer." "Did you even read the message I sent you? Or were you too busy with your 'urgent work?'" Her little flashing sneer made her thoughts about Liam's nightly self-medication sessions painfully evident.

She wasn't wrong, at that, Liam admitted, as he sighed and rubbed his bleary eyes. "You know what? I'll add it as first point in the agenda if you'll pretend I have no idea what the problem is and take it from the start."

Ms Lee shot Liam a glare so sharp you could use it to cut Space Elevator cable. Clearly, pretending Liam was an incompetent buffoon wasn't exactly going to be a strenuous role to play. "The problem?" she said, treating each word like a stabbing dagger. "The problem is you have no right to make us use this damn new app! RedCorp doesn't own women's bodies, damnit!"

Right, the new app. What did they call it again? A complimentary female worker health monitor system? Liam had seen something about it in the mandatory company newsletter. The one you had to scroll down to the bottom of every morning before the interface would let you do any actual work.

"Hey, it's no use having a go at me," he told Lee. "Corporate didn't tell me a damn thing about any new data harvesting app for female employees. I'm on your side here."

Lee started spluttering like a pressure cooker about to explode, but Liam charged on.

"I just need to understand exactly what the problem is so I can fight this for you with Corporate. And I'm not sure what's so wrong about it," he added, fishing the newsletter back out of his interface's garbage bin with a flick of an eye and skimming over the article. "The app's entirely optional, isn't it? And you're getting paid for every day you choose to use it, too."

The temp worker, Mary, nodded at that, and shot Liam a glance full of gratitude. He knew that she certainly wasn't in any position to refuse a pay boost, not on a temp agency salary. Hell, maybe the male workers should be the ones complaining about not getting the chance at a pay raise as well.

"You're joking, right?" spat Lee. "Getting paid for it just makes it worse. RedCorp has no right to demand we track our menstrual cycles and pregnancy data in their app! Let alone treat our bodies like some sort of commodity we can sell them for a couple of credits a day!"

Mary let out a discreet little cough from behind Lee, clearing her throat before speaking. "And the message from Corporate did say that, while we could choose not to use the app, doing so would be factored into monthly reviews and contract renewals. I can't risk losing this contract over an app. So, it isn't really fair to call it a choice, then, is it?"

"Exactly!" said Lee, beaming. "And what about the women who don't have periods, or all the enbies and men who are biologically female? Corporate has done some pretty shitty things to the women here over the past few years, but this is one step too far! Get this sorted out, Liam, or else we're going straight down to the Tulip to sort it out ourselves!"

Damn. When did the words "going straight down to the Tulip" stop being ridiculous and become ominous instead?

"Trust me, Norma. I'm on it."

"You'd better be," answered the tightly wound woman, crossing her sharp-suited arms and leaning back into her chair.

Liam paused for a moment, wary of another outburst. To his left, Job Akintola seemed absorbed in his display—and, Liam noted, decidedly unruffled by the previous night's space-capade. Across the table from him, the show's hulking technician, Barry, smiled beneath his heavy-duty black interface goggles and gave Liam a little wave. Seemed safe enough.

"Right, then. So, everyone's okay for me to get back to the actual show? Only, we've got a primetime feature to organise in six days' time, and it says right here on the agenda that we still only have eleven of our twelve contestants lined up for Season Three. There's no fucking around this year, people. Twelve contestants, not eight, and no grace period. Straight into eliminations after a single week of live feeds. Those are the orders from the Tulip, and we don't have time for mistakes. So, someone please tell me it's just a mistake from the agenda app and that we have our damn contestants lined up."

Barry looked across the table to Akintola, who looked over at Lee, who in turn kept her arms firmly crossed and stared up at the damp-patched ceiling tiles. Akintola waited a second, then shrugged with unperturbable cool. "Listen, it's not our fault. Not really. The damn algorithm is supposed to do all the work, just like everything else around here. But the thing refuses to pick the final candidate for us, no matter how much we fiddle around with the criteria."

The man had a point. There was no way a flagship show like the GiG could run with a barebones crew of five people, out of a dockside warehouse that was crumbling down around their ears, if it weren't for the AI processes doing most of the actual work and the decision-making for them. People were messy and expensive, while processing time had never been cheaper. It didn't exactly promote initiative and responsibility, even when the machine's decision trees collapsed under their own weight and defaulted to "let the humans sort it out." Hell, he'd used the same excuse himself more than once, in the past.

"Right," Liam said with a grunt, not feeling up to arguing a point he didn't really believe in. "There must be something we can do about that. Barry?"

The crappy lighting of the lounge/conference room/storage closet caught the technician's bald crown as he dipped his head, slipping off his goggles. The entire table kept its silence as he wiped them with a cleaning fluid-stained handkerchief, deep in thought.

"Beats me," Barry said at last. "I mean, it's possible to get into the AI's programming and mess with it, theoretically. Brute force the motivation weightings until it gives us an answer."

"Well, why don't you do that, then?" said Lee, with a scoff.

Barry shook his head. "It wouldn't have any meaning anymore. You'd be better off pulling a name out of a hat. It'll be just as meaningful, and at least then I won't have to spend more time fixing all the damage to the programming."

"Well, that might not be the worst idea, anyway," said Akintola, rubbing his face. "If the computer can't decide between two or three candidates, and they're all just as good, then why not leave it to chance and pull a name out of a hat?"

They all started squabbling at that—well, all except Mary, who was staying well out of it as usual. Norma Lee was going on about how they'd all be out of a job soon if that's all it took, but Liam's mind was racing, trying to keep up with the lightning-flash thrill of the fresh idea he'd just had, before he lost the shape of it.

"That's right," he said, inaudible over the raised voices filling the tiny room. Giving himself a little shake, he stood to get their attention and raised his voice. "You're all right. Yes, we could choose the easy route and brute force the programming or let chance do our job for us, but where would we be then? How long until they just let the AI itself sort out any dilemmas with a random number generator and cut out the middleman entirely? No!"

Liam thumped his hands down onto the "table" for emphasis, creating a cascade of cleaning supply boxes under the tarp until they were all sitting around a red gingham-covered mountain. "We're here because some problems need creative solutions, thinking-outside-the-box solutions, the sort only human beings can come up with. So it's a good thing I'm here to sort out your mess," he added, with a wicked grin that felt equal parts unfamiliar and delightful on his face. "And don't you forget it."

At the opposite end of the room, Ms Lee shuffled in her seat, wary and confused as a lion tamer who bumps into one of her charges down at the pub. "Are you saying you've got a solution, then?"

"Not merely *a* solution," Liam smarmed, playing it up too much for his own good and enjoying every second if it. "*The* solution. We can't find a candidate? Then fine. We'll just make one."

"You mean a composite stand-in?" Barry asked, goggles forgotten halfway down his dome of a forehead.

"Right on the money," Liam replied, with his best gameshow bullshitting grin. "The simulation technology's ancient, we just need enough real-life material to feed into it to make it credible. And we have plenty of that hanging around in the rejected applications, more than we could ever hope to use."

The camera techie frowned, breaking his cool composure and coming dangerously close to showing an honest emotion. "But if they're in the rejected applications, doesn't that mean they weren't good enough and we already turned them down?"

"Only because they weren't flashy enough, on their own, to really get people's interest. Too scary or too terminal. Not enough story. But with a composite contestant, we can stitch all those depressing real-life stories together into a fresh new whole. One that'll get everyone tuning in, day after day, to see what fresh misery is in store. It'll be better than the highest-rated telenovela yeastcrap they dish up on the other feeds. Our best contestant yet!"

"What about the other eleven, though?" piped up Mary's mousy voice, reminding everyone that she was in the room too. "Won't they object to competing against a fake person? And won't their own lenses give away the fact there's nobody standing next to them?"

"Well, that last bit at least won't be a problem," Barry replied before Liam got a chance to—and he was more than happy to let the towering technician field this one. "It'd be child's play to sync the composite stand-in into the other outgoing feeds. A bit more processing power, sure, but we've got plenty to spare. And as for what they'll think of it—well, I'd imagine they'd be happy enough to go along with it. One less real contestant to win the prize, I suppose. And it'd be easy enough to force them to play along with the composite, for that matter. It's not like adding one more ridiculous clause to the waiver we make them sign would make any difference. The way I see it, the question isn't if we're able to do it or not. It's whether we should."

All around the nominal table, cogs turned in heads long used to weighing the pros and cons of any decision in terms of how little personal effort they could get away with putting in, and how much risk they'd incur doing so.

"It'd sure make things a lot easier for us," muttered Lee, before catching herself. "Hypothetically speaking, of course. What did the Editor say when you ran your idea by him?"

Of course they'd assume he'd never take any initiative without getting the Editor's seal of approval beforehand. Mars knew he'd never given them reason to think any differently over the past few years.

Maybe he could use that to his advantage now.

"He loved it. So much easier to control than a flesh-and-bone candidate, after all."

The lie came so easily to his lips, he almost believed it himself.

Mary shot him a bright, encouraging smile. "Well, it's none of my business really, but if the powers-that-be are on board with the idea, it seems like there's nothing to lose in giving it a go and seeing if you can get this simulation thingamabob to work. If you think you can do it, that is, Barry."

The technician's frown at the mention of an increased workload melted under in a sudden burst of professional pride. "Of course I can do it! Oh, it'll be a challenge, especially at such short notice, but at least it'll give me something more interesting to do in the lull between the elimination shows than just sit watching dropped packet counts."

Liam had no idea why the man was talking about making a mess with condiment packs all of a sudden, but it sounded like he was agreeing, so the host simply nodded and smiled. "Excellent. I've already got the rejection archives loaded, so I'll handle the materials selection and send the best bits on to you, Barry. The rest of you, make sure there's no issue with all those flights and we don't lose any more contestants for Sunday's big season premiere."

Akintola flashed a blinding white grin back at him. "You got it, Boss."

Boss, huh? As he left the impromptu conference room, Liam tried to remember the last time they'd called him "Boss" and came up with a blank. Maybe things were looking up after all.

Behind him, the AR sign on the door switched back from "Conference Room" to "Supplies Closet."

6

Liam swung open the door to his own little office and breathed in the productivity-stimulating pheromones that were mandatory for all execs, which he just barely qualified as. Even through his monster of a hangover, it still smelled like success.

"Host/Supervising Producer" might be a joke of epic proportions, but it still had its perks. Well, its perk, at least. And this office was that perk.

Sure, Ed had taken most of the fancy furnishings with him when he moved on to a better place at the end of the first season. Specifically, a top floor office at the Tulip, with a view over the London Sprawl as far as the tenacious smog allowed the eye to see. Long gone were the imposing bookcases and their real, paper books, along with the polished faux-stone desk and the drink dispenser that only dispensed water.

But Liam was glad it was all gone. He'd had a hard enough time making the space his own as it was, with so many memories of getting chewed out, manipulated, and generally screwed over by the Editor in this very room. It had taken a while for him to feel comfortable here. But once he'd put in a gaming-spec computer station, had Mary hang a couple of classy Banksy canvasses on the walls—he especially loved the one with the little girl hugging the bomb—and installed a drinks cabinet that had a damn sight more in it than water, he'd finally felt like he'd exorcised the lingering demons of the Editor's tenure there. The space was finally his own.

With a deep, satisfied sigh, he plopped down into the deep foam embrace of the executive smart chair, moulded at the nanomolecular level to the contours of his body. Then he flicked his desktop out of the AR realm and onto the huge physical screen. Nagging memories of shattered bodies at the foot of the Quito Elevator still scratched at the raw nerves of his conscience—but he finally had a real plan to shut them up.

He crackled his knuckles, ready for action. It was time to gather all the rejection folder's most damning Corporate tragedies and wrap them up with a nice bow for Barry.

Instead, the cursed ring of an incoming comms call shattered his resolve and brought back, with a vengeance, the lancing reminder of his early morning drinking session.

The call auto-connected, whether Liam wanted it to or not, after three rings. Which meant it could only be one person.

"Argyle!" barked the Editor, appearing in all his dickie-bowed glory in the comms window. "I do hope I'm not interrupting anything."

"Well, we are a bit busy around here, Ed, to tell the truth. Just got back from that... special assignment down in Quito," Liam said, with only the slightest hesitation, "and we've got the big season launch special coming up this weekend. I'm sure you remember how hectic it gets around here in the run-up to a big show like that."

On screen, Ed the Editor grinned like the shark who just figured out the remora stuck to it are basically handy junk food. "Oh, I'm certain you aren't so busy you don't have time for a little chat with your old mentor, now are you, Argyle? I may have moved on to bigger and greater things here at Corporate, but you know I keep a keen eye on my first love, *The Grass is Greener*. And I'm always here for you especially, Liam."

Liam fought back a gag reflex and kept as casual a smile on his face as he could. The Editor always found a way to make words that should be reassuring sound like a threat.

"You know you can talk to me about anything, my boy. Anything at all."

The balding little man on the screen paused, as if trying to force some expected response out of Liam through the sheer suction power of a conversational vacuum. But damned if Liam could figure out what Ed expected of him.

"That's… That's great," he stammered eventually, when the pressure became too strong and he had to say something, anything, to break the silence. "Always good to know you've got my back." Yeah, just like the rest of him, owned from head to toe by the company.

The Editor nodded but still wore an unsatisfied little frown on his round face. "So, if there were anything going on, anything out of the ordinary you were concerned about, you would tell me, right?"

"Oh, absolutely," Liam lied, trying to strike a careful mix between puzzlement and chipperness in his voice. "You can count on it."

What was the man on about? Had one of his co-workers already figured out he'd been lying about the Editor's approval for the composite candidate idea and immediately ratted him out? It hadn't even been five minutes, which was surely some kind of record, even in this dog-eat-dog Corporate environment.

"Right, then," said the Editor, his frown barely hidden behind an attempt at a condescending, paternal smile. "I won't keep you from your work any longer, not in such a busy part of the season. We're all counting on big numbers for this year's launch episode, you know. Especially with to the big publicity boost we got from your on-the-ground footage from the Elevator. Damn convenient timing for us, that's for sure."

He paused, listening to his own words, then chuckled before carrying on.

"Mars above, if the protesters hadn't chosen such a fantastic time to attack the Elevator, we'd have done well to stage the thing ourselves, just for the publicity value. Theoretically speaking, of course," added the Editor as an afterthought, perhaps in reaction to the expression of horror Liam couldn't prevent from slipping past his professional façade. That the man could not only think, but feel comfortable voicing such a callous, inhumane thought stunned a part of Liam that he had thought long dead.

And speaking of callousness, he'd almost forgotten to ask about the latest RedCorp exercise in tossing shit down to the troops on the ground here at the Mews.

"Actually, Ed, there was one thing, come to think of it," said Liam. He tried not to wince at the eager glint that flared in the Editor's speckled brown eyes. "What's this about a new app for female RedCorp workers to log their health data? Even menstrual periods and pregnancy data, where applicable. Ms Lee just received the instructions from Corporate, and you can imagine how well that went down."

The Editor chuckled, almost wistfully. "The words 'house on fire' come to mind. Ah, I envy you, Argyle. I truly do. Such trifling, down-to-Earth problems to deal with."

Liam gritted his teeth and kept smiling while the man belittled him and his co-workers. At least now they were back in the charted, smug-infested waters of normal conversation with the Editor. And he needed an answer from the man anyway, so best to humour him for the time being.

"You're welcome to come back and show us all how it's done whenever you want, you know," Liam settled for saying, with a fake little laugh to take the edge off the comment.

In the comms window, the Editor adjusted his scarlet bowtie and shook his head. "What, when you're doing so well? Perish[1] the thought! I know you can handle anything the day-to-day running of *The Grass is Greener* can throw at you, including resistance to the

---

[1] *Per/ire*, to "go through." Or, as John Malkovich put it: "*I don't really go through a process, it goes through me.*"

handy new health tracking app we've decided to provide to our workers of the gentler sex. Free of cost, too, I might add, even though it cost the R&D folks a small fortune to design!"

"Yes, and with a financial incentive, too. I know all of that."

"Well, then!" said the Editor with a little scoff. "Where's the problem, Argyle?"

For a second, he had the disturbing impression the Editor was speaking with Liam's own voice, but he was quick to shake it off. "The problem is that you can't just push people to sell us their private information like that."

"Oh, we can't, can we? I think you'll find we can." The Editor's voice dropped to dire depths, all jovial[1] presence gone. "The word 'can't' has no place in a modern work environment, Argyle. No 'can't' in our cant. Even a philosophy fellow like yourself knows that," he added, with a private little chuckle.

"Yes, of course," Liam was quick to reply, hating every word of it. But he reminded himself how vital it was to placate the man if he had any hope of obtaining some concession on this menstrual app issue and preventing an all-out war of the sexes in the central corridor of Tantamount Mews.

"When someone applies for a position with us, or to become a candidate on our show," Ed carried on, "they give us their birthdate, personal history, family information and status, yes? And without any guarantee they'll be accepted, or any form of compensation?"

"Well, yes. Naturally."

"Then tell me. How is this any different?"

"Well—" Liam started to say, but his brain came up empty when it tried to find the words to follow. He paused, flummoxed. Morally, he knew the Editor was wrong. Of course he was wrong. But damned if Liam could suss out why, exactly. Or wrap his head around the words to express it.

---

[1] "Pertaining to Jupiter," because we all know how much fun that guy used to get up to.

"I'll tell you the difference," smarmed the Editor, as Liam's confused silence dragged on. "Our ladies are getting paid for their data, that's the only meaningful difference. They should be grateful."

Still confused, and angry at himself for letting the Editor get under his skin again so quickly after he'd resolved to start regrowing a conscience, Liam grasped at the passing opportunity to divert the conversation onto a new track.

"If you look at it that way, what about discrimination, then? And I don't just mean with the men complaining about not getting the same pay bonus, like you pointed out. There are plenty of women working for RedCorp who can't give the sort of data the app wants, or who aren't biologically female in the first place. And vice versa, biological females who aren't women. And there's a whole non-binary spectrum in-between. Isn't this app just a discrimination lawsuit and PR nightmare waiting to explode?"

"Well, you aren't so slow as you let on, eh, Argyle?"

Liam remained silent while the man laughed, trying to pass the insult off as humour. There's no good answer to a rhetorical question like that anyway, other than a slap upside the head, which was difficult under the circumstances.

"You're right, of course. Legal fussed over discrimination as well when we ran the app project past the Board. But, as ever, etymology is our friend here. It's amazing how many problems simply disappear when we get down to the true meaning of the words we use."

Profits almighty, this nonsense again? Liam had never known someone as obsessed with the "real meaning" of words as the Editor. Especially when it let him twist that meaning to serve whatever point he was trying to make, at any given time.

"Discrimination," the man pontificated on-screen, "is far from the bigoted evil that common usage would make it out to be. As the great Christopher Hitchens so rightly pointed out, discrimination is a skill, a precious facility, a virtue even. It is the ability to observe and to make appropriate, justified distinctions. The exact opposite of the blanket, factless judgments people think of when they speak of so-called discrimination."

Liam was an old hand at the Editor's companyman-splaining, and he could see where he was going with this a mile off. But damnit, he was still fighting off a piercing hangover. He'd had too much to drink last night to face this now—or, perhaps, nowhere near enough.

"So, as you can see, what we're doing with this app of ours is anything but discrimination. We're simply offering certain employees with certain objective, biological features a free tool to help them, and us, manage those distinguishing characteristics on a day-to-day basis."

Deep in the embrace of his form-fitting chair, Liam opened his mouth to respond, then closed it again. What was there to say after something like that? If the Editor were an air traffic controller, he'd probably be able to convince the passengers on a crashing automated plane that their impending impact with the ground was not only the most natural thing in the world, but also highly desirable. They'd be landing early, for starters.

"Well, that's another thing," said Liam, scrambling to assert some semblance of control over the discussion. "Why do we even want to buy the data from all our female workers in the first place? What good can it possibly do us, to be worth all this potential trouble?"

"Dear boy, that's the best part! It's not just an internal measure to follow employee health and prevent hormonal-related conflict. Our R&D branches are desperate to get their hands on such a large sample of data. Those bastards at Triumph and SyneDeal will go green with envy when they see the new digital products, marketing packages, and pharmaceuticals our subsidiaries will start rolling out using these data sets. The possibilities are endless!"

"Yes, and that's the rub with the troops here on the ground," said Liam, trying to sprinkle in some buzz language, hoping the Editor might finally bother listening to him. "Our HR assets are afraid their private information might be used for purposes they'll have no control over, and possibly against them personally."

The Editor scoffed and shook his head in disbelief. "Is that what all this fuss is over? Then I'll tell you what. How about if I give you a symbolic guarantee that any harvested data will be entirely anonymous? Mars almighty, I'll even throw in an official policy memo from RedCorp that the health tracking app will only be used for purposes in strict compliance with our Ethical Mission Statement and Charter."

"You mean the one that's full of meaningless, generic commitments that are absolutely not enforceable, or opposable, by anyone?"

"Precisely," replied the Editor, professionally deaf to the irony in Liam's voice.

Liam rubbed his eyes. It was just the regular dehumanising shit of business as usual. It didn't even matter, really, in the long run. He had more important plans to set into motion. Maybe the Editor's half-assed concessions would be enough to keep the lid on this issue and stop it from becoming even more of a distraction.

Plus, he doubted he'd get anything better out of Corporate, even if he marched on down to the Tulip and kicked up a fuss in person. Not the best idea, anyway, when he was trying to keep a low profile—when he had finally found a way to give his resolve to take action some teeth.

"I suppose I can sell that to the team here at the Mews," he said with a grimace.

"That's my lad!" said the Editor, beaming on screen. "And I'm glad to see you're back on top of your game, Argyle. If anything else comes up and has you worried, you come straight to me. Understood?"

"It's a deal, Ed."

"Righty-oh, then. Just make sure you don't forget it. And keep your chin up in the meantime. Toodle-oo!"

When the Editor ended the call, Liam buried his throbbing head in his hands and tried to remind himself why feeling this shitty about the outcome of the conversation was a good thing. It certainly beat his instinct to just run from his responsibilities and stop caring again.

Liam lifted his head and flicked the screen out of standby, loading up the mess of shattered lives from the rejection archive.

Yes, this revulsion was good. Things were fine.

And soon, if Liam had any say in the matter, they'd finally start getting even better.

7

Goddamn, these stories were depressing. Liam couldn't really blame the Editor for ruling them out for the show. There wasn't any spice here, no suspense, nothing he could mould into conflict to keep the feed-viewing billions around the globe entertained. Just a nearly infinite series of people getting unilaterally shit on by life. Or the nearest Corporate-packaged facsimile thereof.

Maybe Ed was right. People would tune in to look through the eyes of the last human porn star in Hollywood, like poor Spike Bighorn back in Season One, or a musician like Rami Cantor in Season Two. They'd get drawn in to watch the latest gory scene somebody like Suicide Jill or medical enforcer Brad Leigh had to deal with in their line of work. But the unmitigated tragedies that filled *The Grass is Greener* applicant archives would only make them roll their eyes— not in the exasperated teenage-girl sense, but in the AR-interface sense of flicking your eyes upward to change the channel.

How could he succeed in bringing people face-to-face with the devastating realities of the Corporate world when nobody in their right mind would sit through these relentlessly miserable sob stories voluntarily? What was the point of it all, of putting himself on the line, if nobody had the patience to care?

The point, Liam scolded himself, was to stop another Quito Elevator massacre from happening. The point was to help make a world where the Corps couldn't get away with literal murder, where their actions had consequences, and where Liam could sleep at night without drinking himself into a stupor just so he could face going back to work the next morning.

As far as credos[1] went, it wasn't the most noble or selfless ever—but Mars above, it was a start.

If only the damn fake contestant would cooperate, maybe he'd even have a chance of accomplishing something with his new resolve.

"What the hell is it doing now?" Liam moaned, dabbing at the lake of sweat currently defying gravity on his neck. He watched the glitchy middle-aged figure, dressed in genderless floral prints and khakis, stutter-step its way through Barry's hot, humid technological lair.

"It's doing what it's supposed to." The goggled technician sounded like he was trying to convince himself just as much as Liam. "Machine learning takes time. It's not just about jamming a bunch of data into a file and running it."

In their respective lenses, the grey-faced projection in the purple Hawaiian shirt stepped forward once again, smiled at nothing in particular, and started speaking through their audio implants.

"Funny you should mention that. Reminds me of the time security forces broke into our house in downtown Bogotá on some trumped-up charge, with orders to force us out. We were one of the last holdouts of the big Candelaria redevelopment project, and none of their threats had succeeded in making us sell the old family house up till then. I went with my partner to get them to leave, and I thought we could solve everything peacefully, but when one of them shoved Marta out of the way, I saw red and took a swing at the guards. You wouldn't believe how fast an assault rifle slaved to a private security AR interface can shoot. One thought and a twitch of the eye is all it took, and I had a dozen bullets in me, from head to pelvis. I died instantly, of course, and—and—and—"

---

[1] Literally "I believe" in Latin, from the PIE root meaning "heart."

The creepily stone-faced projection started stuttering and twitching, before blinking out altogether, its current iteration brought to a crashing halt of contradiction. It reappeared a moment later on the other side of the room, marching forward again to have yet another go at its introductory spiel.

"Funny you should mention that. Reminds me of the time I went in for gene replacement therapy, but my insurance rang the hospital halfway through the operation to tell them my last payment had bounced and they were withholding coverage. They talk about something costing an arm and a leg, but that would have been cheap compared to what I discovered when I woke up…"

Barry grumbled and said, "It needs to integrate the materials through trial and error. That part's normal; good, even. But the real problem is contradiction. Leads straight to a fail state. And the stories you've sent through are so dramatic, it's hard to find ones that make sense when they're mashed together. There's just too much material there, Liam."

The jug-eared host turned away from the simulation as it came to another crash and restarted once again. "What are you saying, man? That we need to be more selective?"

"Sure, as long as you can find life stories that don't contradict each other at every turn and stop making the AI go doolally[1]."

"How the devil am I supposed to do that? You're the expert, not me. I can just about use the interface to order a pad thai."

"It's not quantum chess, Liam. Just find us some applicant stories that make sense. You know, to the average Jude."

"Right. The average Jude," the host said, sounding more dubious than the program itself, which chose that moment to break into impromptu dub-step stutters.

"And not to be rude or anything," added the technician, spinning away from Liam in his swivel chair, like a boulder on ball-bearings,

---

[1] From Deolali, near Mumbai.

"maybe you could do it in your own office? I'm not sure the machines like you that much."

The feeling was mutual, and Liam was happy for any excuse to leave the sweltering server dungeon. The rattling air-conditioning had never felt so good on his clammy skin as he made his way back to his office, lost in thought.

So, he needed to do some testing. To speak with normal people, try some of his stories out in as safe—and as anonymous—a way as possible. And not just for the sake of their program's digital sanity, either. If they were going to force him to be selective, he needed to know which applicant stories would make regular people around the world sit up, listen, and want to make a change.

Of course, there was the small problem that, other than his little binges where the whole point was not to run into anybody, he didn't really see anyone outside of work anymore. He didn't actually know any normal people to speak with…

There was a knock at the door, and this time, Liam had enough presence of mind to say, "Yes, come on in."

The door edged open, and in wheeled Mary Artworthy's bulky, multipurpose trolley, followed not long thereafter by the Mews's general factotum herself—*i.e.*, the one who gets totally facked over in the workplace.

Liam didn't normally encourage interruptions when he was thinking, but this looked like an opportunity. If there was one thing the contestant archive files had shown him, it's that the one common trait of all "normal people" was how badly they get screwed over by the Corporate system.

"Yes, Mary. Do come in."

Liam rose to his feet, walked around the front of his desk, and sat back down on the edge, in his best attempt at nonchalance.

"Just a second," muttered Mary from behind the stainless-steel trolley, which rattled and shook as she tried to edge it through the doorway and into the cramped office space with a twenty- or thirty-point turn. It made a sorry show, and Liam wished he'd had the presence of mind to tell the agency worker to leave the heavy trolley outside. It was too late now; it was damn embarrassing to watch, and even if Liam offered to help, he would probably only make it worse. So he settled for gazing tactfully away at his Banksy prints until she was done.

The framed picture directly to his left was the classic one with the couple embracing while each looked at the bright screens of their ancient handheld devices behind their partner's back. It was so archaic, and yet so familiar. The birth of the modern age in a nutshell, and Liam always found his eyes drawn away from the couple and toward the screens. As if, maybe this time, he'd finally make out what they had to show.

Mary let out a little sigh of relief, signalling that she'd finished her exertions and it was polite to turn back to face her.

"Close the door behind you," Liam said out of habit, before instantly regretting the words. The sound-proofed metal of the doorframe screeched against the edge of the trolley as a straining Mary forced it closed, almost knocking her cleaning supplies, catering odds-and-ends, and maintenance tools all over Liam's floor.

The host reddened all the way to the lobes of his jug-ears. He fought to keep his composure as Mary finished shutting the door and turned to face him, miffed but smiling.

"Well done, Mary. At least now we've got some privacy. Did you have something you wanted to ask me?"

"Yes, in fact. Yeast-roast or chicken?" the little mousey-haired agency worker replied, still panting from the effort.

Liam blinked. "Come again?"

"On your sandwich. Yeast-roast or chicken? Sorry, I know it's not much choice, but it's all I've got left."

Liam's brain had trouble making sense of the words, but his stomach chimed in with a loud rumble, letting the rest of him know that it, at least, still had its priorities straight. His stomach hadn't felt up to breakfast before work, and a liquid diet will only take you so far.

"Profits almighty, I could murder a sandwich. Roast please, as much as you've got."

"I figured as much," said Mary, rummaging around in a series of small, mysterious drawers. "Everyone else had already come get their lunch, so I saved you a bunch of roast and decided to bring it to you directly."

She handed Liam a little cardboard tray, laden not only with two little triangles of bread overflowing with salad cream and nut-coloured, enriched yeast roast, but also a fresh apple, a few slices of cheese, and a tumbler of vitamin/caffeine water.

It was a thing of beauty to Liam's eyes, and he took it off Mary's hands with eager thanks. She always did make the best office lunches, so much better than the cafeteria slush they used to dole out at his old weatherman job.

He dug into the sandwich with gusto, and Mary nodded in approval, with an artisan's satisfaction at a job well done. "So, you've been busy, I take it?" she asked, as Liam washed down his first chomp. "Is it this silly tracking app business, then?"

Liam swallowed, clearing his throat to reply, but Mary beat him to it.

"I just want you to know I didn't mean to put any pressure on you this morning," she said in an embarrassed gush of words. "That was all Ms Lee's doing. She dragged me into it so it wouldn't be just her and didn't really give me much of a choice. I mean, it was a surprise and all, but I don't even mind having to use the new app all that much. They'll be paying us, for starters, and I'm just glad they decided to include us agency workers in the offer. I could really use any extra bit of pay I can get, is all I'm saying."

Liam sat on the edge of his desk and rocked in the flow of words from the normally unassuming woman. They'd worked together going on three seasons now, and he couldn't remember her ever unloading so much on him, or anyone else for that matter. She was always there in the background. Always busy, single-handedly doing all the thankless little jobs without which the show, and the people nominally running it, would soon come apart at the seams.

"So, I wanted to make sure you knew I'm not ungrateful, and I don't mean to cause any trouble," she finished, with a nervous little smile. Liam's heart went out to her.

"Well, Mary," he said, wiping a blob of salad cream from the corner of his mouth, "don't let on that you already know when I tell everyone in our conference meeting later, but I've secured some serious guarantees from Corporate. That data will stay strictly anonymous and will never be used for anything unethical. Hopefully, that should calm even our formidable Ms Lee and she won't drag you into any more confrontations."

Liam chuckled at that, to show what a genial[1] boss he was, and Mary smiled in response—a real smile this time, not the nervous grimace she'd come in with. It did Liam a world of good to see. Maybe he could do some good for normal people, every now and again.

Speaking of which…

"Ah, Mary. While you're here, do you mind if I ask you a question?"

"Sure," replied the dark-eyed agency worker, wary once again. "Nothing's wrong, I hope?"

Liam shook his head. "No, of course not. But please, have a seat."

He gestured at the empty chair on her side of the desk, then picked up the half-eaten remains of his lunch and carried the tray over to his own, bigger chair. He sat down, with an inner sigh of content as the expensive padding worked its magic and embraced his bottom with nanometric precision.

"Right. Nothing wrong, don't worry, but I just need someone

---

[1] "Pertaining to marriage or (even less appropriately in the workplace) reproduction."

with a… down-to-Earth perspective to test a couple of ideas with. For the show's benefit, of course."

"Well, I've got a lot left to deal with today, but if you think I can help, I'm happy to. What's it about?"

"I'm trying to set down some principles for selecting candidates. Some guidelines, sort of thing."

Mary frowned, confused. "I thought the contestants were already all selected. I mean, you've got me building the set out there to bring them all in for Sunday's big show, is all."

"Yes, yes," Liam rushed to reassure. "Everything's in order for this season. I just wanted to get ahead of things for next year, in the lull before the season starts and we need to monitor twelve different live feeds."

"Well, I'm glad someone has a lull right now, but I've got a lot of work to do before Sunday, so if it's all the same—"

"It won't take long." Liam leaned forward, trying to hold the woman in place through sheer force of will. He needed this, he needed to speak to someone, to give voice to the fresh rebellious thoughts churning around his brain. He needed to do something with those thoughts before routine and the invisible chains of Corporate life conspired to silence them again. He doubted he'd get a second wake-up call like this.

"I just need your thoughts about a story or two I've found in the old contestant archives. Just your off-the-cut thoughts, first ones to pop into your head. It'd be a great help with the process of building the last contestant, and as you know, there's no time to lose."

Mary shuffled in the seat. "Well, if you're sure it won't take too long."

"I'll be brief," Liam replied, donning his professional smile to cover his panic as he flicked through the dozens of individual files open on his screen. It was so hard to decide which one stood out above the others in the general mire of misery that was the candidate archive. "Here, let's start with Mister—oh, never mind the name.

Best left anonymous, just like that app, right? Anyway, this SyneDeal IT guy has a stroke in his little white-collar apartment stack in Busan, forty-five minutes into his high-impact exercise routine. He crumbles to the floor and loses consciousness. And yet, even though he's all alone there, he actually wakes up, so to speak. The blood clot somehow clears itself out after a few minutes and he lives. Lucky, right?"

"I mean, if you can call that luck, I suppose," Mary replied, dubious.

"Well, you're right to doubt it, because he wakes up paralysed all down one side and with major damage on the other. His exercise program is still blaring, on repeat, and when he finally fights through the brain fog and musters up enough energy to shout out for help, nobody reacts. Even though he swears he hears the neighbours passing outside his door all the time. Not just on that first day but every day for the following five weeks, stuck alone on the floor of his apartment."

Mary shook her head in disgust. "That's gross, Liam. And silly, too. He would have died long before the five weeks were out."

"You'd think so," Liam said, nodding impatiently. "The exercise machine had a built-in water dispenser and a cabinet full of protein bars, but that's not the point. Five weeks later, he got lucky—if you can call it that, as you say—because his landlord decided to kick him out as soon as his job stopped paying him and his rent bounced. He's the one who found him there, when he busted open the locked door to empty the place out for the next renter."

"It's a horrible story, sure, but I don't know what it has to do with the show. I mean, at least it ended well for him. He got treatment for the stroke, right?"

Liam frowned. "That's where the story gets really messed up. They sent him off to hospital, but when he got there, SyneDeal's medical insurance denied coverage. The stroke happened during strenuous exercise, making it a lifestyle-choice condition they didn't have to pay for. So the hospital orderlies just dumped him in the nearest homeless shelter. He only managed to send us the application because a volunteer at the shelter took dictation for him. Not that we could have taken him on even if we'd wanted to," Liam added, almost as an afterthought. "There's an update note here saying he died of septicaemia a few months ago anyway."

"God, Liam. That's horrible." Mary looked like she was ready to throw up—good thing she had all those cleaning products in the trolley, close to hand. "Why'd you have to go and keep me here just to tell me that? If this is some sick joke…"

"It's horrible, yes. But it's true, just the same. And what I need is your reaction to hearing the story. What does it make you want to do?"

"What, other than find someplace for a quiet cry? I really don't know what you want to hear me say, Mr Argyle."

Liam wasn't entirely sure either. Some spark of rebellion against the status quo? Some radical new idea, or even an old one refurbished for modern times? Anything that would help Liam fulfil his urge to take *The Grass is Greener*'s special eye implants and shove them so far up the Corporate Council's bottom line, they'd be smelling lens fluid for the rest of their pampered lives. But if he couldn't get a reaction out of someone like Mary, then what hope was there for any of it?

"Let's try another one," he said in measured tones, scanning his open pages for an even worse story, one that might provoke that spark he needed so desperately to see. "How about this file here—

"I don't really want to hear anything like that last one again."

"This is important, Mary. Trust me." He turned away from the screen to look her in the eyes, and something in his voice rang true, maybe for the first time ever in the fluorescent-lit halls of Tantamount Mews. He hadn't said anything that felt so nakedly honest in a long, long time.

"Alright, then," the agency worker said, in a near-whisper.

"Thank you. Now make sure you focus on what the story makes you want to do, what it makes you want to change. And brace yourself, because it's not pretty."

Across the shining desktop, Mary gulped nervously but nodded.

"This application's from New York. A luxury apartment right in the shadow of RedCorp's North American HQ in the Spiral. But the application isn't for either of the Corporate execs who live there. It's for the child who lives with them.

"Not their child—not anyone's child. Just a healthy ten-year-old enbie child sold to Triumph at the age of two by a single mother in Louisiana who may even have genuinely thought she was offering the little one a better future and a better education with some well-off Corporate couple somewhere—and not just trading the child in for much-needed debt relief after all the flood damage to their family soy farm."

"What are we talking about here, exactly?" Mary asked, with a hint of a growl beneath her normally placid tones.

"Legal slavery. Did the mother know they were selling their child into slavery? I'd like to think not, but the application doesn't really say. All we know is that Triumph placed the child with manager parents within the Corporation who got a pay rise and better prospects as long as they made sure the Corp's new property stayed fed and watered in between sessions with the AI.

"The child was more valuable to the Corp than any exec could ever be. Triumph makes its money off independent AI agents, and that illusion of independence doesn't come cheap. It takes hours of human input, and reaction and adaptation, for an AI program's machine learning to reach an acceptably believable level of response. And it's even harder to keep them cutting-edge, able to adapt to the changes in society so they can seamlessly sell all the latest products and shows—shows like ours—to unsuspecting brains around the world. It's a bit of an industry secret, but that's why North American children are by far the most valuable assets to a Corp like Triumph. They can teach AIs everything they need to flawlessly adopt the standard, contemporary human mannerisms that are understood and expected around the world. That's why the child labour sweatshops of our times have moved back to the West."

When Liam stopped reading from the file and looked over at Mary, the woman had a rough tissue in hand, probably grabbed from the nearby trolley. "And these are real people?" she asked, with a slight quiver in her voice.

"They certainly are. We only got to see this child's story in the applications file because the management family thought they could pad their pay with agent royalties on merch deals if they made it on the show. But there are hundreds of thousands like them in North America alone, and nearly just as many all over Europe. More every day, thanks to that landmark Corporate Council ruling back in 2064. So, what do you say about that?"

Mary blushed, and her eyes flicked away from Liam, over to the art on the walls. "Well, it's not really fair, is it?"

It was only a start, a glimmer, but the words were music to Liam's funny-shaped ears. "Go on," he said, leaning forward.

"It's just—nobody should have the right to turn people into things, you know? That's even worse than what they make us agency workers do, and nobody should be allowed to do that. Not even the big Corporations." Mary lowered her voice to a whisper, as if uttering sacrilege. "Someone should do something about it."

Liam grinned, a surge of hope rising within him. Yes! There it was!

"But that's just silly thoughts," Mary carried on, shaking her head as her voice returned to normal. "Everybody knows there's nothing anybody can do about it. Not anymore."

And she was right. That was the rub. Those were the words Liam had sensed prowling around the guarded gates of his consciousness. The ones he couldn't bear to express himself, not even in his present, rebellious mindset.

Life and death in the Corporate Council-run world-state were tragic, but the stories were useless as long as there was no way to act on them, to turn them into a drive for change. The various political systems in the lingering nation-states around the world were just different spins on the same joke, different takes on the same parlour trick to keep people content and entertained.

The only decisions with real impact on people's lives came from the Corporations, and the only say individuals ever had was as a consumer, not as a voter.

Unless you counted placebo votes like the ones Liam himself conned the world with on every Sunday elimination episode of *The Grass is Greener*. And Liam certainly didn't.

But maybe there was a way to trick the system. To switch the placebo for the real thing and see what happened when a body used to sugar pills and tall tales got a dose of real medicine coursing through its political veins.

Maybe the best way to make people realise how badly they've been conned, for generations, was to pull off an even greater con—and then pull back the curtain, so everyone could see how the trick was done.

Across the desk, Mary coughed politely. "Is that everything, then?"

"What? Yes, sorry. Just having a bit of a moment there. Thank you so much for your help."

Mary nodded and rose to her feet, confusion mingling with relief on her face. She yanked the door open, muscled the trolley into position, and made a hasty exit—but not before flashing Liam a little conspirator's smile, which he returned tenfold.

8

A fist pounded on his office door for what felt like the hundredth time that day. So much for Sunday being a day of rest. It opened before Liam even had a chance to respond, just wide enough for Ms Lee to stick her head through.

"The contestants are all done with makeup and ready for the launch show, but they're getting restless, Liam. If you're still plan on speaking with them before we go live, you'd better do it now."

"Sure. Thanks. I'll be right there." Liam rose to his feet, and Norma Lee scampered off, leaving his door half-open.

Best get this over with, he told himself, trying to work up even the slightest degree of motivation, let alone enthusiasm, for meeting this season's crop of losers and lowlifes before they got fed to the existential meatgrinder that *The Grass is Greener* had become. And probably had been from the very start. At least he could admit that much to himself now.

This year, he'd managed to fob off[1]—sorry, "delegate"—the screening interview process to Lee and Akintola. So he'd been able to avoid having to meet any of these fine folks in person. Until now, that was.

He strode into the Mews's cavernous central warehouse area

---

[1] "To pocket stealthily"

where the *Grass is Greener* set, which had taken the ever-diligent Mary days to erect, stood gleaming. A dream in pungent, emerald green nanopaint and cheap plywood that would shine like gold in the AR lenses of viewers around the world.

Beyond the padded green couches where the world would meet its latest sacrifices in about fifteen minutes, there was his own open central platform area where he would address the camera and pace to and fro, dynamically going nowhere once again. And beyond that, in the far corner, the show's gleaming, spotlight-bathed operating table, flanked by the not-so-tender arms of the state-of-the-art surgical robots. Their fancy, modernised new operating theatre was everything their original basic set-up hadn't been: all the best thrills and useless scares money can buy, with none of the humanity.

That's where each grateful candidate would open their eyes wide and try not to scream as they received their very own, proprietary eyeNet lenses—the mandatory ocular camera implant that made *The Grass is Greener* so unique—before the watching eyes of GiGalos around the world. Great fun, and always good for the ratings, too.

In the half-shadows just to the side of the floodlit stage, Mary had set up the usual row of cheap folding chairs for the contestants to use while they were off-stage. And sure enough, there they all were, lined up like bickering, fair-stand ducks.

Liam had thought he knew what to expect just from reading the profiles, seeing the pictures, and having to watch the interviews over and over again as they edited them down to the desired spin they wanted on each candidate in preparation for tonight's big show. But in the flesh, the reality was a thousand times worse.

It was the clash that did it. Not just in their looks, which was bad enough when you had Davy Muriithi, still in his soiled blue Kenyan road service overalls, sitting awkwardly at one end of the row, next to the eye-watering and ever-shifting mobile fashion display that was Sabeen al-Amin. And at the other end, wizened little Hattie Hughes was showing off her latest bundle of pink knitwork to the unnaturally lanky and entirely baffled teenage Neriene Cartwright, their visiting Martian.

It figured their only two native English-speakers this season would band together at the premiere. But everywhere else, the true, stunning clash lay in the sounds, with voices from all walks of life competing to be heard in more languages than Liam had ever heard in one place all at once. Not for the first time, he regretted not pushing back harder—or, truth be told, at all—against the directive from upon high at Corporate for this season. People were complaining about how many Londoners ended up making it onto the first two seasons of the show, and season three had to be truly international to maintain its ratings.

Was it Liam's fault that Greatest London had all nationalities and cultures close to hand and the show could save a bundle recruiting locally as a rule? No, now he had to use the same budget to pay the extra expense of bringing all these candidates into London every week for the live shows. Why keep things simple when you can let RedCorp's almighty Marketing division muck everything up for everybody else? And that's how he ended up with contestants yammering[1] in Spanish, Brazilian, Arabic, Swahili, Russian, Mandarin, Japanese, Indonesian, and Hindi—all dreaming of that grand prize, a one-way ticket to the easy life on Paradise Mars, and all desperate not to miss out on drawing attention and scoring points early on.

At least Corporate had found a solution to the most pressing problem this created—how he was supposed to run a show when he could only speak to two out of his twelve contestants.

Digging through the menu in his AR display, Liam found and fired up the shiny new live translation app Corporate's R&D boffins had sent through for the occasion. It was just a beta version, not yet available on the market, but it already looked as polished as an AR mirror as it loaded up, just for him.

---

[1] "To lament"

Sure, some of the contestants would have their own, off-the-shelf, one-way translator apps. He knew for a fact that someone like Sabeen Al-Amin wouldn't be caught dead without one. But Liam's new toy was something else entirely.

Options and menus appeared in a little window at the bottom edge of his field of sight, and words flashed into existence as AR highlights over the contestants' heads, one by one. From the depth of the off-stage shadows, Liam let out a low whistle of appreciation. Not only was the app translating each contestant's words and displaying them in comic book-style speech bubbles in real time, but it also added little tags identifying the language, along with notes keeping track of all relevant info from what they were saying.

Liam stood hidden in the shadows of the on-set glare and watched the latest crop for a minute or so, making sure the no-doubt hideously expensive new app had enough time to fully work its magic. He had to admit it was impressive stuff—after only a few sentences, it had identified Davy Muriithi's accent and vocabulary as coming from the region around Kibera, southwest of Nairobi, and provided a handy list of cultural, geographical, and historical references. Liam had never been to, or had any real interest in, the area. But there was no denying the info could be very handy in conversation. He soon had the same thing for all eleven of the human contestants, and with his newfound wealth of trivia about everything from Mexico D.F. to rural Iraq to Fiji, he strode out of the shadows and into the light.

The babel of babble petered out as he approached, and he fired off his best, toothy game-time smile.

"I know some of you can't understand me, but as ever, Mother RedCorp has provided." Little green icons blinked into existence in the air next to each contestant as he spoke, confirming that his new app had successfully linked with their own AR displays and was broadcasting a live translation of his every word in their preferred language settings. "Let me start by saying how excited we are that this season *The Grass is Greener* has the richest and the most diverse selection of contestants in the show's history, from all around the Red-connected world."

"So wait, does this mean you can understand me?" asked the social media sin eater Georgi Popov in his native Russian—with his tech experience, it made sense that he'd be the first to figure out that this new app didn't make any sense unless it went both ways.

Liam's grin twinkled in the spotlights. "You bet, Georgi. And the rest of you, too. Hey, if it helps, feel free to think of me as your resident speaker in tongues."

Silence reigned around the busy set as his joke fell flatter than a poorly aimed suborbital shuttle. It was almost enough to make Liam wish they'd all start blabbering[1] again. Then again, judging by the baffled looks on most of their faces, they probably had no idea what he was talking about. The only two to show any sort of reaction were the religious-minded contestants: the flamboyant Jesus Hernández Dzul from Mexico D.F. and the unassuming Shou Ito from Kyoto-ku, and they were too affronted to be amused.

"Welp," said Liam, clapping his hands and rubbing them together to distract from the embarrassment of his first meeting with his new contestants, but also wondering why he even cared, "unless anyone has any further questions, let's get this show on the Red, shall we?"

He turned, giving a thumbs-up to Barry as the man lumbered past with a bundle of ancient-looking hardwired power cables in his arms. The technician nodded back, took a deep breath, then hollered, "Positions, everyone! Going live in ninety seconds!"

Behind Liam, the questions from the rapidly recovering contestants died on their lips, and the very air in the Mews seemed to crystallise into a lattice of eagerness and tension. Liam took the opportunity to flee from the scene of his latest foot-in-mouth incident and step up onto the particle board of the set's centre stage. He

---

[1] "To speak like an infant"

stepped over to the little smudge on the floor that was his usual marker, stood straight, and grinned into the spotlight glare.

It was funny, and probably very symbolic, he thought, as his eyes got used to the glare. Here he was, standing on cheap, flimsy particle board. But in less than a minute now, the entire world would start watching, and through the magic of AR illusion, they'd see him pacing across a floor of shiniest, sturdiest marble.

He took a deep breath, pushing all such musings out of his head. He didn't have time for random thoughts right now. There was only room for the show, and he had to surrender himself to it fully, just like every big weekly show over the past two seasons.

A slight touch of panic rose within him, whispering that everything had changed now, and it had been a long, long winter since the season two finale. Was he even still capable of working the old magic, pushing his own self out of the way and letting the show speak through his mouth?

Yes, damnit, he told himself, quashing the fear. Everything depended on him keeping up appearances here. If he wanted the freedom to take his new work and his ideas on the little test drive he'd been planning for after the show, now would be the worst time to raise suspicion.

So, if they wanted a host, he'd just have to give 'em the most host they ever grossed. First past the post.

Blissfully, the little light he'd been waiting for started blinking above podcam one, and he could stop filling his mind with rhyming drivel to distract from the wait and the stress. It blinked five times, then went solid green—the show was live, broadcasting around the world, and this season, for the first time, beyond.

"Boys and girls, gentle enbies all across the spectrum, it's that time again." He paused, grinning his damnedest into the dazzling light as the canned applause rang through speakers and bone-conduction buds across the world. "It's time once again to put it all on the line, no holds barred. It's time to step into the ring, dip into lives from all walks of life, all around the globe, and find out who has it bad, who has it worse, and where…"

He trailed off, lifting a hand in scripted appeal to a non-existent audience, and nodding as the pre-recorded shout, "The Grass is Greener!" echoed in perfectly artificial chorus.

"That's right, folks. And what a line-up of contestants we have for you this season. Our third year, broadcasting live from Tantamount Mews in Old London Town. Of course, three's a special number, you know. Three atoms in a water molecule. Three bears living in the cottage in the woods. And only three years of claim-free coverage before you qualify for reduced rates on RedCorp's own MediCalc health plan, sign up while the offer lasts!" Liam paused again as per the script flowing before his eyes, while the feed played laughter so thoroughly canned that it was sure to keep its taste until Doomsday—even if that taste was bilious and bitter in Liam's mind. He gave it a mental shrug and soldiered on. "So that's why we here at *The Grass is Greener* have listened to you, our loyal viewers, and decided to make this season, our third year, something special too."

In the corner of Liam's vision, the contestants, lined up in their drastically varying levels of finery, tensed up as one. Their moment in the augmented limelight was finally here. If it weren't for the shepherding presence of Ms Lee on one end of the line and Mary Artworthy on the other, Liam wouldn't have been surprised to see one or two of the most jittery ones stand up and run straight onto the stage. Anything to secure an extra few seconds in the eye of the world, an extra chance to make their claim to victimised fame and earn a life of extraterritorial luxury among the corporate elite on Paradise Mars.

It was time to kick this pile of voyeuristic crap into gear.

"This year," he boomed, larger than life, "we've got an incredible batch of contestants for your viewing pleasure, from all around the world. Never before has our show explored so many different settings, so many neighbourhoods, and so many back alleys of this global village we call home. And even beyond!"

Liam cocked one hand against his hip and waved a finger in the air, almost scolding his imaginary audience. "Believe it or not, we've even got an extra-terrestrial among our contestants this year! The first human born off of Earth, up on Paradise Mars itself. Of course, the whole point of the show is to win a ticket from Earth to Mars, not the opposite. You think she read the fine print upside-down? After all, they say there's no up or down in space."

Liam felt the grin congeal on his face as he paused for the stupid canned laughter again. He'd pushed back against the joke, if you could even call it that. But the Editor had insisted. A little bit of planetary pride never hurt anybody, he said.

But Liam wasn't sure that was true anymore. Over on the contestants' waiting bench, poor gawky Neriene Cartwright—her body twisted a thousand ways by her low-gravity gestation and clone-birth, plus more than a decade of treatments since then—bowed her lofty head, as if trying to draw her stretched-out form into a ball. Her elfin features flushed red, and Liam knew he'd have a crying Martian teenager on his hands if he didn't cut the crap, and soon.

"Aww, I'm just having a laugh, you know me," he said, ditching the other two pages of Mars-bashing "jokes" the Editor had foisted[1] on him. "So, without further ado, let's hear it for our contestants." Liam raised his voice, as if to speak over piped-in cheering that existed only in the viewers' minds. "Your eyes and ears for the next three months. The biggest victims our Solar System has to offer! Come on up here, you lot!"

He waved an arm, urging them up, and the two stewards stepped back, releasing the hounds. Relief positively oozed from both women's faces as the eleven contestants with physical bodies rose to their feet, pushed off from the waiting area, and made their slightly dazed way onto the bright-lit stage.

---

[1] From the Middle Dutch *vuist* or "fist," referring to cheating at dice games by hiding a loaded dice in the palm of your closed fist, hence the current usage, "to work in by a trick."

"Come on, don't be shy! It's far too late for that!" Liam shouted, leaving a gap for the stupid piped-in laughter once again.

9

The men and women from all around the Earth did their best to smile at the cameras as they each followed their own AR arrow to where they were supposed to stand on stage. Neriene Cartwright didn't smile, but moved to stand in her spot behind Liam with gloomy resignation. Liam, who was used to being one of the tallest people in the room, was keenly aware of the towering, low-gravity-born teenager looming behind him.

He was just glad that, true to their waivers and contractual obligations, none of them was paying any special attention to the gap between them all in the middle of the stage. The servers back in Barry's digital den were busy inserting the projection of a gnarled elderly person of indiscriminate gender, age, or origins. The show's final and lowest body mass index contestant stood there in Liam's AR overlay, looking just as shell-shocked and apprehensive as all the other contestants. The illusion was all the more credible thanks to the little details the AI had finally decided to add: the shock of pure white hair, the patched beige suit, and that little shiny silk bow-tie.

If the Editor ever discovered Liam's little game of deception here, maybe that last nod to the man's latest affectations would buy him a bit of clemency. Or at least a few minutes' head start before they set the RedCorp rent-a-cops on him.

"Don't worry, everyone," Liam called out to the invisible crowd, with a nervous giggle to cover his unease. "We know how hard it is to break the ice at a party, and with four billion of you out there watching us right now, this is the biggest party in the Universe! So we've got clips for you lucky viewers, all the best bits from our interviews and selection process, to help you get to know our fine new contestants. To get the conversation started, that sort of thing. Let's have a looksee!"

Liam held his suddenly aching smile for another second or two, until the little light on the side of podcam one flashed from green to orange. They'd be offline for the usual four minutes and thirty seconds, and Liam could give his cheek muscles a blissful rest.

Feeling like he was almost scowling in compensation, Liam waved off the querying looks of the contestants. "You all stay put. We'll be back live in no time at all. Best advice I can give you is to try to get used to the lights and plan ahead for when that light over there goes green again."

He left them standing awkwardly in their assigned spots and stomped over toward the operating theatre on the far side of the stage, with its table decked out in shining *Grass is Greener* emerald and its gleaming steel robotic surgery arms. Barry Fletcher was already there, on his knees, with his head buried in the cable assembly at the base of the surgical unit.

"Hey, man—" Liam started to say, before a loud thump from the innards of the machine and a choice curse from Barry cut him off.

"Damnit, Liam. Mr Argyle, I mean," came the man's muffled voice. "You scared me."

Liam winced. "Sorry about that. I wanted to—"

"Can't hear a thing, you know. Just give me a minute. I'll be straight out."

Grunting, Barry started pulling himself out of the belly of the beast. Liam shifted his eyes to the feed monitor window at the top of his display. It was as good an excuse as any to avoid having to watch the man extricate himself from the cables and machinery. There was something obscene about physical hardware in the era of incorporeal omni-connectivity—the least he could do was avoid adding insult to injury by staring as the man pulled his leg out of a tangle of power leads.

Precious seconds of respite trickled by as the technician panted and wheezed. On-screen, the highlight reel shifted from lithe Fnu Cinta as she crept, in some sort of bulky disguise, into the middle of a rowdy bunch of Komodo Dragons, to Georgi Popov wading through the avalanche of insults and sexist slurs in a Russian celebrity's social media feeds. It had just started in on the footage of stoop-shouldered Gang Luo mopping the floor around the thrashing form of one of the patrons of his VR porn parlour when Barry finally worked his way free and stood before Liam, rubbing at a red spot on his balding head.

"Right," Liam said, looking away from the feed monitor window with a sigh of relief. "Sorry about that, again."

"Oh, don't you worry. Like my own mother says, a good knock upside the head every now and again is just life's way of keeping you honest. So anyway, what can I do you for?"

Liam struggled briefly with the concept of what this poor man's upbringing must have been like, then gave up with a shake of his stage makeup-caked head. "I just wanted to congratulate you on doing such a bang-on job with, you know, contestant number twelve."

"You mean Raja Cassar," Barry added in a stage whisper, still rubbing his sore head.

Right on cue, the construct's own falsified introduction clip started playing at the bottom of Liam's display: the old-timer hobbled down a back alley, reminiscing for the camera the whole time. The scene could have been in New York, Lagos, Guangzhou, or Quito itself, but Liam knew it would be pumped from road maps of Malta, which the computer had decided was the ideal place to base "Raja Cassar," their enbie fictional contestant designed to be relatable for all humanity.

Liam hated the name. It felt so fake to his excessively prominent ears.

"Right, hir. I also wanted to make doubly sure these machines here are ready," Liam added, eager to change the subject and feeling vaguely that causing cranial trauma to one of his employees just for the sake of a compliment wasn't necessarily best managerial practice. "We don't want another incident like last year—the Editor says a bit of surprise blood and gore can work once, for the shock value. But if it happens again, it won't be worth the cost of the reconstructive surgery."

On the stage behind him, Liam heard some multilingual mutters as the waiting contestants shuffled nervously. He pushed down a pang of pity for them—they knew what they were signing up for. He had bigger Corporate fish to fry. "And have they all signed off on their Binns waivers?" he asked, leaning in and dropping his voice to a whisper.

Barry leaned in as well, until his condensation-coated goggles were nearly pressed against the orange stage gunk covering Liam's forehead. "Yup. The last ones came in today. Wouldn't have let them on stage otherwise."

"Well, that's something at least." Liam didn't know if he could handle another contestant like Juliette Binns, back in the first season, who clearly hadn't read all of the fine print and panicked when time came for her to receive her eyeNet lens implants. Last he'd heard, she was finally settling into Elysium Fields, the fancy VR therapy residence RedCorp had pulled strings to get her committed to—she hardly ever tried to escape anymore.

The aptly named Binns waivers Legal had cooked up made sure the contestants were fully aware, consenting, and psychologically ready to undergo the procedure.

In the feed monitor screen in the corner of Liam's eye, rotund Hernández Dzul rose grinning from the sewers of Mexico City, covered in grease, with a fat-filled sampler test tube in his hand. Then the feed cut to *The Grass is Greener*'s emerald beckoning-hand logo, snapping its fingers in time to the rising beat of the intro song.

That was Liam's cue. Nodding at Barry, who returned to his devices for one last tweak before closing them up, the host sauntered back into the middle of the crowded stage, just as the light on podcam one flashed green again.

"Amazing, isn't it! So many lives, so many experiences, and yet so little time to get to know them all. Over the next twelve weeks, you'll get to dive into their worlds, from the fantastic fatberg under Mexico D.F. to the roadkill-strewn motorways of the Kenyan plains. And it is you, with your vote, who will choose who gets eliminated, one by one, until only a single champion is left. Seeing through their eyes, thanks to our very own eyeNet lens implants," Liam said, forcing the grin as he swept a suited arm over to the gleaming operating theatre, "you'll decide who is the worst of the worst off. The most deserving of our grand prize, a life of comfort among the elites from our world's great Corporations on Paradise Mars."

Liam paused, breaking for the virtual applause. But before he could resume reading from his prompter, a more literal break shattered the silence behind him—and someone's skull, too, judging by the crunch and the cry of pain.

"No line crashing! Nobody's getting their implants before I do!" The words appeared in a jaunty font in the translated speech bubble above statuesque Sabeen Al-Amin's head, completely at odds with the splatter of blood coating one karate-chop extended hand and the sleeve of her flowing, rainbow-hued designer gown. Poor Matheus Carvalho, the Brazilian mosquito disease researcher, crouched at her sparkling-pumped feet, clutching his bleeding scalp and letting out a string of curses in Portuguese that were tactfully filtered out by the translation app.

"Wait, there's a line?" squeaked lithe Fnu Cinta, the Komodo dragon sperm wrangler, in Indonesian. It was just Liam's luck that one of them would understand what Al-Amin had said, even without the benefit of the translator app.

"Now, now, there's no need for panic!" Liam shouted, trying to restore a bit of order. He had no trouble picturing what the Editor would have to say if he let this get out of hand. "Plenty of eyeNet lenses for everyone, after all!"

But Liam's words, translated into as many languages as needed to ensure everyone present understood, only served to inflame the contestants even more.

"What do you mean, panic? Are they getting their lenses before us?" asked the willowy Martian-born teenager, nudging forward just one step before squat Georgi Popov shoved her out of the way.

"The first feed to go live always gets the most viewers! Out of my way!" he shouted, before adding a yelp of pain as Hattie Hughes plunged one of her knitting needles into the Russian's forearm.

"Dearie me, whatever happened to common courtesy. Nobody needs that prize more than I do. Old ladies and locals first!"

With many shoves, uncountable kicks, and much pulling of hair, the contestants charged as one toward the operating theatre, completely ignoring Liam Argyle's aggravated shouts and desperate flapping hand gestures.

The sharp surgical arms jerked to life as their sensors reacted to a dozen conflicting signals and almost seemed to mock Liam's own panicked gesticulations as they rose into the air. Polished and disinfected steel gleamed in the stage lights.

Fnu Cinta was the fastest on her feet—a decade of collecting sperm samples from rutting Komodo Dragons had given her one hell of a sprint speed over short distances. She leapt onto the operating table with one eager bound, as if the slavering beasts at her hiking-booted heels were as deadly as the ones she dealt with on a daily basis. And they might well be. At least the giant slavering lizards were acting for their own benefit and not to impress every other dragon in the world.

True to Barry's meticulous programming, the surgical unit registered the patient on the operating table and started in on the eyeNet lens implant sequence, little compartments opening and closing, surgical arms zipping left and right, up and down.

On the table, Fnu Cinta tried to grin for the cameras and relax as the edged metal limbs flexed ever closer to her open eyes, with the dangling little processor and audio unit that would soon be tucked into her tear ducts. But her grin quickly turned to twitchy panic—as ten other irate contestants jostled for position all around the operating table, some to be next in line, others to yank Cinta out of the mechanical beast's clutches. Liam hoped their new construct was keeping up with this nonsense, or else he'd be the next one on the chopping block.

The sight of Barry Fletcher in the shadows on the far side of the eyeNet implant theatre, clutching his balding pate with his mouth forming a perfect "O" of horror, was far from reassuring and would have been comical under any other circumstances. But Liam shared the sentiment—in a few seconds, they'd end up making history with the first lobotomy broadcast live around the world. The Editor would never let him live it down. Especially if it happened before the lenses were even live, to catch it in first-person perspective.

He stepped forward, ready to grab the nearest contestant and whack some sense into them, live feed be damned. Hell, it'd be nice to be the one delivering the blows on stage for a change.

But instead it was the contestants who rushed to meet Liam, with the Mexican fatberg diver Hernández Dzul stumbling backwards, straight onto his shiny Saville Row shoes, while Georgi Popov drove an elbow into the host's chest, cutting short his cry of pain and protest. Liam suddenly wished he'd had his little crisis of Corporate faith sooner, so he could have pushed for all of the contestants to be computer-generated this year.

Through watering eyes, he watched, breathless, as the gleaming metal arms followed the branches of some obscure decision tree deep in their programming, diverting a couple of the sharpest and deadliest-looking limbs from the eyeNet implant operation and swinging them to and fro, creating a whirling defensive perimeter around their visibly relieved patient.

"If we all rush the machine at once, we can still get her down from that table," grumbled the wild-eyed Fijian nanopaint drying supervisor Tanoa Sharma. Luckily, no one else spoke Hindi, and Liam wasn't about to translate for them.

And so, the contestants milled around at the less lethal edge of the operating theatre, patting down ruffled articles of clothing and smiling for the cameras, as if it were all a great lark and absolutely not a momentary lapse of any pretence of civility at the mere thought of someone else getting their live feed up first, Even if they had nearly decapitated one of their fellow contestants, live, before the watching eyes of the world.

Not for the first time, Liam decided it could be no coincidence that live is just evil spelt backwards.

"If you'll excuse me," he said with a sigh as he edged his way through the assembled contestants, as formal and polite as only a stressed-out Englishman could be. Finally, Liam stood at the front of the crowd, staring down the over-excited scalpel blades. He shot a questioning glance over toward Barry, who shrugged his rolling shoulders in response, helpless. Figuring he probably didn't have that much left to lose at this point, Liam tried to look as unthreatening as possible as he stepped forward into the reach of the machine arms.

The gleaming blades paused for a moment, seeming to debate the merits of disembowelling Liam on the spot, before deciding he wasn't worth their time and retreating partially—but not quite completely—into the confines of the central unit.

Breathing a heartfelt sigh of relief, Liam turned to face the contestants and the cameras beyond, with his first genuine smile of the night.

"Gentlefolk of the Red-connected world," he boomed, in time with the little notification that popped up in his display, signalling the end of the first implant operation, "I give you our first live contestant feed of this third and greatest season of *The Grass is Greener*! Come on, Fnu, sit up and let the folks see what the world looks like from your eyes!"

Liam grinned away, in control once again, and watched in his own little monitor window as the Indonesian's live feed came online and took over the main broadcast for a moment. It was an odd experience, looking through someone else's eyes as they blinked in the overhead operating theatre light, cast a nervous glance at the sharp metal still very near their face, then sat up and turned to look at Liam's own, bespoke-suited back. Damn, were his ears really that wide, seen from behind?

"My name isn't Fnu, you know," said the tame voice behind him in translated Indonesian, sending him off-script again the very second he'd thought he'd recovered some hold on the course of the show.

Liam's grin faltered for a moment, and he turned to face the khaki-clad contestant. "What do you mean, your name isn't Fnu?" he said in a whisper, all the more ridiculous for the literal billions of people listening in on the conversation through this lady's fancy new implants—whatever her name was. "If you're not our contestant, we can have those eyeNet lenses back out again in two swipes of a finger, you know."

"No, I'm definitely your contestant," stammered Whateverhernamewas, looking more nervous than she did facing down robotic scalpels and an angry mob at the same time. "But the name's Cinta. Just Cinta. We don't use any other names. Fnu is just some rubbish you Westerners keep sticking us with to make us fit into your forms when they demand a given name. 'First name unknown.'"

First name unknown. Liam gave himself the mental equivalent of a slap upside the head, then fired off a fresh grin, for the sake of all the viewers hidden behind those muddy green eyes. He leaned in toward her, turning his whisper into something straight out of an ancient black-and-white film.

"Well, just between you and me, that sounds like a pretty bad life already, having names that aren't yours forced on you all the time. Bit of a leg up on the competition before we even get started, eh?"

Liam sealed the cheesy persona with a wink, and felt a guilty rush of pleasure when Cinta—as the updated name in the AR display now read—obliged him with a blush.

"Righty-oh," he proclaimed, spinning back around to face the rest of them. "We'll be doing things in an orderly fashion from here on in, people. None of this running around willy-nilly nonsense." They started grumbling and pushing forward again, but Liam raised a silencing hand—and somehow, miraculously, it worked. "The blind hand of the almighty random number generator decrees that the next lucky contestant to get their implants will be... Ms Hattie Hughes!"

Liam stepped aside and invited the little lady forward with a dramatic sweep of the arm, ignoring the other contestants' scowls and the wizened hellion's smirk of satisfaction. To be honest, he was glad to see the back of her. She still had one of those knitting needles left, and Popov was going to need some serious medical attention from Mary before they could retrieve the other one from his arm.

The surgical machine went about its flashy business, unhindered from there on in, and Liam slipped into automatic mode as well. Reading from the AR prompter scrolling before his eyes, he vaunted the merits of *The Grass is Greener*'s iconic eyeNet broadcast lenses, teasing that—due to popular demand, of course—RedCorp was working on an officially licensed, off-the-shelf version that might just be available for pre-order soon. So viewers had to make sure they stayed tuned to the show to avoid missing out!

Poor, salivating bastards around the world. As if Corporate would ever saw off the branch the show was built on by giving this tech to the public and losing exclusive distribution of the world's ultimate voyeuristic drug. There would be no amateur copycats to dilute the show's audience, not on RedCorp's watch.

The script helped Liam keep the easy banter going, providing a soundtrack everybody would be ignoring anyway as they watched the surgical arms slice, thrust, and squeeze, with morbid fascination. Not a single person in the wide world outside the rusting warehouse walls of Tantamount Mews gave two hoots about his half-hearted jokes about the hundreds of throbbing mosquito bites covering Matheus Carvalho's blood-crusted scalp or the lacquered walking-stick in the non-existent hands of Raja Cassar. Liam couldn't see why he should care, either.

At least this lot were eager and willing to submit to the operation and get their eyeNet lenses. The extra waivers had done their job—no repeat of the Juliette Binns incident this year. The surgical unit even did a credible job of pretending there was a physical body on the table to operate on when Raja Cassar's turn came around. Even for the GiG, which was surreal at the best of times, it was a strange experience watching the feed's augmented version of reality, with the surgical arms slicing into the Maltese old-timer's virtual flesh. In the "real" version of reality, the modified eyeNet lens unit Barry had rigged for the fake feed was sprouting the little polymer tendrils that would keep it moving around like a real, hobbling person, both for the benefit of the viewers and to give the servers a realistic base for their falsification.

All these fresh new live feeds would still need intensive monitoring by the Mews's threadbare production team, just like every year—well, except for the Raja Cassar feed, which wouldn't need monitoring so much as digital babysitting. But Liam didn't think they'd get anyone trying to back out of the deal and stop the live feed, like Binns had in the end. Hell, if anything, they should probably be more worried about one of these whack jobs clawing their own eyes out trying to overclock the implants, just to give their feed an advantage over the others.

These new guys, gals, and enbies were lucky Liam was the Supervising Producer at the Mews and Ed wasn't running the show here anymore. Well, at least not on a daily basis, that is. Because the Editor would have eaten eager bunnies like this alive. With him, they were at least going to get a fair shot at making their case to the voting public at large.

Well, more or less fair. Fairish, definitely. Depending on what orders came down from on high. Liam could only resist so much, after all. And he needed to keep up appearances if he was going to have any chance of pulling off his scheme without having the Tulip drop on him like a ton of designer bricks.

At last, the final set of eyeNet lenses was tucked neatly away in the final pair of eye sockets, and the line of feed monitor lights in his display turned completely green.

"And there you have it, gentlefolks of the Solar System! Twelve feeds, twelve lives, all available for you to watch at your convenience, wherever you may be, at any hour of the day or night. So please, once again this year—do your duty! Submit our contestants' lives to your scrutiny! And then vote, massively! Because it's only with your help that we'll be able to sort the wheat from the chaff. To discover who, among the twelve contestants on this very stage, truly has it the worst of us all and is most deserving of our grand prize. It's only thanks to you, with your help, that we'll be able to find out where—" obligatory pause for effect and shining grin— "the grass is greener!"

He paused to leave time for the canned cheer, yet again. Mars almighty, Liam hated it.

"So, get to it, then! Thank you all, and I'll see you right here next week, same GiG time, same GiG place! You're the best!"

With such meaningless platitudes, he rode out the show's blissfully short credits sequence, until the light on podcam one finally went red.

But, of course, Liam couldn't drop the fake smiles, not even then. Not with twelve feeds currently still live and mostly pointed directly at him, along with the eyes of his contestants—and the beady electronic lens bobbing at the end of its black polymer tentacles, marking where he was supposed to pretend "Raja Cassar" was currently standing.

"Thanks to all of you, too," he told them, marvelling at how easy it was to rely on the new translator app to bridge the gap between cultures and continents. "You were amazing. We're going to have such a great show this season. Our best year yet!"

Corporate hadn't bothered to provide him with a script for this bit, but Liam figured a bit of extra, behind-the-scenes buttering for the sake of the viewers behind those eyes couldn't hurt any.

"I don't want to sound ungrateful, but are these things supposed to itch so much?" asked the Martian Neriene in her flat, Corporate-standard English, blinking and rubbing at her owlish eyes.

Liam reached up to pat the teenager on the shoulder. Earth was an alien planet to her, after all. It wouldn't kill him to show a little sympathy—especially since she was still the daughter of a Corporate bigwig, even after leaving the libertarian cocoon of Paradise Mars.

"Chin up, my dear, and don't worry. There's a car waiting outside to take you straight back to the Corporate Council embassy downtown, and I know they'll have all the best meds there to take care of it for you. As for the rest of you," he added, turning to face the ten contestants who at least looked like they belonged to the same species as him, "there's a bus on its way to shuttle you all to Biggin Hill. The same RedCorp supersonic jets that brought you here are still waiting to shuttle you back home, you lucky devils."

"Some of us are luckier than others," said squat Tanoa Sharma, with a sarcastic little grunt. "Four stops between here and Fiji, making the trip three times as long as it needs to be, just so others can get home first. Including our… friend, from Malta, which is completely rid—"

Liam rushed to shush the Fijian nanopaint watcher. "Now, now, let's not start picking on anyone else, especially not Mx Cassar, who deserves all our respect. Just like my old Nan used to say, offer it up for your sins, Mx Sharma! Or for your votes, in this case, if you get my drift."

The giant Fijian had opened his mouth to protest some more, but shut it at Liam's words. They looked for all the world like a giant frog who had just swallowed a particularly juicy fly.

Mary Artworthy and Norma Lee fell into place on either side of the flock of contestants with resigned efficiency and herded them off down the Mews's central hallway and to the roll-up warehouse doors that sorely needed replacing.

It was only when Cassar's nightmarish walking lens frame had finally turned the corner and disappeared from sight that Liam dared stop waving and grinning like a loon.

"Hey, congrats on another great show!" boomed Barry's voice from behind Liam, making him jump. How could a man so large be so discreet?

"Is that a joke? I mean, they called the Great Plague 'great' too, right?"

"Not at all," stammered the technician, with a worried frown. "I mean really great 'great.' Haven't you seen the ratings yet?"

The tired-eyed host shook his head and stifled a yawn. "You know I took that ratings monitor window out of my display ever since the first season finale."

"Oh, that right." Barry's smile made the ball bearing grease stain on his cheek shimmer like a sordid little splotch of rainbow. "Still can't bear to see any show beat the ratings from that big first season finale, eh, Mr Argyle? It's only been a year and a half," he said, with a deep chortle.

Liam nodded, more than happy to leave it at that. It had always been a weak excuse at best, and he was amazed it still held. The truth was much simpler: ever since he'd watched the viewer numbers climb higher and higher as he sent the urn with the ashes of Usnavi Musibay, the charming young man sacrificed live for progress and entertainment at the end of *The Grass is Greener*'s first season, off on their merry way to Paradise Mars, he couldn't stand the sight of the monitor window anymore.

He'd spent the whole of the second season trying not to think about it—or anything else for that matter. To keep his head down, get on with the work, and drown any lingering critical thought in whatever drink was closest to hand. Until his trip back to Quito, it had mostly worked, too.

Standing awkwardly next to him, Barry let out a nervous cough when Liam failed to respond. "Well, anyway, the numbers really are spectacular. Four-point-two billion and change concurrent viewers. That's our best season launch ever. So we must be doing something right!"

"That's one way of putting it," the host replied, with an aching smile he hoped didn't look anywhere near as ironic as it felt. Liam had a sneaking suspicion he, along with the rest of humanity, were the ones getting "done." And the worst part was, it was entirely consensual.

"Got any plans to celebrate, then?" Barry asked, his goggles dipping ever so slightly as he checked something in the bottom of his display—the time, no doubt.

That old thrill coursed down Liam's spine again at the hulking technician's words—his first bit of honest excitement of the evening. He fought to keep his composure as he smiled and said, "Oh, you know me. Any port in a storm. And a cognac, too, if I can get it."

Barry laughed, far more generously than Liam thought his overused joke deserved, but he was happy enough to join in. It was as good an excuse as any to break off, give the man a little wave, and make a hasty retreat to his sleek, waiting vehicle, which had just pulled up outside the Mews's still-open warehouse doors.

Outside, the Thameside night was cold, smoky, and damp as the grave of a kipper factory accident victim. Closing his eyes, Liam breathed it in, listened to the electric hum of the automated vehicle grid, and let out a grunt of satisfaction.

So, this was it. He'd struck the first blow. The construct's name might be stupid and sound pretentious, but with each of hir anecdotes, with every second of hir scripted feeds giving viewers a front-row seat to some of the worst deeds the Corporate world had to offer, the true life-destroying stories the Corps had worked so hard to bury were rising back up to the surface, like so much alcohol downed without proper pacing.

Speaking of which, he'd earned a drink or three. And anyway, he had an image to maintain. Grinning, Liam slid into the embrace of the waiting vehicle, and the door closed behind him in automated silence.

10

Earth, thought Ed the Editor, looking out over the septic rash of concrete and humanity that was the London Sprawl from his window near the bulbous bell-end of the Tulip. This planet didn't even have a proper name—"Earth." That was just a description, and a filthy one at that. At least that much was fitting.

He could not wait to leave this mudball behind. Or maybe that should be "earthball."

His comms suite rang with a gentle little *meep* in his ear—his unobtrusive and utterly non-urgent notice that some underling wanted to speak with him. It was entirely his decision whether to take the call or not; and most often, he didn't. That's what his AI secretary was for.

But tonight was *The Grass is Greener*'s big new season launch, after all. Argyle must want someone to pat him on the back and tell him he'd been a good boy.

And so, without bothering to open the Caller ID tab, the Editor flicked open the call window and said, "What do you need from me this fine evening, then?"

There was a choked pause on the other end of the line. Just long enough for Ed to realise that his caller's face most definitely did not belong to Liam Argyle. Was this another report from that bartender, Sabine, earning her pay by sharing Liam Argyle's latest trials and tribulations as he vented to the safe outlet RedCorp had set up for him so long ago? If so, she was a bit earlier than usual.

"Sorry for bothering you, sir. But there's something you need to know," his mystery caller whispered at last. And something in their tone told the Editor this was one call he would not regret taking the time to listen to.

11

"The usual, sir?" asked country-ready Sabine, manning her Sunday night post behind the antique mahogany counter of the Jenkin's Ear.

Liam started, with a sudden flashback to his teenage years and daily fear of getting caught in the middle of something embarrassing and largely self-referential. Because that was precisely what he was doing here: scanning the *Grass is Greener* discussion forums, which scrolled in the augmented air before his eyes.

"Oh, you know me," he replied with a half-hearted grin.

The bartender lifted a sculpted blonde eyebrow. "Double G&T, elderflower and lime?"

"Ah, straight to the heart." Liam clasped a hand to his chest and swayed dramatically. "Keep this up, and I'm going to have to ask you to marry me one of these days."

"That'd be bigamy, sir. I'm already married to this bar top, right here."

"Ah, well. At least I couldn't lose to a more reliable adversary."

The bartender rewarded Liam's efforts at banter with a professional smile, then turned to busy herself with mixing his drink. Liam lifted himself up onto the tall stool and returned to his chat-delving.

Truth be told, he didn't even want the drink that badly and merely thanked Sabine with a nod when it arrived, ice cubes tinkling against the frosted glass bulb. The juniper and elderberry wafted up to mug his nostrils, and his hand was melting the little sheen of ice covering the glass before he had even registered the smell.

The erstwhile revolutionary sipped and enjoyed this drink far more than any other of the countless G&Ts he'd downed here, night after night, week after week. And Liam suspected that was entirely due to the thrill of rebellion tingling down his spine.

He'd started it. He'd breached the wall, found a way to get the real-life stories out there, right under the noses of all those smug bastards up in the Tulip. Liam usually avoided the comments section of the various *Grass is Greener* live feeds like the plague, but not tonight. Because there they were, in Raja Cassar's feed chat. His people, the ones he burned to give a good wake-up shake. The viewers had seen and heard. They were listening.

"FMS, where'd they dig this one up?"

"Where've they been hiding em more like! Betting on em to win right now!"

"Dude sure has been screwed over. That can't be true about the escape from sexual slavery can it?"

"RIGGED!"

"I mean, it's legal. But to lose your mother to it as well. That ain't right."

"Lot of shit that's legal ain't right imho."

"RIGGED!!"

"Yes, we know. Rigged."

"No spamming!"

"It's true tho. Rigged system, all against people like Raja."

"Yeah, and the rest of us."

"Slavery? Organ harvesting? What gives them the right, anyway? I say we– <THIS MESSAGE HAS BEEN DELETED BY THE MODERATOR AI>

"See? RIGGED!!!"

"Unban or riot!"

Admittedly, they weren't exactly singing the Internationale yet, but Liam loved every second of the scrolling chat text. Using RedCorp's own depraved show to help disenfranchised citizens around the globe realise just how much mindless harm the Corporate world-state did to people, big and small? To them? There was a poetic justice to it. Liam pictured himself as a sort of modern Robin of Locksley, and chuckled as he spotted the famous outlaw's iconic figure grinning back at him from the label of the gin bottle Sabine had left close to hand—out of habit and convenience, Liam had no doubt.

He raised his glass in silent salute, took a swig, and set the chat to archive mode. He wanted to read the whole thing later. Hell, he felt so damn good right now, he might print it out on actual paper and frame it for his wall, if it helped capture even a fragment of this feeling.

His mind buzzing, Liam flagged Sabine down for a refill before she got caught up with one of the other Sunday night patrons and then flicked the Raja Cassar feed into full screen.

"—just stuck there, on the floor," drawled the computer-generated elderly Maltan, sitting in an equally fake airport bus stop and making its own riff on a familiar story from the rejection file. "Two whole weeks, twitching on that damn coffin apartment PVC flooring and listening to my exercise routine play over and over again. Crying for help that never came, fighting for enough control over my arms to get a bit of water into my mouth."

All around the simulated contestant, other people bustled to and fro, as other buses pulled up to the shelter. Were they real, or was the computer generating them as well? Liam couldn't even tell anymore.

"Some people think strokes are a joke, a thing of the past, but not everyone can afford reconstructive nanotherapy. Especially when the insurance finds a way to wriggle out of any coverage. One way or the other, they always get you in the end."

A shiver ran down Liam's spine at that, one that not even the indignant bursts from the feed chat could quell[1]. He shut down the feed window and knocked back the last bit of the second glass he hadn't even noticed he'd been drinking.

---

[1] "To kill, murder, execute"

What the hell did he think he was doing? He had a good life. A great life. Okay, he might not exactly be happy, but what did that even mean, anyway? He was certainly better off than the average working stiff, and a whole lot better off than the poor slobs on his show. Were a few dead bodies on the other side of the world worth losing everything for? What would his poor mother say?

Liam desperately tried to drudge up memories of his mother scolding him and urging him to be practical, to justify his sudden urge to call up the Editor, confess what he'd done with the fake contestant, and try to make everything right again. But for some reason, all he could picture was her cadaverous—though still well dressed—figure reaching out to him and asking why he hadn't been there for her.

Elderberry fumes still tickling his sinuses, Liam flicked his payment to the genial bartender, who nodded in confirmation, and stumbled back out the heavy wooden door into the smoke-filled Southwark night.

Mars above, he couldn't think straight. A good night's sleep, that's what he needed. It'd all seem clear again in the morning.

12

Ed the Editor sat back in his antique leather chair and scowled at the tracking window floating freely in the air.

As he watched, the little dot representing Liam's car stopped blinking green and turned a bright red. And instead of carrying on toward Liam's house in Richmond, it took the next right and started looping back around, deeper into the City.

At the end of its new projected route, a series of black dots were converging and taking position. The welcoming committee was ready.

Oh, Mars take the man. Why had he tried to go behind his Editor's back with what could have been a perfectly sellable idea? Was it partly his own fault, for being focused so much on his future in Paradise Mars that he'd thought he could leave an algorithm to watch over *The Grass is Greener* and keep things ticking over?

Possibly—not that he'd ever admit it, of course. This was all on Argyle, and Ed wasn't about to let anything put his own prospects at risk.

As for Argyle… Well, the whole point of running an extraterritorial, lawless haven like Paradise Mars was that you could do whatever you wanted there—whatever needed doing—without worrying about things like legalities or so-called personal rights and freedoms.

The same absolute liberty that made life on the Corporate

sanctuary so pleasurable for the lucky few chosen to relocate there was also what made Paradise Mars so useful in squeezing wayward— but still valuable—employees back into the mould.

Ed took a sip from his tall glass of frosted water and felt a twinge of regret, but only a twinge. It was a shame that Argyle's first taste of Paradise had to go this way, but there wasn't a damn thing Ed could do about it.

Argyle was in *their* hands now.

And if push came to shove-into-the-recycler, it wouldn't be too hard to find another dressed-up monkey to smile at the camera every Sunday.

13

Yes, Liam had panicked at first. A little. Who wouldn't, when their car started taking an entirely different path than it was supposed to? When they discovered, as if further confirmation were needed, that the car's commands were locked and they were a prisoner in their own damn vehicle?

But now, he was calm. He was focused. He was a rock. He had been through all this a thousand times in his nightmares and daydreams. He was so resigned that not even the approach of the looming, bright phallic[1] Tulip—that sleepless affront to any notion of taste that housed the infighting departments and management strata of RedCorp's European HQ—managed to unsettle him.

Whatever happened next, he promised himself, he would remain unphased, like a willow against the wind. Well, except for in really strong storms. Or if the willow is really old. After all, doesn't wind wear down mountains, eventually? Perhaps that wasn't such a great promise to make to himself after all.

Then the car pulled up outside a conspicuously hidden side entrance at the base of the Tulip, and he saw the private security goons lined up to welcome him. That's when the real fear set in.

---

[1] Referencing, among other things, the Greek *phalle*, or whale. One of those lovely moments where etymology and objective biology converge.

The AR para-police badges on the chests of his muscular new friends gleamed as they rushed out to greet him with military precision, even in the feeble alley light.

Their badges looked a lot like the coppers' badges in the old vids. But even in his manhandled daze, Liam knew these were only virtual. Public police forces were a costly thing of the past, and the "protect and serve" mottos had long since been cast into the gutter alongside the road of Progress.

He had always been a bit uncomfortable with the idea of having the world's policing run by a couple of monolithic private security companies, but one does get used to the idea so very easily—especially when confronted with the grinding halt the new police forces had brought crime to, in less than a decade. Sure, they were constantly trying to find ways of increasing their margins, making them more bounty hunters than police. And yes, some people may have ethical issues with surgically re-socialising any repeat offenders to make them into unpaid police agents. But surely it was a small cost to pay in exchange for cheaper and more effective security forces than the old States had ever been able to provide… Wasn't it?

It was one of those things everybody knew and no one questioned. But the wasp-sting of the neurotaser at the back of his neck made him seriously reconsider the idea of an unaccountable private police force. But only briefly, since the barbed weapon—the evil great-granddaughter of the TENS machine—quickly drowned the entire world in a dark crimson pit.

Blood pounded at Liam's temple in perfect time with the person screaming in his ear again and again. Whoever they were, he really wished they'd go away, along with the lavender and fresh sweat aromas wafting about the place, and leave him to the warm neurotaser afterglow. But then, as if in a nightmare, recognition grew in the host's mind, and he knew that it was no scream, but rather the even-less-welcome buzz of an incoming high priority comm call ringing in his subdermal speaker.

Liam's eyes screeched open like the rusty gate back at the Mews, and the call connected automatically, making him wish he'd stayed unconscious after all. Nobody, not even a man with as much on his conscience as Liam Argyle, deserved to face the Editor's jowly cheeks and brightest green bowtie so soon after returning to the land of the living.

"Argyle!" the insufferable little man barked jovially. "About time, really. Now don't be distressed[1]. You're going to feel a bit of a push, and then everything will be right as rain."

Liam had just enough time to wonder why people still persisted in saying "right as rain" in a world where acid rains made any sort of urban tree growth impossible and umbrellas were made of Kevlar. Then a sudden rush of acceleration pushed down against his abused body, with the G-forces of a couple of extra Earths that just happened to roll in for a visit. Thick straps he hadn't even noticed until now tightened around his chest and waist—as if he could possibly hope to lift himself from the padded seating anyway. Other folks, barely visible lumps at the edge of his pinned-down vision, writhed within their own, identical straps.

Distressed? Liam was so distressed he made Ankh-Morpork pudding seem barely indisposed in comparison. There was only one reason a padded chamber like this would accelerate this hard, and frankly, Liam would rather the RedCorp goons had killed him outright.

But then again, maybe he was wrong. Maybe it was just some form of residual nightmare. After all, if what he suspected and feared were true, they wouldn't be accelerating very long, and he'd soon be—

FWOOMP. The world around him rattled and shook like a sneezing superbug victim's chest.

---

[1] Etymologically, "drawn tight and pulled apart at the same time."

Then the dreaded and fully expected peace of weightlessness buoyed up through Liam's poor, mistreated innards. In the seat next to him, a deep voice let out a sigh of contentment, and Liam turned his now floating head to watch the heavy-set passenger in the tailored suit stretch their arms and revel in the sudden absence of the weight that pulled down on you every second you spent on Earth.

Profits alive. It was true. The bastards had knocked Liam out, shanghaied[1] him onto a shuttle, and fired him off into space.

It made no sense. Was it just torture? RedCorp was thorough with its psychological profiling, just like any of the other major players on the Corporate Council. It had to be. So they knew how terrified Liam was of space, of the total loss of control a Lightway shuttle passenger had over their own life or death. Full credits for style if it was just some maniacal revenge plan after his attempt to shake things up; but somehow, Liam doubted it. There were far cheaper ways of disposing of an inconvenient body where no one would ever find it.

Liam struggled not to spew gin-soaked stomach bile into the weightless air; neurotaser aftershock, mounting hangover, and good old fear for his life had joined forces to mug his brain. And the nauseating, floating AR window with the Editor's smug face was doing nothing whatsoever to calm his stomach.

"All sorted, then?" boomed the man, still live in the comms window and now holding a steaming blue-white porcelain cup. "Capital. And sorry we had to be a bit forceful with you, Argyle. But, frankly, you've been a bit naughty, haven't you, my boy? Trying to hide a whole fake contestant from us? For shame."

Liam wished his boss really was sitting in front of him, or at least that he was on a physical screen, just for the satisfaction of letting loose the roiling mass churning in his stomach. That'd show them

---

[1] Not sure if you should feel uncomfortable with this term? For the record, being "shanghaied" is something Europeans did to other Europeans, drugging them and sticking them on a ship to Shanghai to serve as unwilling ship hands—the good people of Shanghai had nothing to do with it.

all what he thought about the word "shame" coming from any Corporate exec's mouth—let alone Ed the Editor.

But he kept his queasy mouth shut, and just as well. Unless they planned on sending a shuttle-load of Corporate types to their deaths along with him, maybe they hadn't grasped the full extent of what he was trying to accomplish with Raja Cassar.

"Nothing to say for yourself? Good," carried on the Editor, with more relish than a carnival yeast-dog. "I do hate it when they plead. But you're made of sterner stuff, eh, Argyle? I've always said you'll go far. And you still will, once this little peccadillo is all sorted out."

Liam dared a nod, straining against his straps. It sounded encouraging, as long as "going far" wasn't code for a one-way ticket straight off the plane of the elliptical.

"I mean, it was inspired, really. Daring, certainly. A fake candidate, made from all the worst bits cobbled together! Now that's someone you can really work with. The airfare and liability insurance savings alone are well worth the effort. Should have thought of the idea sooner, to be honest."

"Glad you like it so much," gargled Liam through his dry, sore throat. "So, what's all this, then? A surprise holiday, as a reward?"

The Editor fixed Liam with a calculating stare. "Well, in a way, that's absolutely right. You're a lucky man. The Board decided what you need is one of our all-inclusive executive resocialisation courses in the safety, not to mention absolute luxury, of Paradise Mars. I don't think you've ever been yet, have you?"

The man knew damn well Liam had never been off planet yet; but this sounded like a situation he might be able to turn to his benefit, so the host decided to put on his game face and play along.

"No, but I've often dreamt about what it might be like." That was true enough. Nightmares qualified as dreams, too, right?

"Ah, I remember my first time," the Editor said with a wistful gleam in his speckled brown eyes. "Give it a week or two of rest and rehabilitation, and you'll be right back on your feet, thinking straight again."

So, he was getting the VIP indoctrination treatment. Liam was impressed. He hadn't thought he meant that much to the Corporation. "What about the show?" he asked, surprised to find that he didn't care about the effect on ratings, or even about any risk for his own position. His first thought was for his subversive experiment with the Cassar construct and whether it might get cut short.

Not that he wasn't terrified of dying in this tin can hurtling uncontrollably through space, of course. But there was nothing he could do about that—whereas he just might still be able to save the Cassar construct, strapped into a runaway shuttle though he may be.

"Therein lies the rub, of course," replied the Editor, screwing up his face like he'd just licked the backside of an expired yeastcracker. "And the Psychos sure enjoyed rubbing our faces in it this time. You really should have come to me with this idea first, my boy. Everything would have gone swimmingly. Instead, our friends up at the Psychomarketing Division jumped into the breach and used your little act of insubordination to take control of recruiting your temporary replacement—with the Board's blessing. They've been trying to take over ever since the show became such a hit, so don't give them the opportunity to make this permanent, you hear? Go spend a few days cooling your heels in Paradise Mars's micro-gravity, have a few drinks, do whatever the Concierge tells you to, and get back to us as a well-adjusted, mean, ratings-kicking machine, alright?"

Theoretically, Liam probably *could* care less about the infighting between Departments inside the Tulip—but it would require a frontal lobotomy to get there. Still, the host figured he'd do well to encourage this "us against them" attitude in the Editor; Paradise Mars was an extraterritorial enclave where the Corporate Council's word was the only law. Not pissing off his bosses could literally be the difference between life or death.

"Shit," Liam said, putting the full weight of his fear, his pain, and his helplessness behind the word.

The Editor nodded, looking convinced.

"You can count on me to make sure that doesn't happen," Liam said. "We can't have those bastards taking over the show and stealing the credit for all our hard work."

"That's the spirit!" The Editor pumped a tiny fist in the air. "Carry on like that and we'll have you back down here in two shakes of a drone's prop."

Liam started to respond, before freezing, his eyes flying wide open. One hand flew to his mouth, and his other fumbled about in the pocket at the side of his acceleration couch, desperately searching for a vomit bag. The Lightway shuttle was still soaring in serene, acceleration-less zero-G, but that only made things worse. Talking about drone propellers only reminded Liam about the cushion of atmosphere the damn ubiquitous things flew. Whereas the shuttle he was locked in…

HURP! Liam got the bag up to his mouth just in time, before he sprayed the entire padded and upholstered interior of the Lightway shuttle with the sour mash that was escaping from his stomach in graceful, balletic zero-G globs.

"Ah, yes," said the Editor, averting his eyes from the dubious entertainment of a vomiting Liam Argyle. "I'll let you get on with it, then. And even though this probably isn't the best time to say this, you can look forward to some smashing meals when you reach Paradise Mars. The word 'Paradise' literally means 'Garden[1],' after all. Let it never be said the Council doesn't know how to take care of its own. So enjoy, and let me know as soon as the quacks give you the nod, will you? There's a good chap."

By the time Liam's eyes had stopped watering and the vomit bag was full of worryingly mobile sludge, the Editor had finished his rambling goodbyes and cut off the call. Liam sealed the bag and nudged it off, spinning, toward the waste receptacle above his head.

So it was to be torture, then. Well, maybe not torture, but "So it

---

[1] Which is to say, an enclosed, cut-off place. A place that is guarded.

was to be some bizarre pampered Corporate reconditioning, then" didn't have quite the same ring to it. Whatever may come, Liam would be ready. He would stand firm, never betray his principles. He would be a rock.

A little harp-string ping rang through the local AR environment as the speaker system kicked in, with a synthetic female voice like golden syrup spilled over a vintage Alexa unit.

"Valued passengers, thank you for choosing RightTransit, a branch of SyneDeal Corporation—*The Only Way to Travel*." Yes, quite literally, what with their monopoly over passenger transit launches from the budding Space Elevator; it made the bit about "choosing" RightTransit a complete joke. "We will soon be joining the main Lightway beam for Mars rendezvous in eight days standard time. Please direct your attention to the frontal viewscreen. We're proud to share the humbling sight of the Sun rising across the disc of Mother Earth as it recedes behind us."

The screen flicked into existence in the air. Sure enough, there lay the Earth, a dark, urban-speckled dinner plate rimmed with light that grew and grew until it exploded into day, like some cheesy explosion in a classic action film. It was cosmically underwhelming: prepackaged and perfectly timed profundity for the Corporate mindset.

Maybe it was just Liam's newly restored personal pride talking, but this sorry show couldn't hold a Kindle to the genuine, terrifying, and comparatively down-to-Earth experience Liam himself had endured in suborbital transit just a few days earlier. He crossed his rumple-suited arms and floated above the padded chair with a little, satisfied smirk, confident he'd be able to lick whatever Paradise Mars could possibly throw at him.

Then a whoosh of artificial gravity ran through the ship as it hit the main interplanetary beam and accelerated, just like the saccharine announcer had promised. Liam's stomach churned again, and an invisible hand tried to smoosh him back down into his seat with a vengeance.

And worst of all, the free-floating viewscreen stayed front and centre in his display wherever he turned, as the Earth started shrinking ever so slightly, even to the naked eye.

The Earth—solid ground—was over *there*. Which meant Liam was over *here*.

Liam's heart began to race beneath the tightened straps and hot blood pounded in his ears, in perfect time with a beeping monitor-alarm that crept past the edges of his consciousness like a particularly bad AR advertisement.

"Oh dear," chimed the oil-slick shuttle AI again, but this time without any of the slight echoing tones that signalled a public announcement. "Are we having a teensy-weensie panic attack? No worries, sir, we've got just the thing."

And before Liam could so much as open his trembling lips to protest, a hypodermic needle pushed out of a slot hidden deep in the padding of the seat beneath him and pricked the base of his neck.

Profits almighty, not again, he thought. Then all was comfortable fuzz and darkness, and he thought no more.

14

"I'm ever so sorry," said a deep, whiskery walrus-voice, breaking through the jazz tinkle at the edge of Liam's struggling awareness of the universe, "but would you mind passing me the *foie gras* tube? I seem to have dropped it."

For a first thing heard upon returning to consciousness, this was certainly novel. Liam was rapidly becoming an expert in the field.

His eyes were having trouble focusing; there was a half-squished tube directly in front of him, yes, but it seemed to be spinning around, making him even more nauseous than the sense of shifting gravity in the pit of his stomach had already achieved. The tranq shot still tingled from the nape of his neck to the tips of his fingers, so maybe it was only spinning in his head—a drug-induced after-effect.

But no, there was nothing wrong with his eyes. The tube looked like it was spinning because that was precisely what it was doing. And with a rush of horror, he remembered exactly where he, his bewhiskered neighbour, and the other passengers all around him were currently located—strapped into wrap-around seats inside an engineless tin can, listening to tune-deaf pseudo-jazz Muzak as they fell, weightless, through an uncaring Solar System.

Maybe it wasn't so bad for Mr Goo-Goo-G'joob and his ilk. For Liam, it meant the future was either a computer failure in the

Lightway beam someplace and a long, cold death—probably someplace clear outside the disk of the Solar System—or whatever improbable mindfuckery awaited him if they ever reached Paradise Mars.

Liam rubbed his eyes and strained against his straps as he searched around, in vain, for some water to rinse the horrible, pasty taste out of his mouth. All the while, his fellow passengers were clearly having the time of their corporate-owned lives, living the high life—incredibly high, or possibly incredibly low, depending on your point of reference—in weightless bliss.

Liam blinked in confusion. Why were they weightless, anyway? Weren't they supposed to be feeling a gentle 1G of acceleration while they rode the LightWay beam? Was something wrong with the shuttle—had it crashed out of the beam, just like he'd known it would?

A gentle *bing* rang in his ears, and an AR sign lit up on the ceiling. *Please remain calm while the shuttle transitions between the out-bound Earth beam and the in-bound Mars deceleration beam. Normal service will resume shortly.*

Liam breathed a sigh of relief and tried to relax—before wincing in pain. The catheters gripping his tender bits served as a necessary reminder that, even in the vacuum of space, strapped to a seat for a solid week, nature will still call and assert its rights.

But this all-inclusive and all-invasive service was clearly just another perk for his soiled-suited shuttle mates. They were busy stuffing themselves with as many rich foods and heady drinks as they could grab from the over-worked robo-server trolley. Revelling in their powerlessness. It made sense, in a way. They'd never feel the weight on their stomachs here in zero-G, and Paradise Mars's famous tailored microgravity would make any extra kilos easy to bear once they reached the station.

The executive walrus harrumphed from across the aisle, still waiting for an answer and probably at a loss to fit Liam into one of the only two relevant social categories: equals to be ignored or inferiors to be shouted at. A firm believer in "do unto others," Liam pointedly ignored the man's mounting coughing fit of perplexity and hoped he would take the hint.

The worst part was, as much as it pained Liam to admit it, the concept of a pampered life in space had a morbid sort of attraction. Even giving up freedom over something so fundamental—literally—as going to the bathroom might seem a small price to pay for a week of uninterrupted gluttony, without ever having to leave the comfort of your padded seat, as you rode the Lightway to Mars.

Was this the ideal life the consumer-citizens of the Corporate world strived for, then? No stress and total comfort. Freedom from gravity, from toil, but at the price of a renunciation of all choice and all responsibility—other than what flavour of meal paste to try out next. Freedom to enjoy, without consequence.

And hell, if that ever got boring, there were plenty of thrilling, suffering-filled lives out there on the Red, to experience vicariously. That was what *The Grass is Greener* was all about, after all.

Anger flared deep within Liam like a petulant nascent sun. Was that his role in life, then? Pacifier to the masses, and purveyor of regular misery inoculations for the ultra-rich?

Repressing a growl, he grabbed the damn spinning *foie gras* tube and launched it, spinning and oozing little fatty globs into the weightless air, straight back at his shuttle neighbour.

The executive, who had been sitting twisted toward Liam with his mouth open wide, at a loss for words, barely had time to blink at the uncooperative host's burst of movement before the space-faring tube ended its flight by whacking him straight in the whiskered gob. Heavy-ringed hands that had never seen a hard day's work at a virtual keyboard in their lives shot up out of reflex and grabbed the offending object—but not before flecks of rogue *foie gras* had peppered his face with an ablative shield of tortured goose liver.

The man's sunken eyes glared at Liam, confusion, indignation, and terror clashing for control of his jowly features.

"Much—Much obliged[1]," he rumbled at last in best Corporate standard English, before turning hurriedly away, visibly eager to start pretending none of the confusing scene had ever happened.

Liam reclined into his acceleration seat and gave his straps a satisfied little tug. The resident walrus might be "obliged," but Liam sure wasn't. Not anymore. He refused to be, refused to go along with the global charade any longer. If this was what the countless masses on every continent back on Earth were struggling, living, and dying in squalor to create, then he wanted no part in it whatsoever. There had to be a better alternative, one where people had more control over their own lives, over their world; even if that meant harder choices and more responsibility for their own actions. Anything was better than this casual trampling of all ethical principles, this infantilised death of the mind and soul.

On cue, the universe chose that precise moment of resolve to show Liam Argyle who was boss once again. Gravity, the unquestioned bedrock of Liam's life until he was introduced to the tender ministrations of the neurotaser, returned to the shuttle, apparently determined to make him throw up whatever foul-tasting muck they'd forced down his throat to keep his body going while he was out. It reeled and swerved like a drunken salaryperson after a hard day at the office. The painfully bright cabin lights flickered. If it weren't for the straps, Liam would have gone flying out of his seat—probably bouncing off the ceiling and straight into the whiskery embrace of his pinniped-shaped shuttle mate.

Not a single one of the other passengers seemed in the least inconvenienced by the artificial gravity's somersaults; they carried on munching and slurping and chortling in time with whatever AR amusements were currently occupying their executive minds all throughout the ordeal. They did not even pause as gravity returned to what the body insisted on thinking of as normal—roughly 1G, and coming from below the bottom.

---

[1] "To be in bondage." [Takei]Oh my![/Takei]

That damn obnoxious harp strum rang throughout the cabin again, and the mellifluous[1] artificial tones of the shuttle's AI piped up once again.

"RightTransit is proud to announce that we've successfully entered the Earth-Mars decelerating Lightway beam, in perfect time for rendezvous with Paradise Mars. All systems have returned to nominal gravitic operation, and stress-management protocols can now enter back into effect."

Liam felt like he could use a stiff glass of stress management or two. But wait, they didn't mean—

"No worries, sir," oozed the synthetic voice against his inner ear. "We'll have you dreaming sweet nothings again in no time."

Liam let out the breath he'd been holding in a desperate attempt not to spew. "No, wait! I'm not stressed out! Really!"

The AI actually chuckled at him, which was something he'd never expected to hear from a computer. "Then you should sue my pulse monitor for slander, sir. But worry not. We'll get you to your destination in one piece. There's so much to look forward to on Paradise Mars!"

He started to protest further, fumbling at the straps to find a release button, but a familiar hiss and prick at his nape shut his mouth for him as chemical oblivion coursed into his veins yet again.

He wanted to fight it, he really did. But as five generations of snack food addicts stood to attest, there was no beating chemistry.

And what was one more bout of unconsciousness between friends, anyway? At least there was hope, the hope that he'd finally be able to assert some sort of control over his own life when he woke up this time around.

Third time's the charm, after all. Right?

---

[1] "Flowing like honey"

15

Reality came charging back like a low door frame cracking against Liam's head—unsurprising, really, since that was precisely what had happened.

"Oy, watch it with the door," boomed a female voice from somewhere around where his legs should probably be.

"Not my fault they keep the gravity up here so damn low," grumbled a second, deeper voice nearer to Liam's ears. "It's all about the bosses' comfort, isn't it? Never a thought for the poor working Jude who has to lug their unconscious so-and-sos through their lovely arched hallways. I mean, what are we supposed to do? Roll the lanky bastard all the way to his room? But no, that'd probably scuff up their expensive carpeting. I wear, sometimes I just feel like—"

"Shut yer gob," snapped the first voice. Blissfully, the other one obeyed. "They'll all be in the buffet room this time of cycle. Don't want one of them hearing your bellyaching."

Liam's half-hearted struggle to return to the land of the living continued in padded, bouncing silence, broken only by the rare pant of exertion or muttered curse as one of the hands gripping his limp body slipped.

"It's this one," the higher voice grunted at long last. A sci-fi door swish later, Liam's bearers dumped him face first onto a surface so soft that it made him think he'd lapsed into full-on unconsciousness again.

"Blarg," Liam said with feeling, into the cloudy mass. The door swished once again, leaving him, presumably, alone.

"Argleblarg," he added, happy to discover his mouth and vocal cords, at least, were still mostly working. A very familiar, almost comforting tingle was tickling his arms and legs, but he'd suffered enough abuse at the hands of external reality the last few times he'd returned to consciousness. The universe didn't seem to be actively out to get him in the slumberfuzz of the here-and-now, so Liam was in no rush to give it any excuse to revise that stance.

He managed to maintain some semblance of inner peace for a whole minute, which was certainly a personal record since he'd joined *The Grass is Greener*—unless you counted the inebriated[I] whole of the show's second season; but Liam knew full well that inner G&T wasn't really the same thing as inner peace. Nowhere near.

Then his AR display finished syncing with the local network and a whole rainbow of icons and notifications decided to cascade against the backdrop of his closed eyelids, ruining any chance at serenity[II] or contemplation[III].

Ninety-nine-plus new notifications. Not bad. By now, Liam was used to seeing his face on AR billboards all over the Red; he was more or less a household name, in a certain quality of household. But he had never been all that popular with his co-workers or contacts at RedCorp—the only ones who'd be sending him direct messages like these on his professional-issue implants. It filled him with an odd, vain glow.

But then again, if the date in the corner were correct, then that was only about ten messages a day. Going by London time, which was laughable in its own way, it was now early afternoon on the

---

[I] "To make drunk," unchanged from the Proto Indo-European roots. The really important stuff never changes.

[II] "Dryness"

[III] "To mark out a space for the taking of auguries"

Wednesday of the week following his abduction. Had he really been out for a whole ten days back on Earth?

Before he was done wrestling with the thought, an unholy pounding rattled the door that lurked somewhere beyond his bare feet. It stopped after three sharp knocks, leaving Liam to wonder if he hadn't just dreamt it up. He'd started dozing off back into slumberland when the knocker started up again, now hammering away without any sign of ever relenting. Grudgingly, Liam pried his crusted eyes open and bunny-hopped over to the door, fumbling in Paradise Mars's famous designer microgravity like a fish in oil, soon to be deep-fried. But, alien to him though it was, and however much his wobbly muscles had to say on the subject, Liam had to get to that door—if only to stop the infernal metronome knock and save his poor, aching head from further assault.

Rubbing at the faint stucco-print bruise on his forehead, he stumbled to a bouncing halt against the doorframe. The dread portal itself, coated in sickeningly pleasant pink pastel nanopaint, swished smugly and efficiently open at his approach.

"Mr Argyle," declared what was blatantly a butler at his door, pausing mid-knock. "Your suit."

Liam cast a guilty glance down at himself. He'd heard the same reproachful words and tones a thousand times before, from Mary, Lee, or the Editor himself, early on. Whenever he showed up for a show with half of his liquid lunch sloshed down his jacket; which was depressingly often in hindsight.

But he wasn't even wearing a suit this time, just the soiled shuttle overalls somebody—one of the RedCorp rent-a-cops, no doubt—had worked his unconscious body into before they shanghaied him off planet. Liam reeled his glance back in, focused it on the butler, and fired off his wittiest retort.

"Huh?"

"Your suit, Mr Argyle," the man repeated, the way thawing snow repeats mountain streams in spring. For gentle emphasis, he gave the garment neatly folded over his non-knocking arm a classy little shake. Liam had somehow managed not to spot it the first time around.

"Oh…" replied Liam, for want of any better option.

The butler, either tactfully ignoring what an ass Liam was making of himself or simply not caring to start with, continued, "Sir has already missed formal luncheon, but if Sir would don the provided suit, He might still attend the afternoon buffet held in the executive quarters—if Sir is not otherwise… indisposed."

Liam goggled like a lemur.

"Executive quarters?" Visions of horses with Corporate logos pulling him apart flashed into Liam's mind, as uninvited as the very worst sort of relatives. "Wuh? Wha… How would I even get there?"

"The executive quarters are on the eastern wing of the eighteenth floor, Sir," the butler said in a pedantic tone with a meticulously crafted reproachful edge.

"Well, that's that settled, then." Liam lost his stunned calm and decided to strike out, if only to make himself feel a little better. "And what the hell, pray tell, is the point of tasing me, drugging me, and dragging me all the way here, just to invite me to a damn buffet?"

Liam knew full well that it was the bewildered fear in his mind doing the talking and that freaking out was probably the best way to earn another quick lick of the neurotaser, but Mars take it all—he was fed up, and if that's what it took to force the universe to start making some sense at last, then so be it.

"Oh dear," replied the butler, with that sort of disarming tut that can send a rampaging hippo scampering back to its mud pool to hide its rosy cheeks. "Sir has not read the accommodation guide yet, has He?" The man shook his head with masterfully feigned concern. Facing down Liam's best withering glare with the poise of a matador, the butler waited precisely long enough before adding, with a curl of his hand, "Sir will find His copy conveniently pre-loaded into the interface, care of the Establishment."

Since there was no saving face after a conversational collapse that catastrophic, Liam settled for snatching the fantastic-looking suit from the uniformed man's hand and purposefully rumpling its pressed creases as he pivoted and turned his back on the door. The butler still managed to add a killer "Enjoy your stay, Sir," in an unabashedly smug tone before the door swished shut.

Fuming at his fellow Corporate lackey and his annoyingly crisp demeanour[I], Liam took great pleasure in tossing the fresh suit into an untidy heap on the four-poster bed. Only then, grudging every tweak and flex of his muscles, even in the Corporate haven's sad excuse for gravity, he dismissed all other notifications and loaded the blinking priority message from the local system.

"Welcome, fortunate guest!" The smarm of the machine drew a florid swear from Liam, which the AI, despite its perfectly operational speech recognition function, dutifully ignored[II]. "You are one of the privileged few! Kick back! Put your feet up! Enjoy your well earned break away from it all. The Corporate Council is here to make absolutely certain you enjoy your stay to the fullest."

Liam was wholly undecided as to whether this was an offer or a threat, and the labyrinthine schematics and floor plans which the unit then proceeded to impose upon his overlay reinforced his growing tendency to believe the latter.

But he was hungry. And for all the room's resemblance to a four-star hotel suite, everything conspired to indicate that room service would not be forthcoming. His stomach subverted his rational mind and applauded the idea of a buffet right now. The tasering and whatnot had been proof enough that he was going to have even less choice here on Paradise Mars than he was used to back home. And

---

[I] "To manage oneself as one would a herd of cattle." That's also the origin of the word *menace*, as in, yelling threats at a herd of animals to get them to move. Puts *The Phantom Menace* into a whole new perspective.

[II] That's the whole point of employing machines in the first place—they're designed to naturally possess that necessary indifference for others which takes decades of costly training to instil into a human operative.

the fake AR windows trying to hide the lack of any means of escape from his room hammered home the fact that he was no longer master of his own movements.

At his promptly regretted request, a depressing little animation on the AR floor plans showed a stick figure strolling from his room to the buffet area. When it got there, it waved in unmistakable sticky glee and silently hollered "Hello!" in a pink speech bubble. Liam had rarely had cause to think of himself in stick figure terms. But he felt nonetheless that, were he a stick figure, he would not communicate by the intermediary of pink speech bubbles.

Happy to have something else to grumble about as a distraction, he put on the much-abhorred suit, which—inevitably—fit him not only to a "T" but pretty much every other letter, numeral, and semiotic symbol imaginable, too. Damn RedCorp's noncorporeal hide.

When he finally gave up scanning himself in the mirror, trying in vain to find some flaw in the sharp, horribly expensive-looking suit, he made for the door—only to find that it had locked again after the butler incident. A small screen and touchpad lay waiting to the right of the door above a small, shielded opening. An actual, physical touchpad. He hadn't seen one of those in a while. The whole thing contrived to look like a child's drawing of a vending machine.

The screen waited in ambush, unnoticed until then and silently asking a question which he could only assume was addressed to him, by parties, regretfully, still unknown.

"ARE YOU WILLIAM ARGYLE?"

There was a big green YES button, as well as a red NO, at the centre of the keypad. Simple enough. As tempted as he was to refute the long-shunned, unabbreviated moniker, he really didn't see that he had any choice but to confirm that, YES, he was WIILIAM (shudder) ARGYLE.

The slot slid up to reveal a small plastic tab of some sort. Liam read the new message on the display as he reached out to palm the offering, out of reflex.

"TAKE YOUR PERSONAL COURTESY TAG. WEAR AT ALL TIMES. ENJOY YOUR STAY."

Even this thing was getting into it now, telling him to enjoy himself like it was a command, not an invitation. It's all a bit rich, really, Liam muttered in the relative safety of his own mind. If they really wanted him to enjoy his stay so badly, they could have started by giving the physical abuse a bit of a rest. Who were they trying to fool, anyway?

And what was this in his hand? A name tag?

"Hello! My name is <u>WILLIAM</u>!" The font was about as mirthful as the painted face of a post-suicide clown. Out of morbid curiosity, Liam flipped the little white plastic rectangle over to check the back.

Sure enough, the back repeated the imprecations to wear the tag at all times during his "stay" on Paradise Mars, adding the following useful tidbit[1] of info, almost as an afterthought: "Doors on Paradise Mars, including personal suite doors, will not open unless a courtesy tag of appropriate clearance is present and displayed."

Right. It was bad enough that he wouldn't have clearance to go anywhere other than precisely where the people behind this demented rehabilitation program wanted him to be. But now he realised this very same door—the one to what he was supposed to think of as "his own" quarters here in the ruined and mined-out shell of Phobos—only opened for him earlier because of that damn insufferable butler.

Liam slid the horribly cheerful nametag into the discreet pocket built into his new suit's lapel, integrated so cunningly he only noticed it as he fumbled around, wondering how he was even supposed to attach the nasty, demeaning thing without any pins—or anything else sharp, for that matter—anywhere in the white padded comfort of the room.

Liam steeled himself, put on his game face, and marched out the door to face whatever fresh hell the corporate powers-that-be had decided to thrust him into this time.

---

[1] "Tender morsel"

16

Bobbing balloon-like down the arabesque corridors did nothing to reinforce Liam's grasp on reality. The AR arrow leading the way eliminated the need for him to put any thought or attention into where he was going, but he was also locked out of every single entertainment, news, and social media feed in his interface. He had nothing else to distract himself with but the—for lack of a better word—scenery. Like some cosmic Slinky, a line of identical windows inched past him without end; behind them lay day spas, conference rooms, media nooks, beverage dispenser lounges, and every other amenity that a genuine guest of a five-star luxury resort might expect. Was everyone else here genuinely for pleasure? Or were there other prisoners like himself?

The overall effect of the infernal[1] décor was enough to push him to the most desperate of measures, just for an excuse to look away: Liam flicked open his inbox and started scrolling through the bottomless pile of unread messages—notifications all the way down, like the infamous cosmological turtles.

Buried amid the Corporate memos and menial alerts was a single private message: a personal note from the team back at Tantamount

---

[1] "Underground"

Mews. He stabbed a barely shaking finger in the air, and the message flared to life before him.

"Hey, Mr Argyle," chimed Lee, Akintola, and Mary Artworthy with a wave that would have cheered his heavily sedated heart if it hadn't been for the bright-toothed, perfectly coiffed stranger standing behind them, smiling and waving as well.

"Sorry to hear you're not feeling so well, but don't worry!" Norma Lee grinned at the camera—one of the main stage cameras, judging by the angle and the half-disassembled Sunday feature show stage behind them. "We've got everything under control here, and Glen did a fantastic job filling in for you!"

The precision-tooled tool standing behind his crew waved again at this point, beaming his perfect smile—a *Glen* if Liam had ever seen one.

"Take as long as you need to," called out Job Akintola, giving the camera a big thumbs up. "Get better soon, and enjoy your trip to Paradise Mars in the meantime, you lucky so-and-so!"

They all nodded and waved, smiling awkwardly for the camera—except for the gregarious Glen, who grinned more naturally than a circus shark. Then the recording cut off, leaving Liam with a conflicting mess of emotions churning in his belly.

The Grass is Greener might be a soul-rending, perverse, sausage-spewing machine designed by the Corporate world to pacify the masses. But it was *his* soul-rending, sausage-spewing machine, Marsdamnit.

So, this Glen was the one Ed had mentioned ten days and two hundred million kilometres ago—the shiny, pre-packaged Hostinator sent by the Psych/Marketing bastards to take over the show.

Seeing the whole team there, smiling away with his smarmy replacement, reminded Liam that someone—one of his supposedly trusted colleagues at the Mews—must have betrayed him and warned RedCorp about the Cassar simulation. It had to be one of them. He might never know which one, but if they were ready to go over his head instead of taking his word at face value when he told them everything was validated with Corporate, then how long would it take before the Psych/Marketing stooge had them all wrapped around his manicured finger? Before he turned them all against him?

With an angry stab, Liam deleted all his other messages. Then, a choked breath later, he thought better and dived into his virtual wastebasket, fishing out just one of the deleted messages. The regular automated report with the weekly viewing figures and the voting results from the Sunday feature show.

Liam carried on down the winding arched corridors of Paradise Mars, his step picking up as he read through the report. Well then. At least the voters hadn't seen through the Cassar construct's act just yet. Instead, they'd shown the good sense to get rid of that grandstanding, fatberg-diving zealot Hernández Dzul. Even better, the viewer numbers were down slightly, with barely more than four billion people watching Shiny Teeth McGee try to steal Liam's job.

The man could take his bright blue power tie and hang himself with it. Liam was going to ace whatever was expected of him here and then get straight back to the Mews. The man would get one more feature show to try to sleaze his way into his crew, but that was it. After that, it was Argyle time.

It took him a full twenty-five minutes to reach the gold-gilded doors to the Executive buffet. After five minutes there, staring past the suited crowd at the various displays of Mars below, he was wishing it'd taken twenty-five hours. The place was teeming with overdressed pompous pricks of all sexes and genders, stuffed to the brink of implosion with forced cheerfulness and little asparagus canapés; and all of them seemed determined to block his way to the buffet.

A balding, chain-smoking stump named Keith, according to his stool pigeon[1] of a nametag, bowled into him, interrupting his train of thought as effectively as a tactical tree fall.

"Sorry!" The man sprayed saliva, along with heavy drops of sweat, as he gushed his apologies. "Sorry! Hope I didn't spoil your enjoyment!" With those last words, he glanced around in an odd way that Liam didn't know what to make of—was he looking for someone?

"Hehe," the man added, looking about as amused as Queen Victoria on her wedding night and spreading a miasma of anxious fear that assaulted the nostrils, especially in the aseptic and controlled confines of Paradise Mars. "Well, I… err… I sure enjoyed bumping into you! Yessiree! I just love meeting new people! Happy, happy happy…"

Mopping his brow with a monogramed hanky, the man kept on muttering his lunatic mantra as he bobbed off toward the other side of the room, leaving Liam smellshocked.

Then a gap finally opened in the expensive-suited throng, and Liam made a soaring microgravity dive into it before he lost his shot to fill the gnawing hole in his stomach that hadn't seen proper food in a week and a half. But he had barely grabbed a plate and shuffle-bounced his way over to the bread selection before he was beset upon from all parts by strained[II] faces.

The nearest of these faces fired as soon as Liam was within range. "Care for a drink? Here, let me get you a drink." It pressed its advantage when he didn't refuse within the first picosecond. Liam realised the face belonged to what was, by and large, an elderly

---

[1] Tying a decoy pigeon to a stool is a great way to attract a much larger number of pigeons, if that's something you ever want to do. It's something people in the early 19th century wanted to do so often that this strange turn of phrase entered our lexicon.

[II] Quite literally – the latest developments in cosmetic surgery involved surgically removing the face, putting it through an electron 'sieve' of sorts and simply taking out the bits that looked aged or slack, before replacing them with an organic compound grown on the backs of genetically modified pigs.

woman, when her hand reached out to clench his arm as if it were the last lifesaver ring to have survived the capsizing.

He started protesting when she tugged him away from the buffet and over to the drinks table—but then he saw how well laden said table was, and something even deeper within him overrode his aching stomach. He needed to keep a low profile, after all. He couldn't very well make a scene by refusing, now could he?

Sensing an opening, the good half-dozen other merryfakers milling around the gleaming rainbow of exciting-looking bottles barged into the fray.

"Hey there!'"

"Howdy!"

"I'm Alice, sooo pleased to meet you!"

"Hi! Are you single?"

"We're short one for a game of SpaceBoules. Have you played before?"

It soon became evident to Liam that if he wanted the drink he needed so very badly—let alone if he wanted any food—he would have to make some effort to be sociable. It might even be a deliberate part of his captors' plans—step one of his "rehabilitation." Were the bastards really going to make him squirm in social awkwardness for his meal?

"Oh, umm, hi. I'm Liam." Without waiting for a response, he forced an arm through the living straightjacket surrounding him and flailed for a drink.

"Hello, Liam!" came the resounding answer in a perfect chorus, which chilled Liam to the core. What the hell had he landed in? Their hungry stares were slightly comical yet deeply terrifying, but silence wasn't an option; they seemed to suck the words straight out of him. "So, err… what is this place, anyway?"

"Oh, it's just lovely!"

"This is the Executive buffet, my boy!"

"You'll love it, you'll see!"

"It's the buffet, silly!"

"Are you sure I couldn't tempt you with a round of SpaceBoules?"

"What I mean is," mumbled Liam around the handful of canapés he had finally managed to grab and shove into his mouth, "what are we all doing here? The goons with the tasers didn't exactly hand me a programme when they—"

As one, his fellow Paradise Martians all burst out laughing, cutting him short. It was so contrived that Liam stood confounded, lacking even the drive and the good grace to slump against a handy wall or something. They were all nutters. Stark raving nutters.

"What's wrong with you? This is serious! I'm here against my will! Why won't you…" His indignation fizzled, noticing that not only weren't they listening to him, but they weren't even looking at him anymore. Their attention seemed to have wholly shifted to various specks of dirt at their feet, muttering something about how happy they were and very deliberately not registering something that Liam's instincts told him must be somewhere roughly behind his left ear. The increasingly familiar crackle of the neurotaser confirmed his theory even before he had time to turn around and look.

Falling to the ground in microgravity is an exceedingly long, almost cartoonish experience: Liam would have had ample time on his way down to pull out a hand-written sign reading "YIKES!" and display it for the amusement of an at-home audience of mean-spirited children, if only one had been provided in his coat's inner pocket—and if his arms and legs were not twitching around like an epileptic tarantula trying to win a dance-off. As it was, Liam could only watch the party continue around him in deliberate obliviousness as he fell, as if he were Ebenezer Scrooge, unable to be seen or heard, receiving fifty-thousand volts to the cerebral cortex from the Ghost of Corporate Future.

When he finally reached the ground, all he could see were the black trousers and weighted boots of the security types, who grabbed him and dragged him back through the doors, feet first, so that his last sight before losing consciousness yet again was the gap in the crowd of buffet patrons closing in behind him like so much rancid flotsam.

17

The tawdry corridors and fake potted plants gained nothing for being viewed upside-down and horizontally, and the effect was so stupefying that Liam didn't realise that the taser paralysis had worn off until long after his new friends had dumped him onto his bed—again—and left.

Return to room, do not pass dinner, do not collect any further inkling as to what the hell's really going on around here. How in Mars's name was he supposed to discover what they wanted from him before they'd let him get back to London and smack that smarmy git in the power tie out of his dressing room?

As he lay fuming, the insistent flash of a top priority message from the local network appeared in the corner of his display. With a groan, he lifted himself up on noodly arms, sat against the bed's padded silk headrest, and flicked the message on.

"Liam Argyle is cordially summoned to the Concierge's office, immediately upon reception of this message. He will be Escorted."

At least they got his name right this time. But, ouch, capital "E." Not good, Liam noted, and the prompt rap at the door did nothing to dispel his visions of what precisely an Escort might look like in this nut house.

As it turned out, the answer was a five-foot-something brunette of indeterminately young age, wearing a figure-flattering formal dress and a smile you'd damn yourself just to believe might be genuine. Liam reserved judgment on whether this was any real improvement over the morning's butler.

"Mr Argyle," she said, screwing him to the wall with her smile, "I'm Sylvie. If you would." It took a full half-dozen accelerated heartbeats before he realised that the sweep of her velvet-gloved hand was an invitation to step out of the room. And nothing else, added a little despairing voice that the rest of his psyche ignored for good measure.

The corridors were as gapingly empty and bewildering as ever, but the company was infinitely more charming. And somehow, despite his best attempts at cynical resistance, he still couldn't help but be grateful for the Escort's presence. Gravity grew less and less insistent as they went, and soon they were bunny-hopping along through the air. Buoyed by the gradual release of weight and encouraged by the temporary absence of any tasering, Liam dared to ask a few questions.

"So, do you come here often?" Liam chose as his icebreaker, in absolute failure at life.

"I live here, Mr Argyle," came the serene response.

"Really? Well, saves on rent, I suppose. So, what is it you do here, precisely?" he asked, fishing without bait.

"I am an Escort, Mr Argyle." Not a blink. Liam despaired.

"And I don't suppose you know what I'm doing here, by any chance?"

"You are here to enjoy your stay, Mr Argyle."

"Well, I'm doing a piss-poor job of it, then, let me tell you!"

"Yes. This is why you are going to meet with the Concierge, Mr Argyle. Everyone must enjoy their stay." Her tones were as final as the grave, and only half as flexible.

Liam's legs continued bouncing him along, but his mind stopped. Her tone had not been one of idle well-wishing. It'd been imperative. Suspicion wasn't so much growing as landsliding upon him that in this bizarre, self-loving, extraterritorial place, "Enjoy your stay" was an order. One they—whoever "they" might be—were ready to enforce with all and any measures necessary.

By the time Liam resurfaced from the depths of much-belated revelation, they'd bobbed up the gently sloping ramps to an area of nigh-zero gravity, where grand oak double doors marked "Conciergerie" waited. His Escort's gentle rap at the door pulled him reeling and sputtering back into frigid reality. There was no answer, but after a few seconds his companion opened the door regardless and ushered him in.

The bewildering new room was furnished in a pure, authentic nineteenth-century old boys' club style. Its extravagant viewport looked out onto the Red Planet and what could only be Olympus Mons, seen from above even though the viewport was wall-to-wall. The office was unquestionably a parlour of discernment and taste— even though that taste was something like the last drops of a bottle of wine left unstoppered on the counter overnight: not unpleasant, but too ripe, and disconcerting overall. As for discernment, Liam remembered from some cranny of his long-term memory that the word actually means to "judge off" in the strictest criminal sense. But this did him little good other than to baffle him as to why such a random bit of trivia should pop into his mind at a time like this.

"Mr Argyle, Sir." His Escort seemed to announce this to the empty room, before withdrawing, closing the double doors behind her with a wooden creak. Liam felt like a lame old racehorse about to be introduced to the wonderful world of glue manufacturing.

"Ah!" The voice boomed directly behind Liam, giving him such a weightless jump it felt as if he'd just been deboned like an oversized processed chicken. "Liam Argyle! Just the fellow!" A portly[I] chap[II] in a chequered bathrobe used handy brass knobs to navigate his way

---

[I] Rotterdam, or perhaps Hong Kong.

[II] From *chapman*, derived from the old Germanic *kaupman*, meaning "petty tradesman" or "huckster." "Chap" and "Cheap" share the same origin.

around the room and shake a resolutely baffled Liam's hand. "I was just in the loo, old boy. Sorry I wasn't there when you entered, but I had pressing business to attend to!"

"Not at all, I'm sure," muttered Liam, out of deep-grained habit.

"Oh, but look at you just standing there! Oh dear, oh dear, where are my manners?" He waved Liam deeper into the parlour with a wave of a chequered sleeve. "Come! Come, sit down. Put your feet up. What can I get you? Food? A drink? The cabinet's always full!" He chuckled as he edged Liam into a massive nano-imitated leather armchair, which moulded to his body and then suddenly reclined at his host's touch. The man loomed over him like a hunter's moon. "So, what'll it be?"

"Err…" Liam looked around for inspiration. Ah, so there was that bathroom the man had snuck out of. Cunning design, building it into a cabinet like that. "How about a gin and tonic?" His stomach suddenly punched him in the liver, and he added, "Oh, and a nice big sandwich, if you can get one. I'm starving."

"Can't have that!" The Concierge near burst with glee. "You know what, old bean? I'll do you one better."

The jovial man lifted a finger to his display and winked. The first food trolley arrived so fast that Liam didn't even have time to wonder if the long-expected torture instruments were hiding beneath.

Or what the catch was if they weren't.

18

After the third helping of royal couscous, a short-memoried but not inconsequential part of Liam was starting to think it had all been a misunderstanding. Maybe these folks weren't so bad after all. The rest of him was reserving judgment until after dessert.

Even the Concierge's small talk lost its annoying edge once the antipasti hit his stomach. And now, lounging in the reclining chair like some nabab of antiquity, he was thoroughly at peace with the universe, especially this particular corner of it.

As if he'd been waiting for this precise moment, the Concierge leaned forward in his own moulded chair and got on to business. "So, tell me, Liam, what do you think you are doing here? Other than enjoying our hospitality that is—and rightfully so!"

"Well, at first I was afraid I might have done something, I don't know, wrong." The alcohol pounding at his temples did the talking for Liam long before his reason could possibly catch up and edit. "But now... You know, that nice lady you sent to show me up here, she said something a bit odd."

"Oh, yes? What was that?" If the man suddenly seemed alert and surgically focused, it was lost on Liam.

"Something about everyone *having* to enjoy themselves here. You know—or else." Liam chuckled, a bit uneasy now that his better sense had caught up enough to at least be visible in the background.

"A bit silly, I know. But still, if that's the case, then it can't be all that bad, can it?"

Paradise Mars's Concierge leant in toward him, unadulterated seriousness on his features, his joviality all but melted away.

"Indeed, Liam. Let me tell you why you are here. First, like all the other guests in our little establishment, you have been under quite a lot of stress recently. Now, the members of the Corporate Council take care of their people. RedCorp simply couldn't stand by and let an agent of your value suffer without intervening. Without bringing you every bit of support and comfort money can provide. That, Liam, is where we come in."

Here it was, at last. Liam raised his tinkling glass to salute his host, breathing in the rich scents of juniper and aniseed from the other side of the Solar System.

"Officially, we don't exist. I am well aware that is a sorry cliché, and we certainly aren't doing anything secret here—Mars forbid! But the Council thought it necessary to provide a completely neutral, isolated, and above all safe environment to those privileged and most valuable agents who need, shall we say, a clean break from it all."

Liam nodded, sipping in silence and enjoying the burning chill as the after-meal tipple ran down his throat. Damned if there wasn't something to what the man was saying. A clean break? Who wouldn't want that?

"Oh, I won't deny that our methods may seem a bit forceful, but they are tried and true. After all, our guests are very busy and influential people—they'll often fight tooth and nail to stop us from tearing them away from their important functions. Workaholism[1] is, in fact,

---

[1] The *cohol* part of "alcohol" (and, by derivation, "workaholic") comes from the Arabic *kohl*, a powdered antimony ore used to paint the eyes. The fourteenth-century alchemist Paracelsus did a little linguistic alchemy, and a word for something that tricks people into thinking you're more attractive than you really are became a word for something that tricks you into thinking other people are more attractive than they really are. Turning black eyeliner into a substance that leads to many black eyes is probably the greatest true transformation the man ever achieved.

the leading cause of the stress which requires us to intervene. And if our guests don't fight our help themselves, then all their colleagues certainly will."

"You'd think so," grumbled Liam with a forlorn clinking swirl of the half-melted ice cubes, in the shape of the Corporate Council's ubiquitous "Double Copyright Symbol" logo, that floated at the bottom of his tall glass.

"So, as you can see," the Concierge was quick to add, leaning over again to top up Liam's glass, "we don't have a choice but to be a bit more direct than we might ideally wish to. But everyone soon realises that this is the sort of place where not relaxing and enjoying yourself simply isn't an option."

Caught in the melodious waves of his host's voice, Liam looked up, positively spellbound. The man went on.

"My job here is 'Concierge'[1]—the title is only a bit of affectation, really—but my job is to make sure that everything runs smoothly and that everyone plays the game, so to speak. I am, truth be told, a psychoanalyst by trade. That's what the Council advertised for when filling the position."

Even Liam could no longer ignore the massive change that had seized the man. Like some demented social high-performance vehicle, he had gone from all cheer to stony mountain face in aught-point-two seconds.

"Which brings us to you, Liam. Tell me, why can you not relax and enjoy all that we have to offer you here?"

With the audible question mark, it seemed as if the spell keeping Liam silent and attentive had abruptly lifted. A thousand questions, thoughts, and answers surged out of his locked-down mind. So what came out of his mouth was a garbled mess bearing a somewhat remote resemblance to:

---

[1] Possibly "fellow slave," from the Latin *conservus*. But I like my head-canon etymology much better: bearer of a *cierge*, a religious candle. A.K.A. Lucifer.

"Whuzzanuddle-huh?"

The Concierge kept a silence worth his—impressive—weight in gold[1] and urged Liam on with the faintest of nods.

"Well I… the guards, and the tasering… the sedatives… my car… I…"

"Surely, you now see," said the Concierge, interrupting nothing, "how all of that was only in your best interest, Liam."

The man rumbled the words through a throatful of gravel, and then, somehow, Liam did see it.

"I guess I just didn't know." Liam blinked in the reflected red Marslight, as if waking up from an intense daydream.

"A classic misunderstanding. It's quite funny, really, when you stop to think about it, isn't it?"

The man let loose a wild thunderous laugh, and his mirth was so contagious that soon Liam, too, was bursting at the seams[II]. He had to dab at his eyes with his well used napkin to stem the tears.

"Ah!" The Concierge panted for breath. "Oh dear! Oh my! How very silly life can be sometimes. Oh, and look! Here comes the dessert!"

---

[1] Impressive on Earth, that is. But almost nothing on Phobos. There's a metaphor in there somewhere.

[II] As if the Concierge's girth were as contagious as his mirth.

19

Viewed the right way, the facilities on Paradise Mars were nothing short of stellar. Truly top class. In his initial rush for food, on the confused and misguided first day of his stay, he had completely ignored the other indicators on the AR map. Now, with the waypoints carefully set up and programmed to guide him through the corridors, he could set out and really make the most of his time here. His favourite haunt was the zero-G pool-side bar at the centre of the old moon's shell, and that's where he was headed again, with another pleasant day of weightless indulgence waiting for him at the end of the transport tube.

Not that he was a dupe to what was going on. He was fully aware that all this luxury and comfort was designed to resocialise those "guests" who had started to show cracks in the mandatory blind trust they were supposed to show toward their respective Corporations at all times. It was also a way of shoving their noses directly into all the comforts and advantages that came from being a willing cog in the Corporate machine—and showing them everything they stood to lose. Even through the mood-altering drugs the Council's staff had unquestionably laced his meals with, especially that night at the Concierge's, Liam was keenly aware of what was going on and what was expected of him.

But the way Liam saw it, he deserved every single one of these comforts, and he planned on exploiting them to the fullest. And even more importantly, this was what they demanded of him. Playing the game would be the fastest way to get out of this padded marble space prison and back to work again, before he lost his show.

It chafed him that he couldn't view any of the GiG feeds. He wished he could see how his ten remaining human contestants were faring—it would have kept him distracted and saved him time catching up when he got back to the Mews—but it was not having any news from the Cassar simulation's feed that was worst of all. It burned a hole in the pockets of his most vested interests.

He had no idea if the plan was still working, if "Raja Cassar" was still spouting all of the Corporate system horror stories his employers had been so keen to quash. Beyond punishing Liam's attempt at duplicity, the Editor hadn't seemed overly fussed with the principle of the Cassar construct, as long as the viewing numbers were there—but that was the problem. Liam had no idea if the viewers were still as interested in Cassar as they'd been on premiere night. If they were still reacting to the stories on hir feed. If they really cared.

There was a little warning ping in his display, and then the flow of air in the transport tube slowed to a trickle, popping him gently out onto the pool cavern's rugged natural olivine floor, like a newborn babe in red swim-trunks. Free-floating steam billowed over him and scoured his brain of all mundane thoughts. Instead, the shimmering mermaid lights of the impossible, shifting sphere of water hanging over his head filled his mind, as it did every time; an Olympic-sized pool, floating as free from the constraints of gravity as he and the other residents of Paradise Mars. And nestled beneath it, as if a roof of flying water were the most natural thing in the world, sat the Highest Bar. Liam's home far, far away from home.

Even the people here didn't irk him quite as much as they had the night of his arrival; had it been three days ago already? He nodded and smiled at faces he loathed himself for recognising.

"You there!" rang out an authoritative woman's voice from

somewhere above. Liam was the only one crossing the no-Martian's-land between the transport tube and the bar, so unless she was speaking to one of the sprawling potted plants, the speaker must mean him. "Wait right there!"

Liam came to a bobbing stop, floating gently above the wet, rugged cavern floor, and turned to the stern-faced matron who somehow managed to give the impression of stomping angrily over even as she floated down out of the pool overhead.

"You're him, aren't you? The host of that show back on Earth?"

Even out here, Liam couldn't escape the fans. He put on his best humble smile as the elegant older lady landed next to him, her bathing suit so tight and so sculpted she looked carved from marble. "You're correct, of course. And, wow, I knew the show had fans everywhere, but this really is a p—"

He was so busy waffling on, he didn't see her heavy-ringed hand rise until it was far too late.

WH-LACK! The slap hit him like a rogue asteroid, spinning his head to the right and knocking the self-satisfied words right out of his mouth.

Liam blinked his watering eyes and rode through the stinging pain in silence. He was starting to suspect he may have misread the situation, somehow.

"How dare you let those… those ruffians lay their hands on my poor Neriene! And speak about her the way they do, like she was just another dirt-grubbing slum-dweller!"

"Ah," replied Liam, feeling for loose teeth with his tongue. "Ms Cartwright, I presume."

The fearsome woman huffed back at him through alabaster nostrils. "As if you didn't know."

When the ringing settled down, Liam had to admit there was a resemblance there, between this compact, sculpted dragon of a woman and the elongated waif he'd met at the Mews—the same way a string of tortured processed cheese still bore some resemblance to an aged wheel of Parmigiano Reggiano. The same basic ingredients, just shaped by entirely different forces.

Poor Neriene. Having a woman like this for a clone-mother was bad enough, let alone the physical and mental torture of birth and childhood in a place so thoroughly unchildlike as Paradise Mars.

"What, nothing to say for yourself, then? I shouldn't be surprised," huffed the original Cartwright. "Just make sure you put the riff-raff on that show of yours back in their place, you hear me? If I don't see them start treating my Neriene the way someone of her standing deserves, the RedCorp Board will be hearing about it. Your Ms Heath is in my Tuesday night squash club, so see if they don't!"

Oh, Mars almighty. She was right. Ms Heath would be lurking up here on Paradise Mars as well. Liam's backside clenched in instinctive terror at the thought, and the rest of him couldn't blame it. The last time he'd had a run-in with Ms Heath, he'd ended up having to engage in public intercourse with a robotic version of himself. The RedCorp senior executive was the one who had roped Liam into *The Grass is Greener* in the first place, and she took the expression "the show must go on" to entirely excessive lengths. Really, very excessive.

Bobbing slightly in the pool area nanogravity, the Cartwright woman nodded—possibly misreading his clenching fear as due respect for her position. Liam wasn't about to disabuse her.

"Right then. As long as that's clear. Don't make me regret not going straight to the people in charge, you hear?"

"Loud and clear, ma'am," said Liam, only just fighting back the urge to add a sarcastic military salute.

"You don't want to make Cartwright Industries angry, Mr Argyle."

With that last parting salvo, she spun with practiced grace and kicked off, floating back up toward the overhead swimming sphere and diving into it with barely a ripple.

Huh. What happened to the Paradise Mars diktat of being happy at all costs? Did that only apply to abductees in need of a good brain-washing, like Liam?

Clearly, not everyone was equal, even in Paradise.

Lost in thought, Liam scuttle-shuffled on autopilot over to the most familiar, most welcoming place this side of the radiation belt.

"Ah, Mister Argyle, sir!" cooed the bartender. "What'll be your pleasure today?"

"Morning Glory, Arnie." Liam wasn't all that surprised to discover he no longer needed to look at the young man's AR tag to remember his name.

"Right you are, sir," came the consecrated reply as Arnie grabbed some floating fruit and busied himself at the blender.

What came out was a teardrop-shaped cupful of thick gunk weighing nothing and bearing a lovely khaki disposition. Liam took a deep swig, chewed some pulp, swallowed, and let out a sigh of appreciation. Just the right amount of bourbon to offset the healthiness of the fruit. As always.

Nursing his drink, he decided to take it for a bit of a dip in the frothing globe above. He scanned the bright-lit waters for the bit with the lowest saggy-old-person-in-far-too-revealing-swimsuit density, taking especial care to stay well clear of the busy patch where he was pretty sure he'd spotted Justine Manzano, his *Grass is Greener* second season winner[1] and just about the last person he wanted to bump into

---

[1] Excerpt from Ms Manzano's file, from *The Grass is Greener*'s archives: After falling nearly one-million fids into debt earning a PhD in the archaic computer languages needed to keep the U.S. government's many out-of-date but too-expensive-to-replace computer systems up and running, she was two days from graduation when a brand-new AI system crashed into her chosen field like the Hindenburg and automated the entire process. But that was a dime-a-dozen sob story in the modern Corporate world, unworthy of *The Grass is Greener*'s greatest prize. In fact, her minimum-wage job carrying the bulky, out-of-date computers up six flights of stairs to manually plug them into the new quantum supercomputers was considered a success story in the Corporate Council's annual employment statistics as being "within her chosen field" and "union-protected"—specifically, the UAW, or United Android Workers union, which deemed stair-climbing to be unworthy of the wear-and-tear it caused to expensive robot joints and thus restricted to human laborers. Manzano had won the sympathy of the GiGalos and her

here—even less than Cartwright Senior. Keeping his head down, he kicked off from the bar, ping-ponging his way one-handed along the cavern's walls until he could launch himself through the air, straight into the water.

The plan worked better than expected in the zero-gravity—too well, in fact, as he went careening[1], full-body, beneath the frothy water.

His short cry of alarm turned into a warm gurgle, and the entire universe seemed to spin around him. But still, he kept his priorities straight: when his face emerged, spluttering, from the water a moment later, his morning drink was still clutched in the arm he'd somehow managed, out of instinct, to keep safely extended above the water globe's shimmering surface.

The strange jelly-like ripples around Liam were disappointing—nothing like the massive splash his Earth-formatted brain insisted he should have caused—and the cavern around him seemed to have turned on its head. The bar was now part of the ceiling, with ol' Arnie bobbing there like a mojito-slinging fruit bat. The other lucky few bobbing at the surface of the heated, jet-churned globe of water seemed oblivious to the change, as if up and down had always been subjective, everything was relative, and this were the most natural thing in the universe.

---

one-way ticket to Paradise Mars when, live on the feed, she'd been collecting hard drives from the scrubbers that pulled lethal levels of arsenic, lead, and other metals out of the New York City drinking water for use in semiconductor manufacturing in New Jersey, only for a runaway goose to get sucked into the machine's intake and shower her with feathers, blood, and *foie gras*. The destruction of the scrubbing machine having happened during her maintenance, she was promptly dismissed from the job with the cost of the equipment to come out of her future earnings, should she ever again have any. Only after a massive, spontaneous social media campaign by *The Grass is Greener* viewers were the terms of her dismissal amended to specify that she could keep what remained of the goose as compensation for her service.

[1] To turn a ship on its side, exposing the keel"

And maybe they were right, at that. Ah well, when in the new Rome…

The jets caressed Liam in ways he had almost forgotten he could be caressed, as he closed his eyes, took a deep drink, and let the fumes rising off the subtly magnetised chemical mix in the water work their magic. Liam's mind and worries melted to so much mush; the lunch chimes, nearly two hours later, caught him in that same position, for all intents and purposes a vegetable.

After lunch, Liam decided upon partaking of a delightfully retrograde pleasure he'd discovered only two days ago: the cinema. As the historical brochure had explained, in the early days of entertainment, the ancestors of vids required heavy and expensive infrastructure, both to produce and to replay. People would ritually flock to their local "cinema" at a designated hour to watch the latest production on a massive white screen, which, for some reason, they insisted on calling "silver."

This habit lasted long into the era of the first attempts at distributed mass media, competing with the ancestors of modern media such as the "television" and the primitive computer.

Liam could see why; there was something dwarfing, something immersive, something almost sacred about paying homage to the screen and its characters. Everything was so much larger than life, and in an era where the world had been formatted to fit the standard ten cm^2 AR window, it made for a profound and refreshing experience. The brochure mentioned that RedCorp's venture division was planning on reintroducing one or two of these Cinemas in the richer commercial areas of the biggest urban sprawls back dirtside, and Liam signed up for AR alerts on any developments.

Yet another day had passed so amazingly well, and Liam's happy buzz was so complete that even the Concierge's summons for drinks at seven did little to dampen his spirits.

No need for an Escort this time; he sauntered there in the best suit his hosts had to offer, gave the door a smart rap at precisely five minutes before the hour, and entered without waiting for an answer, as was custom.

This time, the Concierge was sitting deep in his sofa when Liam arrived, and by the looks of him, he had already set into the reserve port with extreme, delighted prejudice.

"Ah, Liam! Just the fellow! Do take a seat!"

The host sat and drank his own bulbous glass of port, enjoying himself as required, but not even half-listening to the psychologist's obligatory drivel. Liam trusted the Concierge would get to the point soon enough. And, indeed, so he did—before they had emptied the salted peanut bowl, even. A mark of hurry if there ever was one.

"Well, then. It seems like you've taken to our little establishment in the end, hmm?"

"Hmm," Liam assented. "Haven't seen the time go by, really."

The Concierge took an appreciative swig of port. "And yet," he resumed, smacking his lips, "here we are, three days later. And frankly, you look like a new man, Liam. Tell me, how do you feel?"

That almighty intensity had once again entered the man's eyes, cutting his cheer so short it would have made the good Docteur Guillotin[1] stop and admire how close the shave was.

Liam gulped.

"I… I feel great! I really do. This place is doing wonders for me. Exactly what I needed." He tried to fill his words with as much of the sheer relaxation of the last few days as he could.

The Concierge seemed pensive beneath his flushed cheeks. "I see. Tell me, why do you think you needed this little break, then?"

Liam sputtered like a robot lawnmower long overdue for a service

---

[1] Joseph Ignace Guillotin was a staunch opponent of the death penalty and a passionate defender of human rights, especially for criminals. Contrary to popular belief, he did not invent the head-removing device that bears his name and made him famous around the world. All he did was complain so loudly and so often about France's inhumane methods of execution that someone else built a less painful decapitation machine to shut him up. His one real invention was modern Parliament seating, and therefore, indirectly, the terms "left wing" and "right wing."

and hung his head in embarrassment. "Well, you know, work has been a major pain lately. The hours are a real killer. And then there's been this whole mess with the AI contestant. Yes, of course, I should have had it confirmed by Corporate first. I was rushed, so I tried to cut a corner or two to make the show work. Is that really all that bad? We needed the extra contestant, and it's been great for the ratings."

The Concierge steepled his fingers. "And what about your stay here? Have you been satisfied with the arrangements?" His gaze flicked down to the abhorred "WILLIAM" nametag at Liam's lapel. "Haven't you been tempted to explore, to push the boundaries of where you can and can't go here on Paradise Mars?"

Liam took a deep swig and shrugged, with his mouth full of peppery bottle-aged port goodness. He swallowed it down, then said, "The thought hadn't really come to me, I guess. Why would I do anything like that, anyway? Seems a bit silly, when there are so many amazing things to do and see. The routine soon gets filled chock full as it is—and Mars knows I needed the break, after all the stress from work." He set down his empty port glass. "I just never thought it'd all blow up like this, to the point where they'd send some slick Marketing hitman down to Tantamount Mews to replace me. If they ever took my show away, I don't know what I'd…"

Liam trailed off, as if just catching up with his own words. He looked up at the Concierge and shook his head in apology. "But I wouldn't want to dump all my worries on you."

A glint like a car headlight in the night entered the man's eye, and he passed Liam the glass of cold G&T he'd been silently begging for.

"Oh, but I insist. Please. Go on."

With that, the flood gates opened, and the words came pouring out of the breach in Liam's face, devastating any attempt at structuring or censorship he might throw in their path.

Liam spilled every last bean. The Raja Cassar business, the pressure at work, his drinking, losing his friends, all the way back to that first traumatic season of the GiG and his anxieties[1] at being hired. The Concierge's fingers danced across an AR field only he could see, doubtlessly taking notes for Liam's permanent record.

When the flow finally tapered out and it became evident that the last drop of psychoanalytical nectar had been squeezed out, the Concierge broke his silence with a hearty, "Well! Little wonder that you needed a little break from it all! Who wouldn't, with everything you've gone through?"

For some reason, the statement rung dry in Liam's mind—almost rehearsed—but he nodded, nonetheless.

The Concierge ploughed on. "Let me say how happy I am that I was able to lend a hand, however modest. The stay with us seems to have worked its magic on you, and I think it's time to get you back to the real world. What do you say, are you eager to get back to work?"

Liam rubbed at the stubble on his cheeks, out of long-lost nervous habit. "Well, truth be told, I really wouldn't mind staying here a bit longer…"

"That's what I like to hear!" bellowed the Concierge, with a loud laugh. "Good man, Liam, good man! I'll make sure they keep you a seat on the next shuttle out. And… well, I probably shouldn't say this…"

The reality show host blinked in surprise, truly thrown. For the first time since his forced stay in Paradise started, the Concierge sounded genuinely unsure of himself. Uncomfortable, even.

"It's just that my quarterly company review is coming up, and I would be really grateful if you could put in a good word for me on the exit survey you'll get before you board the shuttle. Nothing extraordinary," the flustered man hurried to add, "but if you could point out how well we've gotten on together, and how much you've benefited from your stay here under my care… well, that could mean a promotion for me, and no mistake."

---

[1] "Anxious" and "anger" share the same etymology, meaning "to choke."

Liam nodded with as straight and compassionate a face as he could muster. "You may count on me, sir. I won't let you down."

The Concierge unfurled from of his seat, rising with a bounce and a beaming smile. Liam followed suit, shaking the man's extended hand.

"I'd say I hope to see you again soon," said the Concierge, "but it's always the opposite, really. Damned terrible part of the job." The man actually sounded like he was on the verge of a sniffle. "Right, then! Off you go!"

Liam fixed a polite smile on his face and floated out the imposing doors. As soon as they slid shut, cutting off the red Mars glow behind him, Liam's smile burst its bounds and broke into a properly smug grin.

Sucker.

Liam's smugness at having fooled the weird Corporate shrink kept him buoyed and bouncing as he headed back to his room, changed into the hated Corporate Council logo-bearing shuttle jumpsuit, grabbed the bag with the suit he'd been wearing when they decided to abduct him—freshly pressed, too, which was a nice touch—and made his bobbing way through the increasingly weak gravity all the way to the shuttle departure lounge at the centre of the station's spin on the side that faced away from the Red ^{TM} Planet.

And that's when his cockiness wilted and died. As he floated about, dreaming of what he'd do when he got back to his show and waiting for the shuttle boarding call, he spied an odd, yet deeply familiar ornament atop the marble mantle over the lounge's mock fireplace: a little funerary urn, onyx black with gold highlights. Some lackey had soldered it to the stone so it would remain in the most aesthetically pleasing place atop the mantlepiece, even in zero gravity.

As if the forlorn little bulb had some old-timey science-fiction tractor beam, it sucked Liam in until he was floating, ghost-like, within arm's reach. He rubbed a bit of the built-up Phobos dust off the urn's lid.

No matter how hard he wished the contrary, there was no doubt possible; it was Usnavi. This is where the poor boy had ended up. He'd suffered every possible ignominy[I], every slight the Corporate world could throw at him for eighteen years, every breach of privacy and trust Liam and *The Grass is Greener* could muster for the sake of global entertainment, and had ultimately been sacrificed on that same altar—all that, only to end up as a long-forgotten mantlepiece ornament for the same Corporate execs who profited from his misery, and the misery of countless millions like him all around the world, before, during, and after his short, miserable, yet always optimistic life.

Mars? Hades, more like.[II]

The boarding call rang like a funeral wail, but Liam was glad to hear it just the same. If he didn't tear himself away from the sorry sight of Usnavi Musibay's worldly remains soon, he knew he'd lose control entirely. Now, more than ever, he needed to keep it together. It wouldn't even begin to make up for his part in what they'd all done to the boy, but Liam swore, with his last glance back at the sad little urn, not to waste his chance to make sure Usnavi hadn't died in vain.

"I do hope Sir isn't experiencing Lightway stress again, is he?" chimed the hated shuttle AI voice as the flow of fellow shuttle-goers, unseen beyond Liam's tear-filled eyes, deposited him into the strapped embrace of his padded seat.

"No, no," replied Liam, swallowing the lump in his throat. "Just something in the air filters, I'm sure."

"Indeed." The AI didn't sound convinced. "Well, just the same, we'll make sure you have a lovely, restful ride back to Old Smoggy, shall we?"

[I] "To lose your good name"

[II] Yes, I am aware that's mixing Roman and Greek gods, but "Pluto" was already taken.

Liam didn't even bother to protest. When the injection-sting came at the back of his neck, he welcomed it like an old, long-lost friend.

20

They wanted a well adjusted, complacent worker? Oh, he'd give them well adjusted.

The first thing Liam did after splashdown back at the London suborbital landing pool was buy a disposable external comms unit from the station's travel vending machines. If the bosses weren't fazed at the thought of hijacking his car, assaulting, and kidnapping him, then a little light surveillance of how he used his fancy Corporate-paid AR suite wouldn't even register a blip on their haywire[1] moral compass.

He took his new off-the-rack toy into a stall of the suborbital pool station's gleaming, rainbow-hued bathroom; five minutes with the unit's hard screen told him everything he needed to know. Then he tossed it straight into the recycler and marched out, eager to get back to work—with a vengeance.

He didn't mind sticking to the cover story cooked up by the Editor to explain his leave of absence, that he'd had some undisclosed and embarrassing health and hygiene issue that required private hospitalisation on Paradise Mars. In fact, ridiculous though it may sound, Liam had to admit the story served its purpose perfectly. Even the

---

[1] "Soft wire for binding bales of hay," sometimes of very poor quality, which led to the meaning of "faulty equipment."

most curious of well-wishers—hangers-on and GiG tie-in publicity people from various RedCorp departmental appendages, mostly—didn't really want to get into the hinted gruesome details once they'd pried enough to obtain the cover story.

Everyone agreed Liam seemed in most excellent shape and spirits, though, and that's all that really mattered from a work point of view. There he was, cheerful and helpful in every situation, despite the long hours he was putting in. This new vitality shined through in all his live performances as well, giving the feed a much-needed burst of energy, which rapidly made up for the GiG's slouching ratings in his absence. (Take *that*, you Psychomarketing bastards!)

He seemed to be putting an impossible one-hundred-and-ninety-percent effort into everything he did—all the more surprising, co-workers muttered amongst themselves when they thought him happily busy handling some AR paperwork, given that he had every reason to be in a blind rage after what Corporate did to his pet project, the Cassar construct.

Those first few minutes after Earthfall, monitoring the feed on his disposable comms unit, had confirmed that, once again, reality had found a way to go beyond Liam's worst fears. Back on Paradise Mars, he'd fretted about whether the Editor would pull the plug on the Cassar experiment or not. But the man had, as ever, found a much more elegant—and entirely more devious—solution.

He'd simply had Barry change the simulation parameters. The amalgamated tragedies of a thousand rejected *Grass is Greener* applicants hadn't gone away, but they were no longer presented in a way that might foster one iota of sympathy, much less rebellion. Instead, Raja Cassar's live feed had become a feel-good, whatever-doesn't-kill-you-only-makes-you-stronger, motivational status quo lovefest, peppered liberally with product placement for RedCorp affiliate merchandise, old and new. He was nothing less than the computer-generated embodiment of the Corporate human spirit triumphing over all adversity.

Drawn in to the Cassar feed by the initial buzz over Liam's gory real-life stories, GiGalos all around the world were now lapping up the Editor's new rubbish like extra-strength branded caffeine water. It made his innards burn with cold rage.

Yet, despite all this, Liam went about his work with smile and zeal, as far as the rest of RedCorp was concerned. He even made a point of taking an active interest in everything his co-workers were doing.

Tell me more about your weekend in Huddersfield with your sister!
Allergic to hazelnuts, you say?
No, I've never seen a bunion the size of a walnut before!

At the next Monday morning meeting, just after Liam's first Sunday feature show back on the job—where they'd all had a particularly satisfying time eliminating Tanoa Sharma, the sullen Fijian "nanopaint drying observer" who couldn't keep a feed interesting to save his life—Barry even spoke up to say as much.

"If I could add a word or two," the traditionally tight-lipped technician mumbled, adjusting his orange insulated overall suspenders out of nervous habit, "I really wanted to say how fantastic it's been having you back with us, Liam, rested up and better than ever. I mean," he ploughed on, in a fit of verbal diarrhoea, "I can't remember the last time you were this interested and helpful with what I've been doing. You should go on holiday more often!"

After a brief moment's silence, as Lee, Akintola, and Mary Artworthy cast a cautious glance his way, Liam led the entire cramped closet/conference room in a burst of laughter.

He was glad they were all laughing. Especially at his own expense.

The blow from the butt of your jokes is always the one you expect the least.

Because Liam was done with trying to change the system from the inside. There was no subtle way to get the truth out there, to liberate minds without risk to himself. The only options they'd left him were either full-on, all-guns-blazing, direct conflict or else going back to moral sleep.

Well, so be it, then.

No more dinking around in bars, no more sullen civil disobedience. Driven like never before, it only took him a few days after his return from "holiday" to boil down the mass of modern-era horror stories from the rejection file into a single bullet of vengeful wrath and indignation, ready to fire straight into the minds of illusioned Corporate wage slaves around the world.

Work became a greater pleasure than ever. For Liam, going to the Mews no longer had anything to do with producing a damn useless, mind-numbing, voyeuristic feed. Now, every visit was a recon mission.

The plan had already existed at the back of his mind, tickling his cerebellum but held back into by his inhibitions—and his lingering sense of self-preservation. But what was the point of playing the Corporate game when they could still abduct you—or worse—at the drop of an RFID tag?

Now that they'd taken Raja Cassar—his last shot, his last hope—away from him, the courage to act came surprisingly easy.

Everything was coming together nicely, but Liam still needed one crucial element: information. He needed to know the ins and outs of every single cog that formed the Mews. Every link in the chain between what they recorded at the Mews and what reached the viewers' AR displays. It sickened him to the core when he realised he'd wasted years of his life slaving away in that media bunker and yet had no real idea how the place even worked.

Barry's enthusiasm couldn't have been more useful to him. He was just so damn eager to show off his electronic babies, to give Liam the grand tour of the palace of towering networks and cascading interfaces that made up his working world. So starved for recognition.

Of course, there were things that Barry simply would or could not show Liam, for all his cajoling and buttering up. Inevitably, these were the most crucial bits if Liam ever hoped to succeed with his plan. Of course, it would have been too much to ask for the Universe to start cooperating *now*, after forty-three years of unmitigated hostility.

But Liam kept himself from letting any frustration show, nor did he let the practical challenges to his mad new project mar his enthusiasm. There were always going to be elements that even the best laid plan would have to leave to informed chance.

It took him two weeks of feigning interest in his co-workers, plus a few covert drone deliveries through the service entrance, and then the plan was set. All the preparations were ready, and the moment was upon him.

Sunday evening.

Showtime.

And if Liam had any say in the matter, his viewers were about to get a show like none before.

21

Liam's co-workers buzzed about, wearing their mandatory anxiety on their sleeves as the hours ticked down to their mid-season elimination show. After tonight, only half of the original twelve contestants would be left. Then, the real posturing, infighting, and good old-fashioned slagging would kick in, with each contestant finally daring to picture themselves as the One, the greatest, the most validated victim the Corporate world had to offer in the Year of Our Profits 2074.

But more power to them, the poor sods.

Every single one of the remaining contestants deserved a break, as far as Liam was concerned. Hattie Hughes, the trans widow literally slaving away to make ends meet until her late husband's succession clears. Young Neriene Cartwright, tortured in body and mind by her birth on Paradise Mars—fighting her way through treatments in crushing Earth gravity to make her "normal" when all she wanted was to be herself, to define her own normal. Komodo dragon-milker Fnu Cinta, Amazon mosquito-bait researcher Matheus Carvalho, tortured-flesh fashion victim Sabeen Al-Amin, Kenyan automated super-highway roadkill clearer Davy Muriithi... They all had their own, legitimate twist on modern misery, their own entertaining yet ultimately pitiful reason for making it into the final half of season three of *The Grass is Greener*—the final sprint to the grand prize.

Of course, there was still the dramatically back-storied but now ever-so-optimistic-and-inspiring "Raja Cassar" to contend with. That made seven contestants still in the running. One more would have to go, this very night, before they'd truly reached the halfway mark on the season.

And Liam had a sneaking suspicion that having a fake, completely controllable contestant win the grand prize would be a lovely cost-saving feather in the Editor's cap.

However, all of these GiGalesque considerations formed little more than mental background noise against the buzz of excitement coursing through Liam Argyle's ethanol-scoured veins at the thought of the evening's true main event—the one only he knew about.

The minutes lumbered past like arthritic mammoths.

Liam clutched his little solid-state data key in the palm of a sweaty hand. He was confident he'd be able to pull it off—or so he kept telling himself, at least. He just wasn't so sure he'd be able to do it without getting caught.

Thus it came to pass, one fine Sunday evening, as the late summer heat coaxed the ever-present smoggy backdrop of the urban London sprawl into an ever-thicker miasma of carcinogenic city "character" and as Red-feeders on every continent[1] sat, stood, or lay with their brains glued to the GiG main feed preshow, that Liam knocked politely on the door with the fritzing "Networks" AR plaque. Without waiting for a response, he swung the lockless door open and fired off a warm smile at the baffled Barry inside.

"Liam? What are you doing here? It's almost feed time."

Liam turned on the smarm, discreetly shuffling his ruck sack a bit farther behind his back. "Oh, I know you're busy. I just thought I'd bring you a little something from the trolley to keep up your strength.

---

[1] Yes, even Antarctica.

And double-check that everything was ready for the feed, sort of thing. We can't do any of this without you, you know."

In case the buttering up wasn't enough, Liam showed the Mews's sole technician the fizzing plastic cup of sugar and caffeine in his hand and relied on substance addiction to finish the work. Sure enough, Barry smiled and rolled his chair to one side of the cramped, server-filled office, beckoning the host in. Liam took great care to close the door firmly shut behind him. Even though everybody else was far too busy looking busy to give a hoot about what Barry was doing and the hallway was empty, it never hurt to be cautious.

Liam handed over the cup and turned to survey the techie's domain. "I won't keep you long. I know how busy you are. After all, you're the one who's here pumping away at the bellows, making sure everything's going smoothly."

"Well, thanks for the drink anyway." For some infuriating reason the rotund techie wasn't drinking yet. Liam smiled all the more desperately and struggled to keep a nervous twitch out of his eye. "We're ready to go here, but there's always more to do, checks to make. It's never finished until the feed is over, and even then, there's more to do, you know?"

"Aye, it's all sweat and hard work in here, I know." Liam decided to push the matter somewhat. "And boy, it sure is hot in here, don't you think? We'll have to see about getting you someplace with a window."

"Hot? I suppose so," answered Barry, puzzled, before taking a reflexive swig of the drink. "Can't say I really notice it very much. Used to it by now, I suppose." He chugged again.

Liam kept an eye on the seconds ticking away in his AR countdown. "Well then," he said, after five seconds' pause, "everything looks in order here. I'd best go make sure everyone else is doing as good a job as you are, eh, Barry?"

"Sure thing, man. You break a leg out there, okay?"

Liam gave Barry a firm pat on the back and made for the door, pausing with his hand on the handle. As Barry started wheeling the chair back over to his main desk, the host slipped his hand into his ruck sack, pulled out a little gunmetal grey transmitter pyramid, and flicked the devious little device's on/off toggle.

Behind him, there was a stumbling thump and a mumbled "Wuzza?"

Liam turned back just in time to watch Barry slump into an ignominious heap at the foot of his chair.

Well, then. The dodgy vendors in the part of the Red you couldn't reach from a classic search engine hadn't been lying. They'd been expensive, but the instant carotid choke-nanites he'd emptied into Barry's drink had done the trick. He'd be fine, Liam reminded himself, if only to quell the rising pangs of guilt. The nanites kept blood flow regulated with infinitely better-than-pinpoint precision. They'd keep him safe but unconscious until someone got in here to turn the transmitter off. Good thing the DarkRed had better standards than the Big Five on the Corporate Council when it came to truth in advertising.

Beyond the bulk of Barry's crumpled form, the main solid-state console screen glowed and hummed with anticipative glee at the technician's desk, but Liam would take care of that later. First, he needed to get the rest of his gear set up. With precise motions honed by many sleepless nights' worth of obsessive mental preparation, he pulled his expensive little treasures out of his ruck sack, plugging, snapping, and fiddling them into place.

The host kept glancing back at the closed door, wishing it were lockable, but locks in office buildings were a cost-prohibitive rarity these days. And in any case, no one ever really had cause to venture into Barry's technological den, so the fear was purely irrational. Or so Liam kept telling himself.

He inserted the final cable into the required port, stood back to survey his work, then stepped over Barry's recumbent form and fell into the depths of the man's statutory padded office chair. Liam didn't know why he suddenly felt so tired, but he had a job to do, and his resolve stood out against the flood like a circus tent atop Mount Ararat.

He pulled the penultimate item out of his bag of tricks and looked it over. To think such a small data key could hold something of such momentous importance.

He ceremoniously interfaced it with the central console, then keyed up the feed control interface. The antiquated and arcane lettering appeared in all its primitive coloured glory upon the black console stage. Such an unwieldy and cryptic interface had evidently been designed to make using it as difficult as possible, and thus keep programmer-kind in gainful employment. But Liam had a map of these wild and dangerous virtual territories, thanks to his time being a good Supervisor and showing interest in Barry's work, so he plodded on with slow, painstaking determination.

The seconds on the clock at the bottom of his display needled their painful way into Liam's brain, and he grew ever more aware of the pressing urgency of his task. Already, beyond the closed door, the usual silence of the pre-feed nail-biting was treacle-thick.

Ten minutes until the show went live. Less than that before someone realised Liam wasn't in his usual spot and sent Mary beating the bushes to drive him out of hiding. The slightest bead of sweat formed on Liam's temple, but he left it there as he focused on navigating through the archaic interface.

Triumph dawned across his face as he finally found the proper command line and location for uploading pre-recorded footage to the live feed. To be fair, it wasn't all that hidden—Barry used the command a good dozen times every show. But nobody other than a certified technician knew how to do anything in an interface this old and unintuitive, so Liam decided to take his glory and bask in it while the basking was good.

However, his grin soon crumbled like a chocolate-chip cookie meeting a jackhammer when an innocent-looking command prompt reared its simple little head:

"Password?"

Blink. Blink. Blink, went the accursed cursor[1].

Out of unthinking hope it would suffice to make the offending prompt go away, Liam's finger pressed "Enter" on the console's virtual keyboard.

"Password?" replied the screen, forever constant.

Oh, bollocks.

Barry hadn't mentioned anything about a password. Liam hadn't seen a single password yet, anywhere on the system! Why was there a password all of a sudden? What point could there possibly be in putting a password this deep within the system? Did some clever clogs systems designer say to himself, late one mountain dewy night, "Hmm, I'll put in a password at the latest possible stage. That way, if someone breaks in, knocks out the technician, and tries to broadcast choice excerpts of their amateur pornographic films over the feed, they'll be stuck going down the shit rapids in an easily capsized kayak"?

Well, congratulations, then! Mission fucking accomplished!

There Liam was, with Barry out cold on the floor, more than a year of his grotesque salary's worth of illicit electronic goodies strewn about the place, and the only thing standing between him and getting his message out to the world were eight fucking letters, an arrogant bastard of a question mark, and that damn blinking cursor of doom!

Liam closed his eyes and forced himself to stay focused. He took a deep breath, then let it out. Deep breaths. That was the key.

Opening his eyes again, Liam stretched his finger into the air and decided to at least try the usual suspects before panicking.

How about… "Barry"? Nope.

"Guest"? Negatory.

"Password"? Niet.

---

[1] "Runner" or "errand-boy"

"Drowssap"? Oh que non.

The five minutes-to-feed alarm rang in his display. Okay, he'd tried. Now it was panic time.

"Aaarrgh!" Liam screamed, his sanity splintering into more pieces than the True Cross... He shook his fist in impotent anger at the stupid physical screen, grabbed it from the desk, then threw it down in despair.

He panted, looking down at the fractured console screen. Hey, that was pretty satisfying. Maybe there was something to be said for these old physical screens after all.

Not that any of it mattered, anyway. He was thoroughly boned.

Should he wake up Barry? Try to convince the big man he'd had a seizure and not been attacked by a psychotic co-worker?

Preposterous.

Wake him up and threaten him with violence until he entered the password? Having been knocked out once, Barry might buy it.

Then what? The nanites would wash themselves down Barry's throat the moment they were turned off; they couldn't be used a second time.

Who still used passwords and not bio-recognition scans anyway? It was just like something Justine Manzano—his second season winner—had to deal with in the bowels of New York City's water treatment plants. Even she could never remember the damn things! She always wrote them down on the bottom of the main—

Liam's heart hammered in his ears as he slipped his fingers under the console screen on the floor and lifted it slightly to see the bottom. Two letters and two numbers were handwritten in bright yellow marker: pw42.

He typed them into the virtual keyboard and hit "Enter" one last time.

"Enter file path," replied the uncaring, because non-sentient, machine.

Liam entered the file path.

"Enter start time."

Liam checked his AR time once more, then set the timer for the very second of the beginning of the live feed.

"Press Enter to confirm and return to root menu," prompted the machine, seeming to agree with Liam's choice.

Liam pressed Enter, returned to the root menu as promised, and then came to his senses. This wasn't some stress-induced delirium. He'd actually done it.

"Whooooooooooooeeeeeeeyyyyyyy," welled up the cry of joy inside him, but he fought it back and shunted it aside for now. There would be a time and a place for that later if all worked out as planned. In the meantime, he refused to tempt fate any more than strictly necessary. His open tab at the pub of Luck was running plenty high enough as it was.

Liam gave the screen one last check, making sure it hadn't changed while he wasn't looking; the concept that everything might actually be going his way was so very alien. Then, as satisfied as he was going to be for the time present, he rose to his expensive-loafered feet, stepped gingerly around Mount Barry, and made his way over to the door.

Before exiting, he pulled out and applied the last item in his ruck sack: a thick nanobot paste designed to harden and jam the door into place, bracing it against forced entry. He tossed the empty sack into a corner, took a few precious seconds to compose himself, then entered the corridor and pulled the door shut. The gentle hiss of hardening nanobots on the other side of the closed door was the sweetest sound Liam had ever heard.

He strode out toward the main entrance, duly anxious but lord of all he saw. Was he not the ringmaster of this strange little circus after all?

"Mr Argyle, sir!" Like a good, infinitely exploitable Agency worker, Mary Artworthy came rushing over, her arms full of power tools and catering boxes. She came to a panting stop when she caught up with him. "Three minutes to showtime, everyone's in place. Sent me to look for you, sir."

It was only fitting that Mary, the most abused and longsuffering member of the *Grass is Greener* team, should be the last one he'd ever see at the Mews. It was the thought of people like her that kept his resolve strong.

"Just stepping out for a breath of fresh air," Liam replied, after only the slightest pause. He gave the tired-looking woman a wink and a pointed nod that sent her scurrying. As he stepped out into the seasonal fog, he completed this thought in silence:

I may be some time.

22

Out in the docklands alleyway behind the Mews, the little plastic vial fell from Liam's raised hands and clattered to the drone lubricant-saturated concrete.

The bitter smell stayed in his nostrils, but the nanobots themselves soon made their way up his lacrimal drainage system and across to the corneal implant in each of his eyes.

He fell to his knees in the wet alley, his vision fragmenting into a terrorscape of shards, blood, and fragmented data as the nanobots went about the job he'd sniffed them up there to do. Pearlescent tears streamed from his ducts as the nanos broke down his fancy, RedCorp-issued AR implants and flushed them out of his body, along with the inert husks of the nanos themselves.

"Let them try and trace me now, the bastards!"

Liam indulged in a little cackle before picking himself up and resuming his mad rush to the second nearest subway maw. It was an extra five minutes' jog, but it was worth the extra time to be that little bit more unpredictable for any potential chasers.

He stumbled, blinking, out of the alleyway. Liam couldn't remember the last time he'd been outside without any AR display. Had the city always been this dark? In his new, unaugmented state, Liam felt like a newborn taking his first timid, uncertain steps into a world that didn't have any signs, arrows, or animated distractions at every step. On the road, cargo trucks and the rare passenger transport zoomed by with automated efficiency, ignoring him completely.

But the soon-to-be-former host remembered, with a thrill, that in all of a minute or two, the live feed would be starting, with or without him. And instead of seeing the seven increasingly hostile contestants they'd tuned in to watch have a go at each other, the four or five billion weekly feature viewers would get another treat altogether: Liam's packaged message, beamed from that little key in Barry's mechanical den straight into eyes all throughout the world.

He'd made it as fast and brutal as he knew how. He just hoped the incoming signal interference units he'd loaded the server room with would buy him enough time to get the message through—a few extra seconds, at least, before they realised the kill orders from the Tulip weren't going through and they found a way to cut off the outgoing feed at the distribution level.

Thrills running down his spine at the mere thought, Liam sped down the docklands thoroughfare. He firmly believed the RedCorp rent-a-cops would be giving chase, and soon. Along with scorn and dismissal slips, it was one of those things the big Corps were very good at giving.

That's where the final little surprise he'd left back in the server room would come in, jamming the physical access and hopefully affording Liam a few extra seconds to make good on his escape.

He raced into a scrupulously tidy alleyway that crossed from one main road to another, and his heart raced even faster. Without his AR display, Liam had no idea how long it'd been since he'd left the Mews. One minute, or twenty? Had his message kicked in yet or not? Or was it going out right now?

Were security cameras scanning the whole city for him at this very moment?

Liam popped his suit jacket off before he reached the far end of the alley and tugged the sleeves inside-out. The inner lining tweed wasn't exactly fetching, but he wasn't headed for any high society event tonight. Or ever again, for that matter. Hopefully, it'd be enough to make recognition harder for the security software—especially with the bits and bobs from the RedCorp standard-issue celebrity incognito kit he tugged out of his pocket and stuck onto his face as he set off again, without any real care for how it looked.

A ridiculous-looking mustachioed professor-type with ancient, non-functional, physical AR glasses and an old-school fMRI interface band pinning his tell-tale jug ears flat against his head emerged from the far end of the alley, darted through a gap in the automated traffic, and made straight for the Underground entrance on the other side.

One flash of his safe and nameless commuter pass later, the chthonic gates of the Underground hissed open for him, and Liam dived into the anonymity of the commuter flow pouring down into the gaping maw.

Only then did he allow himself to breathe a sigh of relief. You could always count on the uncaring facelessness of people, all too busy wishing they were anywhere other than in the tube, to make sure nobody gave two shakes of a pop-up ad about who you were or what you looked like. And who would believe, as they glanced from one blaring, flashing AR window to another, that they might really have caught a glimpse of someone even moderately rich and famous in a sweaty hell-bound sardine can such as this?

Liam had first-hand experience how easy it was for his employers to divert a more comfortable transportation option, like any proper automated car, and bring him in for some painfully pointed questions. The streets up top would be under much tighter surveillance[1], too. He'd have to stick to the Underground for now, buffeted by the jam-packed crowd in the subterranean heat, and chafing about having destroyed his only means of contact with the outside world. His only way of knowing if his plan had succeeded, if the message even went out, and if so, how the world was reacting to it.

---

[1] "Over/vigil," with the original meaning of "devotional watching or observance on the eve of a religious festival."

It seemed such a petty worry, when not five minutes ago he'd been expecting the shout of a guard or the buzz of a taser-equipped security drone at any second. But he couldn't shake the thought. He'd sacrificed so much to scratch his itching conscience, and now—out of necessity, but that didn't make it any less aggravating—he had no way of knowing if his plan had even worked.

Or if anyone cared.

Liam harrumphed beneath his sweaty fake moustache. All around him in the crammed subterranean wagon, women, men, and enbies alike stood slouched in rainbow-irised viewing bliss, partaking of the illustrious wholesale and worldwide mindfuck that was modern mass media.

Were any of them watching his message, right now? Was anyone here starting to open the added material he'd attached to the broadcast, the written records of the true worst lives of the modern age, the ones completely destroyed by a callous and uncaring Corporate system?

Liam tried to guess from the spectral glow in his neighbours' eyes, but it was a waste of time. Augmented eyes gave away no secrets.

As the train flickered through lighted sections of the Underground and back into darkness over and over again, a different glow caught the corner of his own grey eye. A gentle blue screen glow rising from a stooped-over figure halfway down the crammed carriage.

Someone with an actual, physical screen? It wasn't unheard of, but Liam still couldn't believe his luck. He didn't care whether it was due to an eye condition that prevented them using lenses or maybe just a retro, handheld fashion statement. All he could think of was shoving his way through the crowd and grabbing the blessed thing out of their hands so he could see what was happening in the greater Red-connected world.

In a society where a person's digital sphere was the most sacred taboo, it was the sort of behaviour which could well earn him a collective thrashing. But the burning urge for information soon overcame Liam's inhibitions, and he started shouldering his way into the throng, toward the glow.

Muttering apologies that drew no reaction from the AR viewers standing zombie-like around him, Liam waded through, barely daring to breathe until he finally reached his quarry, shining like a LightWay relay station before him.

The screen's owner was short, with long hair and a conservative business skirt. Liam peered over a neighbour's shoulder, his heart pounding against his reversed suit jacket.

They were watching an entertainment news feed, and it was on a rival Corp's network to boot.

Great. His one chance at seeing the fallout, and it wasn't even someone who watched the show.

Celeb Breakdown! Couldn't Face the Heat?

The caption scrolled at the bottom of the little handheld screen, sparkling, undulating, and competing as best it could for attention against twenty other widgets and pop-ups. Not to mention the babbling gossipfeed anchor in the middle of it all.

Oh, Gods. Just his luck. Some halfwit feedstar chose the same day he sent out his message to go off their rocker.

The chisel-chinned anchor was replaced on screen with a bald man with thick glasses, reclining next to a classic psychiatrist's sofa that didn't look like it'd ever had a patient in it.

"Vell," he slurred in the purest of stereotypes, as if the fact we were listening to a psychiatrist had not been hammered home quite enough yet, "zis ees ay teepickle hexample of dealeerium eendooced by eekcessieve vork-reelated schtress. Eet ees ay zeemtum of deeper zycolojeycull eeshoes weech, of course, poot eento daut zee judgment of Red Corporayshun een highuring zuch ay purzon een zee furzt plaice."

Even before his brain had finished translating, the reference to RedCorp made Liam pause, first in surprise, then in horrible doubt.

The feed flashed to the next standardised five-second sequence in the report, and with it, the scrolling banner flashed a new headline: *RedCorp Flagship Feed Host Attacks Colleagues, Escapes*

The video showed supposedly candid footage taken outside the Mews. AR-glazed viewers around the world, with the collective critical sense of a fresh water oyster, were treated to shaky glimpses of an ambulance pulling up, lights flashing and siren blasting. Both lights and sounds must have been enhanced for shock value; they pierced the mind with impossible intensity. Next came a picture of what looked like a corpse, wheeled out on a stretcher by hazmat-clad paramedics—that had to be Barry, shunted out to the ambulance.

Liam had to fight back a sudden, panicky stab of doubt. What if the strangler nanites hadn't lived up to the advertising? Or what if he hadn't set them properly? A fraction more choke on poor Barry's artery than necessary, and Liam might have caused irreparable brain damage. He might have killed the man, for all he knew. That'd certainly explain the ambulance and the sirens…

But no. Liam shook his head in the hot, damp subway train air. He'd double- and triple-checked everything. He'd set it correctly.

Plus, if there was one thing you could rely on a rival Corp's news for, it was sensationalism[I] and hyperbole[II]. If there'd been so much as a bruise on Barry's knee from the fall, they'd be crying bloody murder right now. "Assault[III]" sounded bad but it at least described what had happened.

Yet again, the newsfeed veered off in a brutal new direction, leaving the audiences' minds reeling as they took in the next flashing headline: *Massive Data Piracy–Linked with Radical Terrorist Cell?*

Pictures flashed on-screen, faces from all walks of life, every one of them deeply familiar to Liam—his handpicked spectrum of real victims of the Corporate world-state. His people.

[I] "Aiming at violently excited effects on the senses"

[II] "To throw beyond"

[III] "Leaping onto"

Here were their pictures, sent out to the world with a big, dramatic tag labelling them as victims. The sexual tourism safari trophies from the Balkans. The cheap, short-lived, cloned child soldiers dying in Corporate infighting over ash-filled cropland in the Amazon basin. The organ farm breeder-mothers of Kashmir. The climate refugees in their hundreds of millions—from Chittagong, Shanghai, Vila, Osaka, Alexandria, Glasgow, Hull, Miami, Male, Jakarta, Mumbai, Rio de Janeiro, Los Angeles, Anchorage, and a thousand other cities swallowed by floods, buried under landslides, or gutted by wildfires. Refugees, all equal at last in their misery, their stunned shuffling from one continent to the next, one prefab concrete shanty town to another, at the whim of the prevailing winds of national charity and Corporate humanitarian tenders.

They were all getting recognition as victims, at last. Exactly what Liam had been trying to achieve.

But he'd never intended it like this.

"Dozens of unsuspecting victims of Liam Argyle's unprecedent acts of data fraud," carried on the booming newscaster voiceover, "who didn't ask to have their most personal information shared all over the Red just because some RedCorp host had a breakdown. What is the point of sharing such meaningless private records as this? Is Liam Argyle acting in concert with the data terrorists known collectively as the QTs?"

So he was supposed to be one of these new hacker terrorists now, was he? Liam shook his head. He hadn't seen that one coming—he was about as good with computers as a week-old leaf of lettuce. But still, he thought, it was good to think he wasn't the only one out there pissing off the powers-that-be.

"One thing is certain," blared the muffled speaker-voice on the newsfeed. "After a fiasco like this, who could possibly take the risk of trusting their data to RedCorp ever again? What will the consequences be on the struggling corporation's flagship feed? More on all this as it dev—to win TWO HUNDRED THOUSAND credits!"

The voice rising from the handheld unit's speaker had suddenly turned into a woman on intravenous mood-lifters. A tinned crowd popped into existence from some fresh hell with a well-timed "Ooooooohh!" Liam's screen-holder must have grown bored with the newsfeed's blatant stalling until it had any real news to share and switched to one of the twenty-four-hour gamefeed channels.

Liam would have to do his best to prevent any more information about his capture from "developing" anytime soon. But as much as he wished to find a hole to crawl into and die, even more pressing was the question currently weighing on his mind like a black hole.

What about the *message*? Why wasn't anyone talking about that? All the rest would be fine—the lies, the corporate spin, the demonization. He'd be laughing at it, if only he could know everything had gone off as planned. That the message was out there; that somebody, anybody, had heard it. That this hadn't all been a monumental waste and folly.

But this Mars-begotten person just wouldn't flick away from their stupid gamefeed drivel! On the show's shoddy stage, set up in the middle of a crowded place of worship that could have been just about anywhere in the world, two teenagers were busy torturing each other with an assortment of lit torches and pointed instruments, trying to force the other one to cry out first and break the religious silence.

Ah, fuck it.

Liam had never stolen anything before. Sure, he'd feverishly nicked one of his older cousin's cricket cards as a kid, and he'd also brought loads of office supplies back home, but that was hardly stealing.

And yet, he had no qualms whatsoever at tugging the portable podscreen out of its unwary owner's hand and bolting out the train's open door as soon as they came to a stop. Of course, they started shouting as soon as they realised they were now staring at their own empty hand, but his victim was firmly wedged into the subway train, and not a single person budged to help them. Or even moved to let them out.

The doors slid shut again, and the train darted off along its never-ending route. For the first time in his life, Liam realized what a truly powerful thing apathy is. It was not a pleasurable experience.

23

Liam needed to keep moving—his security depended on it. And probably his life, for that matter, if the fallout for RedCorp was anything to judge by. But he also needed to know.

He managed to contain his burning eagerness long enough to get him, his sweat-stained and reversed suit jacket, his false moustache, and his newly purloined handheld screen through the crowds at whatever station he'd landed in—Stratford, a charitable physical sign eventually informed him—and onto the East End streets.

Then, unable to wait any longer, Liam dove into the first cookie-cutter franchise café he could find, ordered the longest coffee on the little server trolley's menu, and settled down for a bit of serious Red-roving.

It took him nearly fifteen minutes of wading through the interconnected drivel of humanity—the sort of thing he had spent his entire life despising and the most recent part creating—before he found any direct mention of his message and not just his actions.

And it was in a celebrity gossipfeed's coverage of a RedCorp press conference, of all things.

Behind a podium proudly displaying the intertwined Celtic knot of fibre optics, pod relay domes, satellites, and AR lenses that formed the central RedCorp Holdings' logo, a human-shaped slab of expensive legal spokesmanship cleared their throat, locked their glassy eyes on their AR prompter, and started reading:

"The Red Corporation in no way associates itself with and takes no responsibility for any and all declarations made by any person, persons, synthetic beings, or other units or entities, gifted or not gifted with legal status as an individual, in Red Corporation's use or employ, at any past, present, or future time."

A shiny PR Department rep smarmingly elbowed his way into the feed, meeting little resistance from the matte-suited *Homo Legalensis*, who, having said their mandatory bit, was more than content to stand there, looking grave[1]—and no doubt watching in AR as fees trickled into their offplanet account. The shiny one *hrummed*, then picked up the ball.

"Of course, we at the Red family are proud to be the creators of products which have been household names for generations." The tinned applause cued as planned, and PR boy beamed as he waited a whole two seconds for it to die down. "And so, we offer out every apology to viewers concerning tonight's unfortunate incident. If any of you, our esteemed viewers, were unsatisfied with tonight's product, then please return the defective employee responsible, or any information concerning his whereabouts, to your nearest Red retail point or police station, and we will be happy to offer you a substantial RedPoint reward as compensation."

The press conference window started shrinking at that, until it was no more than a backdrop to a glitz-covered studio set, where two overdressed celebrity feed hosts sat shaking their heads.

"What a load of old toss!" scoffed what sounded and looked like a cross between a boar and an elderly elephant. His co-host, a comb-thin harpy sporting a permanent face-lift smile, nodded in dramatic agreement. Behind them loomed the ever-classy SyneDeal corporate logo: large SYN passant on a credit-green globe background.

---

[1] As in, about six feet from top to bottom and prone to attracting every kind of worm around.

"The Reds have lost what little credibility they had," carried on the ur-mammalian host, "and now they're trying to cover it up like the wimplings they really are."

"How right you are, Sean! Only an idiot would tune into a feed from RedCorp from here on in!" piped in the ever-smiling scarecrow lady. "I mean, just listen to the things their trained monkey was spouting!"

Liam was both excited and horrified to finally get confirmation that his message had gone out. The need to find proof was like a physical urge—but under these circumstances? Was this what he had worked so hard for?

"Freedom! Freedom!" The classical music background to Liam's message kicked in, just as he'd planned it, and a tinny shadow of his voice rose from the speaker. There he was, so much tinier and yet larger than life at the same time, sitting at his wooden desk back home.

With RedCorp so desperate to get hold of him, would he ever see that desk again?

"Hey there, folks. Sorry to interrupt your regularly scheduled brainwashing power hour, but we're experiencing some technical difficulties. No need to adjust your lenses, I'm only here for a moment, and I'm certain the regular programming will resume as soon as they find a way to kick me off the air."

The on-screen Liam smiled—not his usual wide, manic smile, but a softer, warmer one.

"Technical difficulties," he repeated. "You know, the word *technical* has been around a lot longer than electricity or anything we'd consider 'technology' by today's standards. In the original Greek, it meant any sort of system devised by the human mind. Today, the system is broken. We're having technical difficulties with society, at every level."

Lifting his eyes from the screen, Liam scanned the crowded café for Corporate security forces or anyone who might be alarmed by the tinny, seditious[1] words rising from the speakers. They rang as loud as sirens in Liam's ears, but nobody else seemed to be paying him any attention whatsoever.

"What's that you say?" carried on his stream-self, dramatically cocking an overlarge ear. "You're doing just fine, you don't have any problem with the modern world-system, thank you very much? Glad to hear it! But tell me, would you say someone who believes in things that don't exist has a problem? How about if they believed in the imaginary things so much that they started treating them like people? And what if they took that belief so far that they let their non-existent people take over every aspect of their lives and their future?

"You'd think someone like that is overdue for a bit of psychological rehab. But that's exactly what we do, all of us, every single day. The corporations on the Council have the same rights as people, far more rights and power than any of us really—but they don't exist. That's why they spend so much time and money just to shove their damn logos in our faces all the time. They have to maintain the illusion that they actually exist, in the real world."

In the background, the feed's music swelled, drowning out the café's own atmospheric tuneless elevator jazz.

"But they don't. It's that simple. They only exist in our minds and in our laws—which is just two ways of saying the same thing, when you think about it. And yet, we're all so used to the idea of big Corporations running and deciding everything in our name, the idea of being small and powerless before these beings who are far greater than any individual, than any nation could ever be. We don't even question it anymore."

On-screen Liam shook his head, downcast. On-the-run café-Liam realised it was probably the first genuine emotion he'd shown in a broadcast—ever. He remembered how the madness of it all had welled up inside him at the words. The lives destroyed in the name

---

[1] "Going apart"

of short-term Corporate gains, the ones he'd seen and known himself, flashed through his mind like earthquake aftershocks. Usnavi Musibay. Azar Acquah. Juliette Binns. Carpentiere's daughter.

Himself.

"Of course, it's the easiest thing in the world to understand. It's so much simpler to just give in, to give up, and let someone else decide. We don't have to take any responsibility for how fucked up everything becomes, even when we all hate it. Why bother speaking up for what's right when the Corps have all the real power and there's nothing we can do about it anyway? Why even bother looking at the lives that are destroyed as a result?

"And no, I'm not talking about my dear contestants on *The Grass is Greener*, the so-called victims my beloved masters and mistresses at RedCorp have decided to let you see so we can all have a good laugh and feel better about our own lot in life. I mean the real victims. The ones they'd never let you see in a million years of Corporate world-state. These are the ones you need to finally face, and this message is your only chance.

"This is our wake-up call, folks. We're only going to get one."

Café-Liam couldn't help but let a smile creep onto his face as the solemn version of himself on screen ran through the last few words. He'd done it. He'd said it. The idea seeds were out there.

However, the former host's grin was cut short as the SyneDeal pundits cut back in.

"Yaw-awn!" neighed the horse-faced lady. "I mean, how boring can you get? Can you believe the Reds put hundreds of millions of viewers through that borefest? Or, should I say, millions of their ex-viewers?" She laughed as convincingly as a hyena, drawing deep on her reserves of injected-lithium mirth.

"It gets even worse when you have a look at the junk this Argyle sent out attached with his nonsense," the hippowalrus host added with a growl.

"Are you joking?" The stunted tree-woman goggled in what may have been actual emotion. "I trashcanned that without even batting an eyelid."

Her massive counterpart chuckled. "You and half-a-billion viewers who'll never even glance at an advert for a RedCorp feed again, I'd say!" A snarl rang out through the busy café, and it took Liam a moment or two to realise it had come from him. Luckily, everyone was far too absorbed in their own little augmented world for his outburst to draw any sort of a reaction.

"Still," carried on the louder of the two hosts, "your humble and devoted servant gritted his teeth and actually looked through the files. Just so I could spare all of you the pain and let you know how stupid and boring it all was."

He crooned, flourished, and pulled out a piece of actual paper—always a preferred dramatic prop of anybody claiming authority.

"Hrahum!" he coughed, doing anything but clearing his throat, which, incidentally, looked to Liam like it would easily be able to pass anything smaller than a basketball.

"Wait until you see some of the so-called 'testimonies'[1] he's got in here," said the presenter, with a sardonic laugh and his very best of patronizing grins. "There's so much crap here, I don't even know where to start. Oh well, might as well bite the bullet and go straight for the one our Mr Argyle himself singled out. 'The true, greatest loser of the Corporate era,' he labelled it."

His co-host laughed her equine laugh and said, "What is it, his memoirs?"

The stark mugshot of a gaunt-looking Korean woman loaded in the glitzy studio background for all to see. A sign printed beneath her orange work overalls read, "Revenue Corporation Involuntary Employee no. 736f727279: SHIN Ha Yoon, Grand Theft Data, 96-month Labour Rehabilitation Sentence, LEO Polyvalent Industrial Station."

---

[1] Originally, the Ten Commandments—ironically, given by God when no one else was there to bear witness.

The prisoner looked out of the picture with piercing, night-dark eyes, as if desperately trying to communicate something to the viewer by empathy alone. Those eyes burned into Liam's mind once again, just as deeply as they had the first time he'd fished the young woman's application out of the trash folder.

Text also started scrolling across the bottom of the screen at breakneck speeds, tearing the eye away from Shin Ha Yoon's face and bombarding the viewer with infographics highlighting all the wrong words, the most ridiculous and belittling terms possible. Even the fastest of speed readers couldn't have kept up with it, so Mars only knew what the typical audience for this sort of feed would be left with.

But Liam knew the story by heart.

24

Shin Ha Yoon. One of the last surviving descendants of the Zainichi Koreans shipped from Japan to North Korea after WWII. The scion of a family that had survived everything fate could throw at it: forceful deportation, discrimination, genocide, famine, despotism… even rising tides that flooded what little subsistence farmland they'd managed to hold onto and drove them into the cities. Into resistance.

Little surprise that a young, idealistic, frustrated, and thoroughly alone Ha Yoon—after drug-resistant tuberculosis did what the regime enforcers never could and finished off her parents—decided to use the hacking skills that had kept her so-called "hostile class" family off the grid and safe; she put them to good use, stealing public records about the realities of life in the enclosed, self-contained, and openly authoritarian appendix of the Corporate world-state.

The newsfeeds loved the info leaks. But she'd broken the greatest taboo of the modern time: she'd lifted the veil and rattled the fundamental trust in the inviolability of the almighty data that was the basis of the whole Corporate house of cards. Even if it was only in an isolated backwater like North Korea, barely even a member-state of the Council, that was intolerable lèse-majesté. It might inspire others.

And so, the same Major Players who owned the news stations lapping up Ha Yoon's leaked data also tracked her down, swooped in with dramatic primetime rent-a-cop drama, and sat in judgment as the Corporate Courts threw everything their Code allowed at the downcast, life-abused North Korean hacktivist.

After everything the Shin family had endured, eight years of "rehabilitation" labour probably didn't sound all that bad.

That was without factoring in the bottom-line optimising wizardry of the Revenue Corporation, long-time holder of the world's penal system public tenders. A young, technically savvy political prisoner was the perfect candidate to ram into a cargo pod and ship up the Elevator launch track to their orbital, low-gravity rehab commune and manufacturing plant.

And even then, Liam doubted Ha Yoon ever complained; her official prison record certainly showed no further acts of rebellion and uniformly satisfactory production figures. For someone who had dreamt of getting out of North Korea her whole life, anything, even a tin can prison up in orbit, must have been a welcome change.

The factory station would have seemed like Paradise Mars itself compared to the climate refugee shantytowns of Chongjin. Sure, they didn't bother even trying to build in any spin gravity or anything else that might help compensate for bone loss and the other debilitating effects of years stuck in space. But they also didn't bother with any other extra expenses, such as any particular security measures, guards, or even separation between convicts based on where they fit on the sexual and gender spectra. The prisoners were already up in space, after all. They weren't going to try to escape out the airlock.

So Ha Yoon was, for the first time in her short life, free to do whatever the hell she wanted to during her eight daily hours off the clock, as long as it didn't impact productivity and RevCorp's margins. Even three-hundred kilometres up Earth's gravity well, girls will be girls, boys will be boys, and enbies will be whatever their natures tell them; and so, before her first six months of incarceration were up, Ha Yoon's regular weekly blood tests confirmed she was pregnant.

This was not a rare occurrence on the low-gravity factory/prison stations, nor was it an unwelcome one—least of all from RevCorp's point of view. After all, the penal system contract entitled the winning tenderer to everything the prisoners produced, for the entire length of their term—*everything* they produced.

And while a prisoner would provide fruitful indentured work for a few years, a child born into indenture would bolster the Corporation's bottom line for life. Generations, even.

This was understood by everyone involved. Your average female factory-inmate was eager and excited to get pregnant so they could earn their ticket back to Earth on the next re-supply shuttle, and maybe even time off their sentence for Corporate services rendered if their child was born without any of the genetic defects that were all too common, given the copious doses of radiation the foetus would have suffered in orbit.

It was part of the deal, expected.

What was absolutely unexpected, and unprecedented, was to have a fresh inmate like Shin Ha Yoon, with everything to gain from a quick ride back down to Earth, refuse to submit for processing and kick up a fuss, demanding to keep the child. It was confusing and vexing for the Corporate powers-that-be. The foetus was legally the Revenue Corporation's property, of course, but there was the look of the thing to take into consideration, if only from a public relations angle.

So, the orbital prison-factory's Corporate minders pondered and dithered[1], pushing the matter ever further up the organigramme, and ever deeper toward the bottom of each executive's To Do list. The weeks turned into months, the months into trimesters, and the inconvenient biological clock ticked onward, regardless of how the Corporate schedule was irremediably stalled.

The baby's inmate father ranted and railed at Shin Ha Yoon, urging her to take RevCorp's generous offer, to think of the baby as much as herself. What if she went into labour before RevCorp has sorted it all out? Nobody knew exactly what happened when a child

---

[1] "To quake," hence "to vacillate in opinion."

was born into zero gravity, but there were horror stories. Why couldn't she just take the ticket back to Earth and count her blessings?

Ha Yoon just shook her head and never stopped working away at the low-gravity assembly line—she couldn't have stopped if she wanted to, not if she planned on eating. But she grew more and more desperate as her pregnancy moved into the third trimester and the baby inside her grew stronger, more responsive, one nightless day-cycle after another. Only pressure from outside could stop RevCorp from taking her baby away the instant she went into delivery, but all private communication was locked down and censored. She had no way of contacting the world down below, of letting anyone else know about her situation and the inhumanity of what the Corporation was about to do.

She only found one loophole in the censorship system: inmates could submit freely to Corporation-run contests and raffles. Providing opportunities for ill-founded hope has always been, after all, one of the keys of maintaining peacefully subjugated masses. Shin Ha Yoon's application to *The Grass is Greener*'s inaugural season was a masterpiece, laying out the details of her life, her predicament, her hopes, and her dreams with all the more strength that it didn't use any exaggerations or self-pity. It didn't need to: the young woman's situation spoke for itself.

Naturally, the filters set up by the Editor sent her application straight into the digital waste bin, unopened.

By the time Liam woke up and fished the file out of oblivion, two whole years had passed. The host had immediately dropped everything and started searching for info on where Ha Yoon and her child were. Two years too late to do Ha Yoon any good.

In the end, her fate was sealed not by her own third trimester of pregnancy, but by the Revenue Corporation's second-trimester financial reports for 2072. A rough quarterly report, by all accounts, which had led their Board to commit to downsizing labour costs to protect stock value.

An easy decision, and an emotionless one, since nobody around the virtual table would need to even think about the actual firings, let alone speak with another human about why they were losing their livelihood. The HR algorithms worked their statistical magic and did all the work, finding the objectively least valuable agents and issuing them their little pink AR message.

Sadly, the algorithm programmers hadn't bothered teaching the program to tell the difference between an employee down on Earth and one three-hundred kilometres up in space. This oversight had never mattered before: why would any AI think to fire an employee who RevCorp didn't ever need to pay? Especially when there were nigh-infinite layabouts and slackers down on terra firma.

But if there's one person a short-term productivity-optimising program hates more than a loafer or jobsworth, it's a pregnant woman near the end of her term.

And so Ha Yoon earned her place in the Corporate history books: the first person ever, in the history of humanity, to get laid off in space.

It was a sad affair, and an embarrassing one, too, by all accounts. Losing your job down on Earth was bad enough, but at least there were always the employment centres and Corporate surplus food banks to keep you fed until the job-bot figured out where and what your next position should be.

Up in orbit, there was only the collective shock of the dozen free-roaming inmate-workers when the pink notice came in, which was soon followed by the collective realisation that air quotas and food quotas—barely adequate for twelve—had been immediately scaled back for eleven.

They were all, slowly, suffocating.

Every breath Shin Ha Yoon took after opening the redundancy notice from the bosses was a breath stolen from everyone else's cut-rate, survival-level Corporate allotment. And there'd be no pricy ticket back to Earth for an employee who, on their books, was no longer RevCorp's problem.

It took all of five minutes for the powers-that-be to realise she was an embarrassment to the system. Rather than admit the almighty redundancy algorithm had made a mistake, it was far easier for RevCorp to simply ignore her queries and pretend she'd never existed.

Ha Yoon did not even fight her shipmates, her friends, not even the father of her child, as they apologetically but resolutely explained that they had no choice. It was her or them. And it was time for Ha Yoon to take a short walk into the long black.

The work stress therapy testimonies from the unfortunate co-workers all agreed, after the fact: Shin Ha Yoon didn't cry, didn't argue, didn't protest at all. Her only request, through trembling lips, was that they get her baby safely out into the world, such as it was, before they tossed her out the airlock.

They agreed it was the least they could do—both in honour of their months of friendship and to avoid having time added onto their sentences for destroying such a valuable RevCorp asset. The inmate in charge of crew health and safety, a Cuban doctor and tax dodger, told the others to take Ha Yoon directly to the airlock for the C-Section.

It was the cleanest part of the station, and most of the mess would be sucked out into open space anyway, reducing clean-up. After all, sewing the doomed Korean girl back up after the C-Section would just be wasted labour.

The operation was butcher work by all accounts, over in less than five minutes. In between the cries of pain and loss, Ha Yoon uttered her final coherent words, repeating the child's name and making sure her former co-workers and present murderers got the spelling right: Iseul, meaning "From the Dew." She said it reminded her of happier times, the last happy times she could remember, early in the morning on the family pine mushroom farm by the Orang river.

The others nodded and looked away as they wrapped up the new-born Corporate asset and vacated the blood-covered airlock. The new mother, crying soundlessly and airlessly in tune with her baby on the other side of the sealed door, swelled to the size of a 3D printer and roasted in the unfiltered sun. Blessedly, before long, her brain finally gave in to the lack of oxygen and released its grip on a life too strong and too defiant to fit the bounds of the Corporate-era mould.

25

As Liam said, closing the sequence, "Shin Ha Yoon's story won't be the worst life of the modern age for long. If we let things carry on the way they're going, if we continue to let the value of all of our lives be set at best bargain economic price, Ha Yoon's story will be terribly, tragically normal. Commonplace. We all have to do better."

There was nothing else Liam could do for poor Shin Ha Yoon. Not anymore. Not even singling her story out among all the others in his message could make a jot[I] of difference for her.

But for her daughter: there was still a chance that might be a different story. Even as he sat in the busy café, waving off the serving drone as it pestered him to order a refill on his coffee, Liam hoped that his message might make all the difference, if only for one person.

Ha Yoon may have become an embarrassing Corporate liability, but her daughter, Shin Iseul, was another matter entirely: a genetically hale Corporate slave-child, the potential start of generations of free labour. By the time Liam had tracked her down, she'd been swaddled up and shuttled off to a RevCorp crèche[II] facility in Klin, outside Moscow. The educational and biomedical enhancements they were pumping into the infant there were top notch—enough to

---

[I] "From *iota*, the smallest letter in the Greek alphabet.

[II] Christmas manger scene

make anyone consider Corporate slavery as a valid choice for their children.

For a big Corp like Revenue, no expense was too high to give their legally bonded progeny every chance to live their most productive, most value-producing life.

A tragedy[1], yes, but perhaps one with a silver lining—especially if, as he hoped, Liam's focus on Shin Ha Yoon's story in his hijacked feed message might draw some attention to the daughter. Might help get her released from Corporate bondage and back—as the looping background music hinted not-so-subtly—into freedom.

Still, no silver lining could justify the reaction from the gossipfeed hosts, as the words of Shin Ha Yoon's pitiful life petered out at the bottom of the handheld screen.

"Well, boo-fricking-hoo," drawled the horse-headed host, sneering and pretending to wipe away a tear from ducts that had probably lost the ability about five facelifts ago. "Did she fall down and bang her knee one day, too? Shit happens, that's life. Get over yourself. Gawd, what a crybaby!"

Her walrus of a co-host guffawed in agreement. "And what kills me is that this Argyle person thinks we should give a damn about some criminal scum's poor shattered dreams! All I hope is that RedCorp will have the balls to sue the man for all he's worth. Then again, that can't be very much anymore, so they probably won't bother!"

The sitcom laughter cued and melded with the cackling of the two buffoons on-feed.

"And here's the clincher;" carried on Liam's fellow *homo hostis*, "do you know what Argyle—the man who just attacked his co-workers before bolting—dares to call this steaming pile of digital garbage of his? Any idea? 'On Responsibility!' That's the title he stuck on all this trash!"

The living skeleton opposite him let out a shrill laugh that sounded

---

[1] Literally, "goat song," as in Satyric plays.

as hollow as winter's wind through a summer camp flagpole. "What a (MEEP)ucking hypocrite!"

The hulking newsmound turned to stare directly into the feed's main podcam. "Mr Argyle. If you're watching us tonight, I'll tell you one thing. If you turn yourself in and face your 'responsibilities' before the Law, then I solemnly promise to take full responsibility for every single one of the laughs that will gush out of my throat as I watch them fry your sorry ass to a fine crisp."

Liam had had enough. With the canned laughter buzzing in his ears, he looked away and fumbled for the handheld screen's off button. After a terrible, cackling moment, the device finally fell silent. Liam took a steadying breath, his mind in turmoil.

Were those bastards right? Was his message a laughingstock, best ignored by everyone and anyone? The thought surged forth again and again, an obsession[1]. Had he gone through all this, thrown his comfortable life away, for nothing?

The idea was unbearable; it gnawed at the back of his mind like a starved rodent.

"What!" he snapped, turning to face the squat box of the robo-waiter trolley as it nudged his shin for the tenth time, trying to get his attention physically since he could no longer be flagged with an AR message like a civilised person.

How will we be paying today? flashed the little physical screen built into the serving drone, like a withered, vestigial limb.

Come to think of it, how *would* he be paying? In his burning desire to check the newly purloined handheld device to see the fallout from his hijacked broadcast, he'd completely forgotten to pick up his stashed on-the-run bag before doing anything else. And now, without his AR interface, he had no way of paying. He certainly had no way to access his comfortably padded bank account—which was probably for the best, anyway. There'd be no better way to instantly tell the

---

[1] "Act of besieging"

entire RedCorp security brigade where he was hiding, and they'd probably already locked down his accounts at the in-house bank, anyway.

At a loss, Liam stalled for time by making a show of patting down the inside pockets—now the outside pockets—of his inside-out jacket. He might not be able to afford the coffee, but what he could afford least of all was to make a scene that would get him shocked again faster than a robo-pollinator bee in a thunderstorm.

Sweat brimming at his forehead, Liam opened his mouth for some bit of fast talk that would never work on a drone server; then he paused. His fumbling hand had actually found something hard and round—a shape his generation would probably be the last in human history to associate with money.

Lifting a finger with his free hand to get the machine to wait, the fugitive host reached into the awkward, inside-out pocket and pulled out a pair of green plastic charity tokens. His usual two tokens, the ones he took with him every day to fend off the buskers[1] and transients who littered the city—especially the disused dock buildings around the Mews.

He hadn't even stopped to think before grabbing them out of the box at home and stuffing them into his pocket that morning. And now, here he was, two strips of plastic all that stood between him and having to pull a runner from the shop—and in a secure commercial area like this, that could only end one way.

Through the Looking-Glass? Lewis Carroll, eat your heart out.

"Here, I think this will do," he said, fighting to keep the quiver out of his voice as he slid the two sweaty chips into the tray on top of the server drone. The machine sucked them in with a loud, end-of-smoothie sort of slurp—followed by an unpleasant buzz.

"Mandatory Consumer Alert: This unit does not compensate for difference between physical tender and price of goods. Do you wish to proceed with this transaction?"

---

[1] From *busk*, "to cruise as a pirate."

"Hey, no worries," Liam replied with a grin far more genuine than any he ever wore on the *Grass is Greener* set. There was an old expression for situations like this. What was it again? Oh, right. "Keep the change."

The little machine buzzed in incomprehension; Liam could only laugh. And damn if it didn't feel good. Genuinely, honestly good.

"Don't worry about it," he repeated as he stood up and dusted some non-existent crumbs from his trousers. "It's nothing."

He left the machine to sort out its idiomatic[1] confusion. The grin was still well at home on his face as he stepped back out into the smoggy London twilight.

Liam had work of his own to attend to, and for the first time since he could remember, he was eager to get started.

Change might be nothing—or it could be everything, and Liam couldn't wait to find out which.

---

[1] "One's own thinking"

26

All the gear was still there. As Liam rooted through his spare rucksack in the shiny automated luggage room at St. Pancras, his basic optimism and faith in humanity were restored. If you could put valuable items in a train station locker room and find them there days later, then there was still some good left in the world. Also, the plastic jingle of the sack of charity coupons he'd stashed away was as merry as a mischievous hobbit's grin; it went a long way in helping him think these happy thoughts.

Thankful for the empty locker room, Liam wedged the door shut, then stripped out of his work clothes. He then tugged a ridiculously colourful top out of the bag and, reluctantly, pulled it on, his lips pursed and nose flared. Calling the shirt "Hawaiian" would be about on par with Pearl Harbour in terms of aggression and malicious intent. The trunks and flip-flops he fished out of the bottom of the bag fit in perfectly with his new style. A pair of wide disposable convenience store AR glasses became the perfect yeast-cherry on top of this tasteless sundae.

His bag slung over a shoulder in classic middle-aged backpacker nostalgia, he toddled back out into the open station and blinked in the neon glare. The size and bustle of St. Pancras made him dizzy, even before his cheap, anonymous new glasses interfaced with the station's central pod and filled every solid-coloured surface with advertisement AR windows. Stumbling around aimlessly for a while, he painted the picture-perfect tourist: desperately trying not to look too much like one and failing miserably. Soon, his rolling eyes happened to land upon a handy orientation arrow pointing over to the ticket booth, and so he wobbled his befuddled[1] way in that general direction.

He'd spent quite some time considering the best way of disguising himself after the act—or was it only now that the act was starting? After the Cassar fiasco and his abduction by the RedCorp rent-a-cops, Liam realised that movie-style cloak and dagger stuff would only serve to make him more conspicuous; he just wasn't good enough at the whole sneaking around business to pull it off. His best bet, he realised, was to aim at sticking out like a sore thumb. Even *he* should be able to pull that off, and it would be sure to throw the security cameras and goons off his tail long enough for him to move on to the next phase of the plan.

Of course, it would have helped if there *were* a next phase to the plan. But if so, Liam hadn't received the memo. He knew well enough where he was going right now: his old friend Kyla's apartment in Newham. The show, and what Liam had let it do to him, had cut her off from his life so effectively that it'd be ages before anyone thought to look for him there. And if anyone knew how someone could slip off the Corporate radar, it would be Kyla.

But would she even open the door for him after so long? Where that might take him if she did, and how he would survive if she didn't, were also excellent questions he had no answer to. He hadn't dared risk any sort of message to her before tonight's fireworks—not after years without speaking to her. It would have lit up like a broken lens pixel for anyone monitoring his comms log.

Plus, at some level, Liam felt like he needed this leap into the unknown. A wild dash for freedom. It was neither possible nor

---

[1] "To confuse with strong drink or opium"

desirable to know how it was going to turn out. Where would the fun be in that? It was enough to know that he had enough untraceable touch-money to get by, for a little while at least. For now, he just needed to get to Kyla's—the rest would sort itself out.

"Can I help you, sir?" The young girl behind the bomb-proof armoured window looked him up and down as if she were about two seconds away from pressing the panic button, calling in the security drones, and lowering the blast shutters. But then again, that was probably just how she was trained to deal with all customers.

Somehow, Liam had reached the front of the ticket queue without even intending to enter it. Maybe he was taking this baffled tourist act a little too far.

He gave the booth-jockey an awkward toothy grin and waffled some foreign-sounding gibberish as he took his leave and headed off to wait for the next City line train to East Ham station, which was in walking distance of Kyla's place without being the closest stop—on the complete opposite side of the central sprawl, right past the Mews again.

Hopefully, his zigzagging through London would at least help shake the security goons off his trail. Then again, as he stood waiting for his train to finally pull in, Liam was sure the armed guards patrolling the station were paying him more attention than anybody else. Were they surrounding him, getting ready to pounce? Or was it just that his hapless tourist disguise was still working its magic, and he looked like a mugging waiting to happen?

As long as they didn't pay too much attention to his face, then everything would be perfectly alright. Probably perfectly alright.

Damn, he needed a drink.

It was only once he was firmly wedged into a corner seat at the rear of the train, in constant danger of ending up smothered under someone's leaning tower of luggage, that he allowed himself to breathe.

He'd done it. His message was out there. Sure, the Corporate wheels were busy dealing with it and turning it into a joke, but that was the thing—they had to deal with it. It existed.

It might not be the great spark of revolution he'd been half-hoping for, which was both a disappointment and a relief, since violence was the last thing he wanted to inspire. Or at least in the bottom five. But it'd get people thinking about what they were a part of, about other worlds that might be possible, about responsibility and democracy. And that was worth sacrificing his comfort and his position a thousand times over.

Liam rode out the train ride in quiet, smug dignity. His self-satisfaction was so complete that he didn't even start worrying about what Kyla would have to say—or what he'd do if she wasn't even home that night—until the train announced their imminent arrival at his stop.

27

Liam sashayed out of the train, admiring the damp murk of the East London night as he bumbled about in his touristy way.

He'd always been amazed that anyone would *want* to be in a place like the London sprawl any more than strictly necessary, let alone go through the cost and legendary mither of travelling here. The best explanation he'd come up with so far was that "one born every minute" was enough to sustain a tourism industry. But now that he'd run the subterranean London rat maze in a tourist's blister-prone shoes, he supposed that, to folk hailing from the marginally less urbanised-to-death parts of the Red-connected world, the City must hold some sort of morbid fascination: a terrifying edge which, while repulsive, might well contain some twisted romantic charm that would naturally escape anyone forced to actually live here.

Well, the only romantic charm Liam needed right now was of the bathroom stall variety, so he made a hasty bee-line[1] for the nearest public washroom, hauling his bag along with him.

With the AR signs guiding him once again in his cheap glasses, it didn't take long for him to find the gleaming, stainless steel pod of the public toilets. It sat at the end of an alleyway, between two fast food printer joints, like an extremely lost space shuttle.

---

[1] Did the person who coined this expression ever actually see a bee fly? They communicate through dance, for Pooh's sake!

As Liam approached, the toilet pod's AI pinged to life. "Welcome, good enby-madam-sir! Congratulations, you have located the proactive answer to all of your sanitary deliverables!"

It was probably just Liam's nerves, but the computer's gibberish sounded a little desperate, if that were possible.

"Thank you for choosing your hyperlocal InSanitation solution!" carried on the chipper, if slightly manic, voice. "Please input your preferred payment method and service paradigm of choice."

Liam sighed. The only paradigm he wanted was a room without any cameras so he could finally use all of the stuff in the heavy bag he'd been lugging around.

But luckily enough, "Value-Added: Privacy" was one of the items on the glorified Porta-Potty's floating AR selection menu. Liam had his doubts, but it was probably still the best option, so he swiped a one-use payment chip and selected that one.

"Excellent choice, valued user. Please prepare for onboarding with our best practices sanitary experience."

The stainless-steel pod rumbled as the mad machine shifted components around. Then the door unlocked and slid open.

After all of the computer's corporate-lingo bluster, Liam was almost disappointed to see what was, after all, just a toilet stall. But he counted himself lucky; it was both clean and big enough to turn around in, which suited his needs just fine.

He propped his bag of props atop the little hand-washing basin and fished out a grey business suit, along with a slightly worn white shirt and an off-grey tie. He wasn't bothered about the wrinkles—they'd just add that extra-worn look to complete his last disguise of the day.

After a quick chuckle about how fun this subterfuge business was, Liam dabbed a bit of expensive camera-fooling gunk on his face and donned his most grim and exhausted expression—which took far less acting than he had expected.

He flushed the stall's toilet for good measure, then sauntered out, feeling like a new man.

"Your business is appreciated," chimed in the machine again, oblivious to the double meaning there. "Please share any takeaways with the InSanitation change management team."

That last bit of corporate-speak was too much, even for Liam's hardened stomach, and he wretched a little bit at the mental image it conjured as he made his escape from the buzz-word infected public washroom.

Thirty seconds later, he had fully recovered and was invisible in the crowd; just another suit in the endless tides of late-night salarymen, women, and enbies who were the elemental cogs that made Corporate society go 'round.

Twenty minutes of standard crowd-elbowing later, he stood before the flecked door of Kyla's flat on the fourth floor of a typical run-down East London apartment building, trying to catch his breath. Here was the dreaded point where he left the relative comfort of planned risk and leapt more or less blindly into the hands of fortune. It would not do to meet his destiny while short on breath.

Liam also thought that, from here on in, he should seize every chance to take a breather that he could get. He had no idea what might be coming and when—or if—he might get the chance again.

When he was satisfied, and didn't dare stall any longer, he knocked.

Vague noises came from behind the door, then the gentle whisper of the security camera whirring to life. There was a gasp he knew could only be Kyla's, and Liam gave her the best smile he could muster as she threw the door open. The fugitive knew right away that something was on her mind—she was still wearing her work clothes, for one. Normally, at this hour, you could be sure to find her in her jammies, probably curled up in bed with her library app, reading something thought-provoking. She sputtered at him.

"Liam! Are you okay?" He broke his grin and started to answer, but apparently the question wasn't all that urgent after all, since she cut him off. "Gods, don't just stand there, get inside!" She bustled him in, glanced around the hallway, then locked and bolted the door.

Liam's old friend marched straight into the kitchen nook, head down and frowning beneath her emerald green-hued bangs. "Go sit down. I'll fetch you a cup of tea," she added, almost as an afterthought.

Sitting in Kyla's comfortable den, Liam realised for the first time that he hadn't really expected to make it this far. At some level, he hadn't expected to make it out of the Mews at all—at least, not unless you counted hearses or ambulances.

He'd sacrificed everything. His job, his home, his status, his future in the RedCorp ranks. Say what you want—and should—about the Big Five, but they sure knew how to take care of their employees, for life.

Not that he regretted it one second. He didn't have any choice, really—not if he wanted to remain himself. But the thing about sacrifices is that you don't expect the sacrificee to end up sitting down on a comfy faux-leather couch, waiting for a cup of hot tea.

And yet here he was, in this sitting room where he'd spent countless nights of fun and laughter with Kyla and their other friends, remaking the world. If only that damn wall-mounted vidscreen in Kyla's bedroom would stop blasting its mind-numbing drivel for two seconds, he thought he might just be able to convince himself that he wasn't completely screwed, after all.

Kyla came back out of the kitchen nook with two steaming mugs with simple floral designs. She put them down on the granite-top coffee table, and only then did she look up at him. Her eyes may have had a slightly pinkish tinge to them; Liam couldn't tell for sure.

"Right. So, how are you, Liam?" The words, so often spoken without any kind of meaning, took on a consistency that strummed a chord deep within Liam. Her first concern wasn't about what had happened and whether or not the news reports were true; it was about him, about how he was doing through all this, whatever *this* was. If they hadn't ruled out that kind of thing long ago, and if Liam hadn't valued friendship more than any sort of formal romantic labelling, he could have fallen in love with her right there and then. She commanded honesty.

"I'm sort of shell-shocked… and a bit scared. But mostly I'm excited. This had all been building up inside me for so long. And although I very nearly didn't, I needed to act. I would have exploded otherwise. I'm just sorry I kept you away so long, that I didn't wake up sooner to what that job was doing to me. What it was turning me into."

She nodded through the steam of her tea. The intensity of her stare as she inhaled the vapours made her look like a Greek oracle.

"Yeah, me too," she replied, with a deep sigh. "Alright then, I won't say, 'I told you so.' Even though we both know I did." She smirked, then blew on her tea before taking a sip. "So, tell me, what happened exactly? You know I'm never one to take what you hear on a feed at face value, but the things they're saying, Liam…"

He let loose and told her everything—it felt so good to speak about it with someone else, and even more so since it was Kyla. Their old openness and transparency were still there, still intact.

He didn't stop at that day's events, either. Or even over the past weeks. He went all the way back to the day he got hired for the damn job as host of *The Grass is Greener*. The day their fellowship broke.

He told her everything he'd been yearning to ring her up and say for the past three years, but at first hadn't dared, and then was no longer able to. At every step, he had to force himself to tell the whole truth as it first came to his open mind. He was so ashamed of himself, he had to constantly fight against the urge to modify some bits, tune down some others, to pervert what had actually happened. What a base, self-serving bastard he'd become, actively participating in destroying lives for entertainment—just because the bosses told him to.

As he continued the tale, he discovered the most curious thing. Insights he had never consciously dared to recognise came out when he had to make the effort to put the naked facts to words. He found himself confessing how he'd fled into the job out of fear of seeing life pass him by, of dying as a nobody. He laughed at how ridiculous, naive, and conceited his first attempts at rebellion were. He even ended up recognising, with no prompting from Kyla other than her complete attention, that everything he'd done was probably nothing more than an idealist's folly. But even if it all amounted to nothing, he was still better off now than he was this time yesterday, and wouldn't take it back for anything in the world.

Kyla remained silent the whole time he was talking. Even after he was definitely finished, she still kept her peace a moment or two longer, as if wanting to make sure she'd finished wrapping her head around every detail before commenting.

"Well, Liam, I don't know whether to congratulate you or slap you upside the head. I was watching the show tonight, so I already knew there was more to it than the spin doctor feeds were letting on. I also had a good look at that file you attached. I haven't had time to finish it yet, but there's a lot there. Those are terrible stories, Liam, terrible lives. They needed to be shared with the world."

She paused and seemed to be uncertain as to whether she should say any more or leave it at that. Or perhaps she was fighting to avoid saying what she knew must come next.

"The real question is," she finally said, having drained her last excuse to put it off along with the dregs of her tea, "is it really worth it? What are you doing to yourself, Liam?"

The former host sighed. Good honest doubt, coming back to haunt him. He wet his lips.

"I'm doing what I should have done ages ago, Kyla. I'm doing what I almost lost the ability to do. Think for myself. Do what my brain and my gut tell me is right. Be who I really am, not what RedCorp says I need to be, because that's best for their bottom line." He paused, mustering up the words to corral his thoughts and emotions as closely as possible. "Is it really worth it? I don't know. And I'm not sure I have the luxury to think in those terms right now. I just know that if I'd turned down this last chance, if I'd turned my back and buried my revulsion down deep, once again, it might never have come back up again. And if that happened, I wouldn't be *me* anymore. If we're lucky, you won't be the only one to read those life stories and want to fight to stop it from happening again and again. If not... well, it's done now anyway."

Kyla weighed him up, and most likely down as well, then said, "Fair enough for now, I suppose. What are your plans?"

Liam frowned. "From here on in, I don't really have any plan to speak of. I just knew I needed to see you. And not just to lay low for a while and make them think they've lost me," he was quick to add, "but also to make sure I hadn't gone completely insane. Sometimes, I'm not so sure anymore. I'll be able to rough it some way or another. I've got a bit of cash with me. You know, charity tokens."

Kyla smirked again at that, and it warmed Liam's heart to see it. "Well, I don't know if it's charity or not, but I can get you in touch with someone who might be able to help you. Point you in the right direction, so to speak. All off the record, of course."

Relief rushed over Liam like the waters of a poorly maintained dam. "Thank you, K. I knew that, if anyone could help me figure out how to survive now, it'd be you. Is this contact anyone I know?"

Kyla's emerald hair shimmered as she shook her head. "Like I said, Liam, it has to be off the record. I can't tell you their name. All I can do is make the call, try to set something up. But I can't even guarantee they'll decide to show up, especially if the RedCorp security goons are sniffing around. And if they end up grabbing you, sooner or later, then it's better if you don't have any names to give them."

Mars almighty. Was this his life now?

"Wait, what about you?" Liam asked. "If they know I came here, then aren't you at risk? And doesn't that put whoever else you might know that's trying to fight the Corporations at risk as well?"

A dizzying vision of toppling dominos and cascading Corporate security raids filled Liam's mind. He hoped Kyla would tell him not to be silly, say something to reassure him—but, as usual, the

Universe showed just how little it cared for Liam Argyle's hopes and expectations.

"You're right," she said, with a shrug. "But there's no going back on that now. Not since you decided to pull that stunt and then come running straight to my doorstep." Liam opened his mouth to apologise, but Kyla cut him short. "But Liam, you can't stay here tonight. If they're really serious about finding you, they'll check here before long. If you're still here when they do, that's the end for you. For all of us." She gasped for breath, having blurted all this out in record time. Liam figured that his own breath must be prancing around the Kenyan savannah someplace, it was so very far from caught.

"So, take what you need and go. And after you do, don't come back to my home again. At least, not for a while. If you need to tell me anything, do it through the contact. You know I'll do all I can to help, but just… don't come back here, okay? I can't afford to take the risk. You know what I mean."

Indignation[1] rose like fireworks in Liam's chest, but died just as fast. She was right, and he did know what she meant. She hadn't chosen to get into this mess, and he had no right to drag her into it against her will. What was he expecting, for her to jump for joy and join him in his crusade against the perverters of human nature? Come to think of it, yes. At some level, he had assumed exactly that, in coming here. How foolish.

It just didn't work that way. In time, maybe, if he and others could prove that another way was possible…

"I understand, K. I won't try to impose. Fat lot of good it'd do even if I tried, eh?" He chuckled and gave her a ruinous shade of his former grin, remembering all the time they'd had together: the games, the complicity, the sharing, the good-natured head-butting.

She chuckled a little, along with him.

"Why don't you go grab a shower, Liam? And have you even

---

[1] To feel indignation is to regard something or someone as "unworthy"—more often than not, yourself.

eaten?" Liam's stomach had remained silently buried under the flow of adrenalin for the past few hours, but now it punched through with an almighty gurgle that sent a blush up his cheeks. "Guess not, then. I'll get something hot and stodgy ready for us."

And off she herded him into the bathroom, without further ceremony. It was only when he was in the shower, washing off camo gunk and rubbing a handful of Kyla's fragrant shampoo into his messy hair that a frightening thought crept into his mind, through the back door.

What if Kyla were calling the police or RedCorp at this very instant? What if she'd already called them and they were on their way? Wouldn't telling Liam to take a shower be the perfect excuse to get him out of the way so that a certain doubt-prone friend of his might place the call that would protect her from any repercussions?

After all, she hadn't asked for him to come, and was none too happy about it. He'd just shown up. How long had it been since they'd seen each other properly? Well over two full years. Could he really expect her to put her neck on the line for him now? After what she'd said?

He hurried to rinse out the shampoo and jumped out of the shower, water dripping everywhere. He got half-dry before losing patience and just hauling his clothes on anyway, then stomped out, his hair all a-tussle. By now, he was firmly prepared to feel the good ol' sting of a Corporate police neurotaser the moment he stepped out of the bathroom.

Instead, a piping cup of hot chocolate awaited him on the coffee table, and Kyla called out from the kitchen.

"That was fast! I had some of that organic high-concentration cocoa you love at the back of the cupboard, from Mars knows when. I figure it'll go well with some cheese on toast. Comfort food, what?" Her laugh rang loud and true, and Liam's earlobes burned with shame at the thought that, only a moment ago, he was ready to brand the woman as a traitor.

That little voice was still there, whispering that she must have put something in the cocoa, that they were on their way, urging him to club her with the lamp and then run, run, run… but it was now pariah[1], the submitted drummer, thumping away to complete ignorance.

Wrapped in only a damp towel, Liam took his usual seat and raised the rich cup of cocoa to his nose for a good long smell. The chattering vidscreen in the bedroom was now mercifully silent. Kyla must have turned it off before she placed the call to her mysterious contact—whoever they were—while he was in the shower.

The food was good, the cocoa even better, and the laughs they had—completely forgetting today and remembering the good ol' days and nights—were like aloe vera on his sunburnt mind.

But none of that changed the realities of the situation. When Liam stepped out of the apartment, fully dressed in his freshly steamed suit and with the tentative meeting time and place in his cheap AR glasses' calendar, he still had to find some scummy hotel to bunker down in. Under a false name, hopefully, if he could find a coffin-stack hotel or cheap motel with a human receptionist he could bribe. And wouldn't it be just his luck to come across the only honest hotel desk clerk in East London?

For once, his expectations of humanity were not disappointed; the first nameless crumbling dive motel he found had a human desk clerk who was depressingly easy to bribe. "Monsieur Lucien Artois" was soon safely installed, over-the-top fake French accent and all, in his ratty closet of a room. The night ticked by peacefully—disturbed only by the pattering feet of bugs and rodents and the niggling voice of his subconscious, yelling things Liam might have been able to understand if he'd only allowed his thinking mind to face them, as it faded off to sleep.

---

[1] From the Tamil *paraiyan*, or "festival drummer," which was the function of the lowest caste of southern India.

* * *

He was falling. It was beautiful, it was exhilarating. It was absolutely terrifying.

The wind ruffled his wings, but they were just for show, and he couldn't help but wonder how good they'd look when he hit the ground.

He wasn't afraid, though. Well, not too much. He had his sprue, so he would be fine.

He breathed deep, forcing his eyes open against the wind, taking it all in. He was at peace with the universe. How amazing life was.

All too soon, the ground below grew big and looming. Oh well, time to use the sprue and stop his fall.

He pulled. Nothing happened.

He realized with world-shattering horror that there was not, never had been, and never would be such a thing as a sprue[1].

Kyla had set the meeting for half past noon at a posh little café by a busy market in Roman Road, a click or so south of her place.

It was perfect—the time of day when everyone in London who was in any kind of position of authority would be skiving off to have a nice bite to eat. This most certainly included any conscientious Corporate goon who, given free rein on day two of an all-out search, could be trusted to seize the opportunity to taste the kind of lunchtime freedom normally reserved for their employers. Liam and his mystery anti-Corp resistance contact would have plenty of cover. There'd be no real risk of getting spotted as long as Liam didn't walk his goofy-moustached face directly into any security cameras and stayed out of the drinking holes the Corporate flunkies would be sure to go wallow in.

The fugitive former host crossed the open doors of The Popina

---

[1] Except apparently there is. Go figure.

five minutes early. When nobody reacted to his presence, he headed over to a far corner table of the rustic-looking café and ordered a mineral water from the serving trolley. For twenty agonizing minutes, he sat there nursing a glass of water that soon grew unpleasantly warm in the sweltering heat of the day. He'd just about come to terms with the idea he'd been stood up, and had moved on to despair over what the hell he was supposed to do next, when a tweed-clad Middle-Eastern[1] man made his way through the throng. He seemed to have spotted Liam without difficulty—was he that obvious?

The man sat down and let loose a nervous laugh, and it was that laugh that shook two years of cobwebs out of Liam's mind, making him realise who he was sitting next to. Professor Fourka laughed again, no doubt at the startled expression on Liam's face.

"It is you!" said the former first season *Grass is Greener* contestant—one of the few who survived that eventful opening year. "I've been wagering with myself all day whether or not you would actually be here. With the ruckus you've started, I'm surprised you're not either holed up or in a whole different country by now."

"Professor Fourka?" Liam knew he had no time to waste, but he was utterly boggled by this apparition from a past he had worked so hard to leave behind. "How—What are you doing here?"

"You know, Liam, I have asked myself that same question many times, ever since I received your friend's message." He shrugged, then smiled at Liam under his new, bushy beard, shot with silver. "I have reason enough not to want to get entangled in any more Corporate business, as you are well aware."

"Listen, Professor Fourka—Ali, if you don't mind."

The professor nodded and urged Liam to go on.

"I know you have every reason to hate me, and I can't express just how sorry I am for—"

---

[1] In most people's minds, the term no longer referred to a rich historical and cultural identity, but simply to a time zone for calculating feed broadcast times. I'm not certain that can be called "progress."

"For what?" cut in Professor Fourka with a chop of a hand through the air. "Liam, I am not blind. I knew what I was getting into when I signed on with that show. To be made a mockery, no doubt, but also to have one last shot at getting people to think before political science was washed out of the universities once and for all. Whatever the personal costs have been, I like to think I did some good there."

Something in his tone told Liam he wasn't talking about random viewers. They fell silent and tried to pretend they weren't bothered in the least as the waiter-trolley swooped over on squeaking wheels, plonked down the Professor's lens-ordered mint green tea, and rushed off to the next table without a word.

"I saw that message of yours, Liam," the Professor added, breaking the silence.

"Well," said Liam, blushing with pleasure at the idea of his old Professor hearing what he had to say and taking it seriously. "It's no great literature, but I wanted to do my part—"

"You are a fool, Liam," cut in the Professor once again—but not unkindly. "You realise this, yes? A fool to have squandered such an opportunity to act, to make a difference—but a well intentioned fool, nonetheless." He paused with a sigh before carrying on. "Since Birkbeck closed the PoliSci Department and made the last of us redundant, I've had a lot of time on my hands. I've been known to help out a poor soul at odds with our Corporate overlords from time to time."

"Kyla thought you might be able to hook me up, get me in touch with other… people like me. Is that right?"

"Well, I don't know anything about that." The man's tweed jacket strained as he had a casual yet thorough look around. "I'm just a humble, forcibly retired professor, trying to make a living. You know how it goes."

Doubt gripped Liam once again. Had the Professor just been stringing him along, keeping him busy while the rent-a-cops homed in, just to laugh in his face and get his revenge for the humiliation he suffered on the show, after all?

"What I do know is, if you were to go to the address on the back of the card I'm about to give you, you might find a few people with interesting ideas. You might enjoy speaking with them." He slid the physical business card over. Liam pocketed it without looking at it just yet, but was otherwise at a complete loss as to how to react. Was a "thank you" in order?

The Professor downed his tea and stood up. "One thing I don't know is whether or not I'll be able to join you there so that we might talk a bit more." He leant in and almost whispered, even though the gesture was completely superfluous in the combined din of busy café patrons and equally busy AR displays. "But I hope so."

With that, he elbowed his way back out toward the door, just as conspicuously as everyone else. Liam decided to fiddle around with the display in his cheap glasses, to let his racing mind settle a bit and to put a few minutes between Fourka's exit and his own.

On mental autopilot, his fingers danced their way to the main *Grass is Greener* portal, and he chuckled as he read the first headline there.

Well, at least he'd done someone some good with his act of defiance. RedCorp had been forced to cancel the big weekly elimination feature show, giving all the remaining contestants—he had to struggle against the habit of thinking of them as *his* contestants, which they weren't any longer—the reprieve of a guaranteed extra week in the implant-fuelled spotlight.

As an AI construct, Raja Cassar wouldn't care, but the other six seemed well pleased, each back in their respective natural habitats and busy milking the boost to viewing figures his little scandal had caused for all it was worth.

On the face of it, none of them had any love lost for Liam—but they couldn't very well come out in support for him, not with the RedCorp censors breathing down their backs after the previous night's fun and games. Hell, they'd probably forced the Editor down from his bulbous ivory tower at The Tulip and back into his old office at the Mews to manage the crisis.

Liam wondered what the little man would make of his Banksy prints, and smiled even further beneath his sweaty fake moustache.

And yet, even though none of the contestants were coming out in favour of their former host's call-to-arms against the Corporate world-state, Liam was surprised to see that it was Mars-born Neriene Cartwright and Welsh spitfire retiree Hattie Hughes who were the most sympathetic, always tempering their words with kindness and barely veiled support as they ate their lunches—the gawky tortured teenager in a gloomy Corporate hospital cafeteria, and the slave-contracted pensioner-in-waiting in the sunlit and doily-strewn kitchen of her isolated cottage.

In contrast, contestants like Sabeen Al-Amin and Fnu Cinta, who'd seemed quite sympathetic all in all, were laying the blame on him heavier than a Jupiter breeze. Anything to get a sympathy boost and survive elimination just one week longer.

How strange, to be watching the feed, *his* feed, as an outsider, and yet with himself as the main topic of conversation. It wouldn't last more than a day or so at most, he was sure, so he was glad he'd worked up the courage to tune in now.

Let the extra week's reprieve and any boost in ratings be Liam's parting gift to all the *Grass is Greener* contestants, then. Mars knew he wouldn't be able to do much more for them from here on in—not that he'd been much help to them when he was still working at the Mews, mind you.

Five minutes of mindless browsing turned into ten, until Liam looked up from the screen to see the robo-waiter's dead fish-lens eye giving him the withering sort of look that even mechanical serving staff reserve for podjockeys who only order a bottle of water and insist on occupying valuable table space long after they've finished drinking.

It had been long enough since Fourka left, so Liam decided to take the hint and went to the back of the café to find a toilet stall with enough privacy to finally have a good look at the Professor's card. Curiosity and excitement flared up in his mind like long-lost friends as he pulled the little cardboard rectangle from the depths of his jacket's inner pocket.

The card itself, Liam was surprised to read, was from a Chinese restaurant called the Mandarin Square. It boasted a showy AR mascot—a flowing duck far more colourful than any that ever lived—as well as two separate non-smoking areas. The address was on "Norton Road," which Liam had never heard of. But his glasses picked up the address and, one flick of a finger later, displayed a map showing that the self-styled "Home of Dim Sum" was in a residential part of the London Sprawl northwest of where he was now; easy enough to get to.

As for the back of the card, it held only a few words, scrawled in pencil: *5th floor, third on the right.*

It took Liam a good minute or so, and many flips of the card, to decide there hadn't been any mistake and this wasn't some cruel trick played on him; they did want him to go to some random place above a Chinese restaurant.

He needed a community, a home, and prospects of survival. Not noodles, damnit. Why did everyone have to make things so damn complicated?

As unlikely a base for an anti-Corporate counter-culture as this seemed, Liam wasn't precisely faced with an embarrassment of options; right now, it was either follow this card's pencilled instructions farther down the rabbit hole, or start a lucrative career in panhandling and underbridge homebuilding. Put that way, seeing how far this cloak-and-dagger business could take him suddenly seemed a lot more attractive.

It probably wasn't wise to rush straight there, however, and his stomach had started complaining as soon as he thought about noodles, so he fished a handful of plastic charity coins out of his sack, adjusted his moustache and inside-out suit sleeves in the bathroom mirror, and then stepped back out into the busy East London street.

Out on the pavement, Liam paused, breathing deep. The rich

scents of roasting rubber, post-consumer air, and chip frying oil joined forces to mug his senses. Ah, London. Truly, a city almost—but never quite entirely—identical to the rest of the Red-connected world.

With a fresh saunter in his step, Liam headed out to find two things: first, something greasy and battered for lunch, and second, his destiny.

28

It was well past two of the clock when, suitably stuffed, Liam set out for this Dim Sum fellow's place. He decided it best to keep to the neon shadows of the Underground, so he fought his way to the nearest maw.

The directions to the meeting place seemed relatively straightforward on the map, up until the last bit where he'd have to navigate through a criss-crossing mess of side streets to find the restaurant building. As long as it wasn't too rough an area, he didn't think he should have any problem. After all, he wasn't looking all that snappy himself anymore; he was sure he'd blend right in.

The sun was already struggling to get a few rays down into the crevices of these huddled tenement blocks by the time Liam reached Norton Road. Sick to death of plodding from one end of the city to the other, he finally stood before Mandarin Square, deeply disappointed.

His mood was not helped by the fact that he had passed in front of his destination once without seeing it and had to backtrack once he realised he'd missed the number. This was because the only distinguishing feature of his destination, as opposed to the hundred identically built crumbling brick eyesores up and down the street, was an ancient backlit plastic sign—an actual physical sign!—which had long since faded to white. The few remaining flecks of orangey colour did absolutely nothing to inform the passer-by that this was an eating establishment.

Chinese food had never been his cup of oolong tea. He would've had to be starving before he would have resorted to pushing open the cracked glass door of this dive. Fortunately, there was another entrance to the building in the far corner, and as he entered, he was in luck: The area was just poor enough and just safe enough for the residential buildings not to be equipped with AR security scanners at the doors. Unfortunately, this also meant that his chances of seeing an elevator were about as good as seeing a field mouse spontaneously give birth to a duck-billed platypus.

Five flights of stairs later, Liam was thoroughly convinced he was wasting his time here. He didn't think he could have imagined a crappier, more non-descript apartment building if he were being held at gunpoint by a homicidal architect[1].

But he had come all this way, so Liam swallowed his disappointment and took the right-hand corridor, stopping at the third door. He paused for a moment or two, pretending to be deep in thought and decidedly not thinking about how winded and badly out of shape he was. When he felt ready, he gave the door a polite little rap, just to get it done with and confirm this was indeed a dead end before leaving to start sorting out the rest of his life on the run.

He wasn't surprised to hear a muffled groan and a ponderous shuffle, followed by a curt male bark at the door, asking, "Who's there?"

"Delivery for you, sir," Liam said, inspired by the absence of suitable post boxes or intercom system down at the entrance. "From a Mister Ali Fourka." He hoped he wasn't overdoing it, but was confident this wouldn't mean a thing to the man anyway.

"Don't know 'im," spat the voice on the other side of the door.

---

[1] Which happens more often than it seems—why do you think they build all those convenient sniping roosts?

Ah well, at least I tried, Liam thought as he nodded and started to walk away. However, the man inside the room wasn't finished.

"If you've got a parcel for me, though, I'll take it. Come on in."

Liam froze for a second, then pulled out his purloined handheld tablet. He'd get the guy to sign off for the package on the screen, and then he'd go fetch it for him—all the way back to his rathole of a motel. At least he'd be able to rest assured there wasn't some powerful anti-Corporate organization hiding behind the curtains in this guy's bedroom.

The door opened halfway, so Liam pushed it a bit wider and entered. Three things became evident as he did.

First, it was very dark in here. Even at this late hour, there should still be some weak sunlight coming in.

Two, there was an almighty musk making a mad dash to escape from the open door. Either his host had the worst body odour and hygiene in the history of mammals, or else there was more than one person in here and none of them got out often.

Three, and perhaps most importantly, there was an oddly shaped object prodding into his side, and at a guess he'd say it probably wasn't a vintage Pez dispenser.

"Walk slowly into the next room," said the voice from the door, speaking close enough to the back of his neck for the sour smell of whisky breath to reach Liam's nostrils. His legs went as watery as North American beer, so he wasn't too sure about the walking bit. But "slowly" sounded good right about now. He could do slowly.

He dragged his leaden feet across one dark room and into the next, and considering that all his important bits still seemed to be inside his skin, alcohol fume-man must have been at least nominally satisfied with his performance. Personally, he felt that a round of applause would be more than justified, but he suspected his captor or captors would probably think otherwise.

At least two pairs of hands grabbed him from behind, flipped him around, and pushed him down into an empty chair in the middle of the room. They could have simply asked, but this perhaps wasn't the time to be pointing that out. Even facing his captors, he could make out no more than silhouettes. One slipped behind him to tie Liam's hands to the rungs of the chair, behind his back… with what, to Liam's amazement, felt a lot like a shoelace.

The brewsome doorman swaggered into view before, above, and all around Liam. He pointed a tubular object at him, and Liam just had time to recognise it as a pocket torch before the intense light flooded his retinas and brain.

"What is your naaaaaame?" asked a nasal voice somewhere behind him, in tones so ridiculous they could only be the result of years of training. Nothing less would achieve such a perfectly stereotypical villain persona.

"All my papers say William Argyle, but call me Liam. Please." He added the last bit in a rush, hoping that they wouldn't think he was trying to be funny or taking them lightly. He was too busy squinting into the light to convey this with his expression, but the load currently threatening to force its way into his already well worn, day-old undergarments was there to testify that he was treating the situation with the utmost gravity.

Disincarnate whispers buzzed around him.

A good enough start, all things considered. He still hadn't been tased or shot, so he had that much going for him. But Liam couldn't stop himself from conjecturing what a person speaking in such terrible nasal tones might look like. The words "handlebar moustache" sprang unbidden to mind. A monocle wasn't out of the question, either. Possibly affixed to the face of a cartoon frog. The thought did nothing to help him push back the nervous laughing fit he was desperately trying to contain—especially not when the voice spoke up again.

"Tell us then, Mr Argyle, what brings you here?"

"A card," Liam replied without thought. "Well, the back of a card, really." He dug deeper, failing miserably in his attempt to clarify.

He took a nerve-resetting breath. Best start from scratch. He might as well go for broke while he had the chance. He really didn't have that much left to lose.

"Listen, you know who I am. And chances are you know what I did last night. For better or for worse, I'm on the run from the Corps now." He gulped, surprised by how much effect saying that out loud had on him, even now; some fears and taboos ran deep. "I figured my only chance was to hook up with an anti-Corp group, if they aren't just urban legends. That's why I got in touch with—" Oh, what the hell, the good Professor must be working with these people, whoever they were, so best tell them the truth. "—with Professor Fourka, and he gave me this address."

The worst possible reply met the end of his little speech. Utter silence[1]. Liam sweated it out, not daring to speak further.

"I see," said the droning voice, so thoroughly nasal that Liam's mental picture switched from frog to giant floating nose. "And what led you to believe that Mr Fourka was in a position to help you find what you seek?"

Liam sighed into the blinding glare. He knew what a terrible liar he was. This next bit was probably going to get him beaten. Or worse.

"I knew Professor Fourka's reputation from university. That's why I had a common acquaintance set up a meeting. It was all arranged before the big night yesterday, and I told her it was just for old times' sake. She didn't know anything about why I really wanted to speak with the Professor."

To think, only last night he had—almost—been ready to brain Kyla with her own table lamp, convinced she'd betrayed him. His lie today was wafer-thin, but he just couldn't bring himself to rat her out; not if there was still a chance, however slim, of keeping her out of all this. He was already racked with guilt at having gone to see her

---

[1] As opposed to udder silence, which isn't so bad since it can usually be treated with anti-inflammatories and plenty of fluids.

in the first place. He wouldn't be able to live with himself if he got her into even more trouble now.

A short cough rang out from behind him. In other circumstances, where it didn't sound far too much like the gunshot he kept expecting, he might have called it a chuckle. His shadowy captors seemed to be reaching a decision.

"Okay. Let's search him."

Having been body-searched before, and not just in airports and shuttleports, Liam was tickled to realise the hands prodding and groping at him now were rank amateurs in the art. They missed a good half-dozen nooks and crannies about his person. He could have hidden something. Anything! Hell, Liam could probably do a better job himself. Was this crew embarrassed at having to invade his privacy or something? For a second, he was tempted to complain about the unsatisfactory service to the management—but only for a second. In moments of complete powerlessness, Liam realised, the line between light-headed giddiness and pants-defecating fear became surprisingly thin, much thinner than the chair he was strapped to. And that was so minimal, he seemed to have one buttock firmly planted on each side.

The light finally stopped burning into his skull and moved to his scant possessions, now spread upon some sort of table. In the new half-darkness, Liam's eyes could finally start adjusting, and he squinted at his surroundings. At the same time, he strained his prodigious ears, trying to listen in on the muttered exchanges behind him; but on both accounts, his frazzled nerves left his senses reeling.

He did hear some excitement over his handheld tablet—well, the subway rider's tablet, but what was it they said about possession and the law? There was some tense activity which ended in an openly relieved, "It's clean"—followed by the crunch of plastic and silicone fighting a losing battle against the steel walls of a domestic waste compactor.

It was not long after this that a new, gentler voice said, "Brace your eyes." Before he truly could, light flooded the room, such as it was. At some instinctive, fiction-fuelled level, Liam had a relatively clear idea of what this sort of room should look like—one born of the primeval soup of popular culture references. Gothic vaulting would have been nice, although the location admittedly didn't really allow for it. He would have settled for an operating table with the mandatory tray of terrifyingly unfamiliar surgical implements. Oh, and perhaps one of those nifty little gonad electrocution devices that were all the rage. What he wasn't expecting was a worn-out but still tasteful sofa, an oil painting of some tranquil forest scene, and a little table with a coffee machine and a tidy pile of printer-plastic cups. This was taking psychological torture to a whole new level.

Someone was fiddling at his wrists—untying him? A long and lanky figure stalked into view and helped him to his deeply slumbering legs. The newcomer smiled behind their half-moon AR spectacles. Their shaggy black hair hung over their eyes like a sheepdog, but the rest of their body was distinctly birdlike, as if a particularly gangly emu had been gifted a cable knit sweater for Christmas and was too polite not to wear it.

"I think we owe you an explanation, Mr Argyle."

Liam wished he had a proper AR set-up and could ping the speaker for pronouns as they wheezed in a voice Liam was not surprised to recognise as The Nose. Now, however, they took Liam's unresisting hand and started shaking it. The baffled fugitive would have shaken it back if his hand and attached arm weren't as unresponsive as a well salted slug—as it was, he had to settle, not for the first time, for a smile and a limp flop.

"I'm Nate Fryer. The man who met you at the door is John Small—"

"Ello!" came the rumble from the hygiene posterchild to Liam's right.

"—and the final member of our little team here is Pete Sanders."

A grinning fellow with a mop of red hair like over-sauced

spaghetti stepped forward and shook Liam's hand. He almost felt it this time.

"The three of us are in charge of running the safe house this week," carried on Nate the Nose, clearly the spokesperson among his abductors. "I'd like to apologise for the security measures we have to take, but there have been cases in the past where the Corps have tried to infiltrate us with fake requests for help. And it isn't every day we get someone of your… prominence in the Corporate world."

The individual words made perfect sense to Liam, but he seemed incapable of linking them together into coherent ideas. They were all looking at him as well, which made him feel a bit like a man who can't pee because he's being watched.

"Not anymore," was all he managed to utter through his bafflement and lingering expectation to get tasered or shot at any second.

The Nose shook their wild mane of black hair and said, "I'm not sure which was more noble, Mr Argyle. Sacrificing your position in society to get that message out last night, or not turning in your friend when your back was against the wall today. Oh, don't be so surprised," they added, with a twinkle in the grey eyes behind the half-moon specs—not entirely unlike Liam's own eyes. "Mr Fourka arranged everything with us long before the two of you met today. As you will have surmised by now, this is the gateway into our little resistance group."

They could have said, "This is the North Pole strip club where Santa's elves like to relax after a hard day's work building toy trains," for all the effect it had on Liam. He was beyond it now, in the land of the shellshocked and the just plain apathetic[1].

"No shit," was Liam's only reply. The smug grins froze on the three faces—perhaps they were expecting something a bit more enthusiastic—but they rallied admirably.

"No shit," agreed Sanders the Red. "And sorry about trashing

---

[1] Population: 11.6 billion and rising.

your tablet there, but we needed to make sure nobody could trace it, even without you knowing." He grinned even deeper, showing a surprising variety of coffee stains on his teeth. "Where we're going, we don't need tablets."

The Nose cut in. "If you decide to come with us, that is. Now that we're pretty sure you aren't a Corporate plant, or at least that you can't do much harm if you are, we're happy to tell you that you've reached the right place. If you want to know how you can live off the grid, we can show you. But you need to know that it's hard work. Nothing comes for free. And we never force anyone to join us, because we can only have people ready to put in the work to support our community."

These folks sounded a gherkin short of a yeastburger—you couldn't live as a community outside of the Corporate system. A single person could squat in an abandoned apartment and steal just enough food to survive, maybe. But a group would get picked up by neighbours right away.

And, if the quality of their body search was any indicator, Liam would probably be safer begging for charity tokens in Leicester Square—with an empty hat in one hand and a "Will Disparage the Corporate System for Food" sign in the other—rather than hiding out with them, wherever it is they'd be taking him.

But the voice of curiosity inside him was seriously piqued. And there'd always be that career as a bridge troll to fall back on if push came to shove—or at least to shove off.

"Alright, then," Liam said with a sigh. "You've got me. But wherever it is we're going, you're buying dinner when we get there."

Red chuckled. "You won't need to worry about that, not anymore."

29

Liam didn't need to worry about anything much anymore—at least, none of the things he was used to worrying about.

Food was both delicious and worry-free. Sure, the roster had him down for stints in the fields and the kitchens over the next few weeks, just like everyone else, but that seemed a more-than-reasonable price to pay for such gorgeous fresh squash, field peas, green beans, asparagus, cabbage, and more. Not to mention the gorgeous damsons and cherries from the orchard. You couldn't get food this fresh and tasty from the Corporate H-Mart delivery drones anymore, not for love and/or money.

Even in the golden-hazed days of his childhood, he couldn't remember ever tasting anything as... *lively* was perhaps the right word. The tomatoes alone were worth giving up his personal car and AR lenses for. None of that frankenfood you got all over the place now. And none of the cancer-feed pesticides or fertilisers the big agro-plants had their crops bathing in, either.

There were a bit over fifty of them living and working on the Farm, Nathan the Nose had told him in the back of the van—a manual drive van, the first Liam had seen in decades!—on the way here, sitting amidst the remains of the produce they'd taken the previous day to the some of the City's finest Corporate dining places.

They'd left London, driven out of the sprawl, passed the rest of the amalgamated urban mess that was the Home Counties, even past the West Midlands ManStoB'ham sprawl, until they reached the rolling south Shropshire hills. To Liam's eyes, it was like landing on another planet, or at the very least on the set of some historical drama; he kept expecting the curtain to drop and reveal the illusion. But somehow, it never did.

For the first day or so after he arrived, Liam had felt lost, walking around the grounds of the Farm, getting his bearings. He was safer and more comfortable than his wildest expectations after tweaking the Corporate system's nose in front of billions of viewers, so he couldn't figure out where his unease was coming from; not until he figured out what was wrong.

For the first time in his life, he was in a quiet place. Oh, there were people talking, farm vehicles doing their thing, and more animal sounds—and especially smells—than he ever thought possible. But, for the first time ever, there wasn't that constant hum of drones and vidscreens, of AR adverts and piped in muzak that had accompanied and dulled his every thought for his whole life.

In fact, he had yet to see a single connected device on the whole farm. They must have them someplace, because they were always aware of all the latest news, such as it was. But here, it was clearly an object to use in private, then put away, as opposed to the constant manifestation of a dependant personality it had become in the world at large—a sort of secondary umbilical cord.

Liam planted his hoe down into the dirt of the row of potatoes he'd been hilling—alien lingo for him up until two days ago, but the most natural thing in the world now. He closed his eyes to the green rolling slopes of Wenlock Edge and the raw beauty around him, and breathed deep the earthy scents of the place.

In the distance, down the hill, he could hear the braying rumble of animals that looked nothing at all like their cartoonish representations on the Red and in popular culture. Who would have thought that pigs were so long and so imposing, like round, pink tigers? Or that cows were so stoically intimidating?

Liam had spent over half an hour that very morning trying to tactfully shoo a spontaneous bovine assembly away from the gate outside his door so that he could get down to the farmhouse for some breakfast.

They'd set him up in a little one-room guest cabin built next to the Farm's meeting hall—an old hunting lodge framed with timber and floored with ancient stone; some of which, Liam had been alarmed to note as he walked on them, bore names and burial dates!

The meeting hall was set in a commanding position atop the high hill at the eastern edge of the fields—just far away enough from the braying and bustle of the main farm to take a step back from the sweat and toil of the day, and come together of an evening to enjoy a meal and a drink. They'd sit there and eat, drink, laugh, play games, sing songs, or just talk, remaking the world into the wee hours of the morning with the uniformly weird yet fascinatingly diverse people who, like Liam, had fallen through the cracks of Corporate society.

Nate and his other interrogators from the City were a typical part of the ragtag bunch of academics, activists, former union officials back in the days before they were banned, and general misfits who had found a place where they could fit in and contribute to a community, in their own fashion.

The Farm was nominally owned and informally run by Cassie, a third-generation farmer, and her teacher husband Matt, who had started it all off with a few friends of theirs who were in hot water for not toeing the Corporate line. This was thirty years ago, back when the last independent farm holdings were going under, pushed along by the mob-style practices of the big Corporate agribusiness branches, after they all agreed to block seed sales and restrict market access to any farm that refused to be bought out and brought into the fold. An effective return to Middle Age serfdom practices, under shiny new brand-name banners.

And yet the Farm, alone, had managed to survive. When the writing on the AR takeover notices became clear, the first half-dozen residents decided to get in what supplies, stocks, and parts they could, then cut themselves off from the rest of the economic world. They produced for themselves, and what they couldn't use, they sold in ever-popular black-market farmer's stalls in the nearest bits of the urban sprawl. People who still remembered the charms of the old village market and the variety of crops—old, non-GM strains you just couldn't find anymore—guaranteed them an always-eager clientele.

That's how they'd managed to keep their holdout farm safe while the heat was on, never ordering a single seed or machine part that would put them on the Agricorp radar. And then, after five years or so, when independent farms were effectively dead and one of the Corps inevitably betrayed the others and broke their tentative cartel, Cassie and Matt emerged from the ashes to start carefully placing small amounts of their goods onto the open market again—but only ever through specialist brokers who sold their rare produce as valuable, home-grown throwbacks to a bygone era.

It was enough to keep them in the green, with a bit left over for a few luxuries—and to back the odd bit of anti-Corporate activism. After all, fresh food and healthy living can only take you so far, right?

In the meantime, their little commune had grown to over a dozen, friends of friends who were in need of help, attracted not only to the sanctuary but also to the principles behind it, the alternative it offered to the Corporate world-state. The commune had carried on growing, as slow and steady as the crops it was based on, ever since.

The fundamental idea behind life on the Farm wasn't a new one, and it certainly wasn't the first time it had been done: From each, according to their ability; to each, according to their need. The survival of their commune, against all odds, showed the old ideas could still work as guiding stars, even with the system stacked so heavily against them as it was today—and perhaps all the more so because of how inflexible that system was.

In practice, everyone living on the Farm had a set of duties—all the same, except for the two children and five elderly persons amongst the members—with a rotation between the different tasks and chores. One day, a resident would have to devote a few hours to the fields; another day, to the kitchens; a third, to household cleaning and maintenance; another, to training, either as a teacher or a trainee, one-on-one or in groups. Special tasks, such as accompanying the van to market every other week, as well as manning the safe house in the city when needed, were on a strictly voluntary basis and did not exempt one from the normal tasks.

In exchange, the food was plentiful, the housing on the rambling farm simple yet extremely comfortable, and the many remaining waking hours between tasks were also catered for. The old hunting lodge boasted an extensive paper book collection, scavenged from closed-down public libraries around the country. Music, play, and good old-fashioned conversation were always there for the joining, from sunset to sunrise, by the roaring woodfire in the feasting hall.

No subject was taboo around the long wooden table, from passionate debate about some point of politics or philosophy to relaxed chit-chat around food, or perhaps alcohol or weed brought in from the city. It was not that far off the ideal life laid out for the monks in More's *Utopia*, Liam realised with a bit of a shock. Even the spiritual side was there, with Matt leading a non-denominational sort of mass on Sundays for the benefit of those who wanted to explore the spiritual side of community, each in their own fashion.

Decision-making was on a strictly consensual basis: Carrie and Matt got on with things, but nothing was secret; nor would the Farm, as a whole, do anything if one of the residents objected. This obviously led to regular arguments, especially when writing the bi-weekly list of items to bring back from London when the van went out. But since everyone knew they had a veto on any decision, no individual person's privileges could ever become a threat to the others.

Some of the most regular consumers of the Farm's honest,

anachronistic produce were high-placed Corporate executives, and the restaurants that fed them. Even a few Board members. To calm Liam's protests and panic, Cassie had assured him that their highly placed customers helped ensure the Farm's security rather than threaten it. The Farm had a *place* in the Corporate world, a legal and useful place, that at least a few of the powers-that-be had a personal interest in preserving.

Liam spent his first two weeks there in a complete daze, one that had nothing to do with his increasingly frequent evenings with the pot-heads around the blazing wood fireplace. This world was too alien for him to fully register, and as he went from task to rest, from day to day, it all seemed too good to possibly be true: a fragile dream. And if he were to seize it too roughly with his consciousness, it would surely break and disappear into nothingness.

But as the days, then weeks, went by, the Farm made no sign whatsoever of pulling a disappearing act on him. In fact, the rough realities of labour in the fields and around the house comforted him in the knowledge that this was no dream, just a reality that shouldn't be possible anymore. In fact, with every passing day, the ultra-urbanised sprawl way of life began to seem more like the dream out of the two. Here, there was no trace whatsoever of the teeming billions in their concrete hives, their dismal[I] world hidden away behind an Augmented Reality veil of entertainment and constant communication.

Here at the Farm, there was only life. Rough, sweaty, pungent, and utterly delicious[II].

And one day, as he sat reading at the rickety old writing table they'd moved into his cabin earlier that week, he looked out the window at the pouring rain and a thought rose to the forefront of his mind like a bubble in a lava lamp:

[I] From *dies mali*, "the evil days."

[II] "That which lures away," as in the French *délit*, or criminal offense.

This is the place for me. This is where I belong.

The long-time residents of the Farm were chuffed in the extreme to have him as part of the team.

"Living proof that the rot is reaching the diseased heart of the Corporate world itself," said Matt. Before adding, after a pause, "No offense, Liam."

Liam laughed it off, but not because of any perceived offense. He laughed at the notion that anyone could consider him the "heart" of the Corporate world, diseased or otherwise.

No. After so many years making a public ass of himself, and being a dick to both his contestants and the public, "heart" was just about the last organ Liam would compare himself to.

He'd been an ass, in every sense of the term. A deluded, cowardly ass.

But here on the Farm, maybe even an ass could pull his own weight at last, and finally do some honest good.

30

Professor Fourka came to visit the farm sometime during Liam's third week there—trivial things such as days of the week had already turned into a meaningless blur, revealing just how artificial and unnatural Time, that butcher of human freedom, truly is.

The good professor gushed about how overjoyed he was to see Liam there and assured him he'd be honoured to carry a message to Kyla for him. Then, a steaming mug of strong tea in hand, the first contestant ever eliminated from *The Grass is Greener* took his place by the crackling open fire. Word quickly passed up and down the Farm, and before long most of the crew sat gathered around Professor Fourka in the firelit feasting hall as he treated them to an impromptu PoliSci lecture, expounding on the theme of change—and explaining why, in his mind, it was inevitable.

"It's a law of nature that no force can be denied, not in the long run. You can't just lock up humankind's yearning for freedom behind an AR window and expect that it'll be the end of history. That things will never change again. Human beings are living things, and so are our societies. We are meant to change or die, and no human system can survive unless it creates the means of its own change.

"In fact," he continued, puffing on a ridiculously cliché carved clay pipe that drew laughs from all around, including from himself, "the crises[1] we're seeing today seem to be, all other things being equal, an expression of the sclerosis of the present-day Corporate-run global system. Of its inability to change. That's what leads to uncontrolled, excessive, and ultimately self-destructive growths."

Cassie cocked an eyebrow and tipped her bottle of pitch-black country ale toward Liam. "Like our Mister Argyle's big show?"

Laughter rippled through the smoky hall, and Liam knew it was good-natured. But he found he couldn't join in, and just sat there, rubbing at a raw patch of skin on his hand.

"That was my show as well, remember," Professor Fourka said, with a final laugh. "For a little while, at least. And we can both tell you one thing that show wasn't short on is control from on high."

Liam looked up at the professor, surprised.

"But our show is just further proof," carried on the professor, deadly serious once again, "that the Corporate system is getting desperate in its attempts to keep people quiet and distracted. It can no longer ignore its critics, its victims, so it mocks them. Invites the whole world to laugh at them. Turns them into fools and jesters. So be it. It's a necessary step on the path to change. 'First they ignore you. Then they laugh at you. Then they fight you. Then you win.'[II] We've reached the ridicule stage of our journey. The Corporations invited me to share my thoughts on their little show because they know my ideas aren't anything new to their employees and slaves. Everyone is already thinking them. And thus, the Corporations must acknowledge them—and seek to assure the restless masses that such rebellious thoughts are idle, childish fancies deserving of mockery and not serious attention.

---

[1] As used by Hippocrates in the original Greek, and all the way through to late Middle English, a *crisis* was a medical term. Specifically, the turning point of a disease, where change would either mean recovery or death.

[II] These words were never actually said by Mahatma Gandhi, although he did echo the sentiment behind them from time to time. The true source is American union boss Nicolas Klein.

"And then, of course, there's you yourself, Liam. How many others like you are out there? That's what is keeping the Corporate bigwigs up at night, much more so than your message, which they are professionally trained to ignore. How many of the human cogs in their machinery have developed an immunity to their bullying, their bribery, and their mockery? Who is out there, right now, thinking genuinely subversive thoughts and formulating dangerous plans beyond the ability of their algorithms to predict? Who's next to rattle the worldview of billions of individuals?"

"Oh, is that what we're doing?" Liam was shocked to hear someone shoot back, sarcasm dripping from the words like rain through a leaky barn roof.

He was even more surprised to realise, a second later, that that someone had been him.

"I mean, just look at us," he added, his splayed ears flushing with embarrassed heat. "We're not exactly making the Corporate Council quake in its designer shoes, now are we? And the only thing rattling around here is the water in Matt's bong. No offense."

Matt coughed from his seat next to Cassie. "None taken."

"I know what you're saying, Liam," said the professor, in maddeningly friendly tones. "But you have to take the broader perspective on this. The very fact that we are all here, today—that we can exist, and that you yourself are here with us—is proof enough that the bases of our modern Corporate society are crumbling."

Liam opened his mouth to protest further, but shut it again. There was no point arguing with the professor when he started breaking out the Marxist social analysis.

Fourka was a scholar. A brilliant scholar, and a courageous one. It would certainly take a greater mind than Liam Argyle's to fault his sociology. But that didn't stop the niggling little voice in the former host's head from insisting that they weren't really doing anything of value here at the Farm.

Could simply existing outside of the Corporate system ever be enough? Wasn't life here just as selfish as the rest of his existence so far, including the last three years at *The Grass is Greener*? Happier, certainly. And less predatory, without a doubt. But could he really be satisfied with doing no harm, if it meant not doing any good, either?

Liam didn't have an answer to that, so he decided to drain his bottle of ale instead. Fourka took this as a sign of agreement and carried on.

"Your show, Liam, is just as much a part of the Corporate-era social superstructure as our anaemic[1] client governments and the Council itself. Let alone the so-called Paradise Mars station, which is a literal Corporate superstructure!"

The dozen or so older residents of the Farm, who had learned Marxist theory before it was squeezed out of the Corporate-run universities, humoured the professor's attempt at witticism with a chuckle. A few of the others joined in, if only to avoid feeling left out.

Liam forced himself to laugh along with them, and to rejoin the conversation. "I still can't believe the Corporations chose Phobos to hollow out and turn into their demented extraterritorial haven for retired execs and SpaceBoules fans. All those clever people, and not one of them thought to speak up and say that maybe building their lawless new paradise on Fear itself might not be the greatest idea ever? Symbolically, if nothing else."

There was another round of gratifying chuckles at that, but once again, the professor seemed to take the idea with terminal seriousness. "Maybe they just didn't dare speak up, Liam. That's how fear works. And that's how a system fails." He paused for a moment, puffing at his comical, old-school clay pipe, seemingly lost in thought. "Tell me, does anyone know what the single biggest contributor to RedCorp Holdings' global revenue has been for the past two years?"

There was a general murmur of reflection at the Professor's

---

[1] "Without blood"

question, and a few of the attendees, including Matt, glanced over at Liam, who knew the answer and decided to stay well out of it. Whatever doubts he may have, Liam liked Fourka. He wasn't going to deny the professor his bit of fun.

"Has to be Redlink premium[I] access fees, right?" hazarded[II] one of the mechanics who usually hung out in the Farm's tool hangar.

"Lens leasing fees?" asked Cassie.

A third resident piped in with, "Drone Chow?"

Professor Fourka shook his head to all their guesses. "Over the past fourteen years, the single biggest income source has been advertising and product placement revenue from whatever feed RedCorp has designated as its main, flagship entertainment product. And for the past two years, that's been our Liam's little bit of global voyeurism."

Cassie, Matt, and the rest of them turned to Liam as if he were personally responsible for keeping one of the world's biggest Corps in the green.

It was a stupid way of looking at it, of course. If it hadn't been him, it could and would have been literally anybody else. But then again, the matter of the fact was that it hadn't been anybody else. It was Liam who had gone up in front of those podcams every week, selling the global wallow-in-the-muck-humanity-had-made-for-itself that was his show.

And so, with a little grimace, Liam took their glances in silence. Thankfully, everyone soon turned back to the professor when he carried on, hammering home his point at last.

"When self-destructive entertainment becomes the system's most valuable product, the end can't be far off. Marx had it right, really. He just vastly underestimated the ability for the capitalist system to survive by consuming itself, over and over again. For making capitalist culture itself its main source of value.

[I] A "reward," "taken before"

[II] From Arabic, possibly *yasara*, "he played at dice."

"Of course," he added, after a sip of tea from his no-longer-steaming mug, "if you follow Marx's reasoning, that's not enough to spark any real change. Even the weakest, most self-consuming system will remain dominant, at least in people's minds, as long as they keep control over the means of production. And today, that means the power to produce and curate the entertainment that keeps minds calm and consuming."

Professor Fourka smiled at that, the snarl of his beard curling up into a welcoming nest. "You know, Liam, that's what had me most excited about participating in your show. Those eyeNet lenses are the next step in getting entertainment production back into the hands of individuals around the world. It nearly happened fifty years ago, in the early days of the proto-Red "internet," before the Corporations caught on and clamped down on truly independent production. But once those lenses are out in the world, I don't think there'll ever be any going back."

Liam only shrugged as he cracked open another bottle of the rich dark local ale. "I guess that explains why RedCorp keeps putting back the public release of those eyeNet lenses, then. Someone up at the Tulip must have caught on to how dangerous they were for the Corps."

"Maybe," replied the professor, draining the last of his tea. "But you can't hold back historical forces forever. And once one person gets through the system's controls, it all starts accelerating from there. The old snowball effect, you know? Just a matter of getting the ball rolling, I suppose…"

Professor Fourka popped his clay pipe into his mouth and puffed away, the ember-light casting shadows across a chiselled face lost in thought. This signalled the end of the PoliSci lecture as surely as any class bell, and Cassie turned the conversation over to the latest books the Farm's away team had salvaged from an abandoned cellar in the old Shrewsbury Castle Gates library. Liam was particularly excited about an odd, forgotten Russian science-fiction novella that claimed on the cover to be the inspiration for Orwell's *1984*, although he hadn't had the opportunity yet to look beyond the cover and judge the claim for himself.

The former host joined in the discussion with pleasure, happy for the distraction from his nagging doubts as much as for the company and good cheer.

The good professor just puffed the rest of the night away in silence.

A few days later, Liam screwed up the courage to go find Cassie when she was alone, moving the cows in from pasture under building grey storm clouds, and ask her the question that had been wearing a worried path in the shag carpet of his mind.

"Hey, Cassie. How're the beasties doing today?" he asked, sidling up, hands in the pockets of the overalls he'd inherited from some previous member of the commune.

"Same old, same old," she said, flicking the backside of the nearest of the comfortably shambling bovines with a long stick of some sort of spring grass. Then she peered at him from under her rag of dirty blond hair. "What brings you out here?"

"Ah, well. To tell the truth, I have a question I've been meaning to ask."

The commune's unofficial leader raised an eyebrow, looking grim. "Shoot away."

"It's just that, all the talk back in the lodge has got me wondering." *Nothing for it now, Liam.* "Are we the only ones out there? Are there any other communes like ours?"

She nodded, but whether she was answering him or confirming something to herself, Liam would never know. "Oh, sure, there's others out there. Not so many set up like us at the Farm, mind you. At least, not here in England. But there are people in all the big sprawls who live off the grid."

"The QTs?" Liam blurted, before his better sense could cut the words short.

Cassie's grimace turned positively sour. "Some of them use that name, sure. They survive in their own way, and we keep going in ours. But we try to keep in touch." She paused to pick up a stray piece of long-popped bubble wrap, blown in from Mars knew where, before adding, "It's nice to know there's someone else we can turn to for help if we ever need it. And we've lent them a hand now and then, too."

The imposing woman turned to face Liam, eyes locked onto his like a missile's laser-guidance beam, waiting for his next move.

"Oh, well, that's good to know. I guess I was just curious about how many of us there were, all together. You know, all this talk about change and such…" Liam faltered, having said far more than he intended to.

"Yes, I know very well. Now listen here. You aren't the first to come here and start thinking about setting off a revolution." She cut off his protest with a calloused hand. "Hell, we all think it at one time or another. I don't think we'd have made it here in the first place if we didn't. But there's a world of difference between thinking about stuff like that and actually doing it. A world of difference."

She paused, making sure Liam was listening and taking it all in. For all intents and purposes, the former host was a deep-sea sponge.

"Now just you mind you don't start confusing one thing for the other. You wouldn't be the first, if you follow me."

Awestruck, he remained silent.

"Well, do ya?" she prompted, with another gentle whack on a bovine rump.

Liam nodded with vigour. After a second, Cassie nodded as well, with a grunt—hopefully, of satisfaction. She turned back to her cows but went on speaking nonetheless.

"You know, we have a good thing going here, Liam. And it relies on a careful balance. To fight a thing, you have to get close to it, if only in your mind. Who is it that Matt's always quoting about that?

Neetchi, was it? Anyway, we're just about as close to the madness out there as I'm comfortable with. I won't let anyone drag us in any closer than we need to be. The world will change in its own good time. We just need to make sure we're still around when it does."

Liam didn't know what to say as they walked along with the ambling beasts. A part of him, one that sounded more and more childish every day, was raging against what it felt as weakness, as betrayal. Yet, he was mostly impressed by Cassie's strength, the measure of what she was saying, every word natural and spontaneous, but the underlaying ideas as solid as the earth beneath their feet. And hooves, he added for the benefit of the cow who turned around to give him an evil look at that precise moment.

Cassie must have sensed this turmoil, because she answered the question he wasn't quite able to put to words.

"Don't get me wrong, I'm not saying we shouldn't do all we can to help things along a bit. I'm just saying that isn't what we here at the Farm are about." She turned to face him again, her eyes blazing in the grey glare of the approaching sunlit storm clouds. "Just promise me you'll have a good think about it. And if you still can't shake the feeling that life here at the Farm is lacking something, then I'll see about setting up a meeting for you. With some of the other groups who have a more… what's the word… proactive stance toward bringing about change."

That was the end of the talk, and over the next weeks, neither of them said anything more on the subject. The simple possibility of further action was enough to put the questions out of his mind for a while and let him fully enjoy the charm and joys of life at the Farm. It was only rarely—always at night, and particularly if he'd been partaking a bit heavily of the communal joint—that Liam's thoughts strayed back to dreams of flames and glory, feeding the seeds of the strange wanderlust rooted deep within him.

31

Liam's mental itch grew and grew. He made sure to read the weekly *Grass is Greener* recaps, desperate to keep reminding himself just how much better off he was at the Farm, how glad he was to be well out of that mess. The dispatches from his former life were uniformly pathetic, from Sabeen Al Amin's flamboyant hissy fit when she got voted out to Neriene Cartwright's catastrophic immune system collapse after they tried to bolster the show's flagging ratings with a live crowd. *Damn it all to Mars, didn't anyone read H.G. Wells anymore?*

But, if anything, that just made his longing worse. People were suffering and he was doing nothing, save enjoying his own life.

He'd given up one life of comfort to fight back against the Corporate world-state, only to find another even more comfortable. Somewhere out there, without him, people were pushing back against the Corporate system, striking against it in its diseased urban heart. He kept returning to that thought—poking at it like a mouth ulcer.

Nearly a month after that first discussion, the former host finally gave in and went back to see Cassie, asking her if the offer was still valid—if she wouldn't mind setting up that meeting with the city resistance folks for him.

"Just so I can see what's out there and put my mind to rest," he babbled in justification. "I wouldn't want you to think I had anything against the Farm. Or any plans of leaving. I love this place."

She answered him a knowing nod and went on with her work.

The meeting happened the following week. The QT contacts insisted it take place at the Farm—apparently, they weren't as trusting as Cassie and company when it came to revealing their base of operations.

When word got out about the meeting, Liam started getting quite a few pointed stares from his fellow Farmers. Some of the ones closest to him took him aside to have a private talk, saying they'd be sorry to see him leave and asking him if he knew what he was getting into.

He tried to chuckle his way out of it. "I'm not gone yet, you know. I'm just curious about what other groups are out there and what they do. There's nothing else to it, really."

They frowned, and their unofficial spokesperson, Nate the Nose, said what they were all thinking. "That's just what Tom said, and three months later we heard he got himself shot trying to break into a Corp munitions depot down in Priddy's Hard. The bastards brought him back here to be buried, and he was so riddled with bullets you could have used him as a colander."

The worried enbie let this sink in, then went on. "It's always the same, you know, Liam. Once one of us takes that step and has a good look at what's on the other side, they never come back. At least, not all of them."

These words rang in Liam's mind like the caw of a bird of ill omen as he made his way to the disused barn where he was supposed to meet the city folk. He must have dragged his feet a little, because they were already there waiting for him: a quartet of matching gaunt figures perched like crows on empty crates and bits of machinery. Judging from their expressions, they weren't the kind of people who enjoyed being kept waiting. Cassie had been having a quiet word with one and gave Liam a sad little nod on her way out.

Liam had the sudden impression that he was in front of a court, on trial for some crime he had no knowledge of committing. Or perhaps a firing squad.

"Ah, the infamous Mister Argyle," crooned a woman on the left. "We've heard so much about you."

"And seen so much," chimed in the man next to her. "After that stunt of yours, your face was on every newsfeed for a good week. I guess that's how long it took RedCorp to convince the rest of the Council it was bad PR to show that the Corps could completely lose track of someone. Especially one of their own."

At those last words, their collective expression seemed to grow, if possible, even more grim.

"We can't help but wonder," fired off the woman on the far right, "why someone with your background would ever seek out a group like ours."

"Because you're a Corporate plant, that's why!" barked the last man, the one Cassie had been speaking with. His eyes bored into Liam's, trying to catch his off-guard reaction.

Liam's balls shrivelled with ice-cold terror, but he had nothing to hide. "What? No! How could you think that? After all I did—"

"What you did," came the growling reply from the last speaker, cutting him off, "was both foolish and futile. It didn't hurt the Corps at all. The perfect ploy to infiltrate you into a proper anti-Corp movement."

"Whu—? Wha… I don't know what to say. I poured my heart out. I couldn't stand by and take it anymore." Tears threatened to well up, but Liam fought them down, drawing on years of practice. Where did these bastards come off, accusing him like this? "I did what I could, okay?" he half-sobbed. "And I'd like to think it'll do some good. Maybe not today, maybe not tomorrow, but those stories are out there now. And ideas die hard," he added, in a flash of the old lyrism[1].

The gargoyles perched, sizing him up altogether too long for Liam's liking, even though in truth their stare may only have lasted of a few heartbeats. At last, the man at the end of the line spoke up again.

---

[1] Apollo once turned King Midas's ears into those of an ass for not appreciating his lyre playing. So be warned.

"There might be hope for you yet, Mister Argyle."

Without leaving Liam time to crack a smile at this apparently positive judgment, the woman on the far right snapped his attention back over to that end of the barn, and his neck along with it.

"Cassie tells us you have questions about who we are. What we do."

Liam nodded, struggling against the urge to wipe away the sweat tickling his temple.

"Then ask away, and we will answer if we can. But know that if any of our answers leave these walls, we will kill you." This last statement sounded more like a promise than a threat. At least it made where Liam stood painfully clear.

"Well, I suppose the main thing I want to know is, what do you do, precisely? What are your goals?" Liam added a little smile to help relieve his own nerves, if nothing else, and hoped the sweat wasn't about to start streaming down his nose.

"Two very distinct questions," said the man in the middle, in tones as smooth as a pitcher plant's nectar. "First, our goal: We aim to bring about the fall of the Corporate world-state. Of course, we will not be the cause of its inevitable collapse. We simply aim to speed up the process, and to prepare for the new beginning which must come in the aftermath, like day after night."

"Without getting all poetic," said the woman at his side, sneering a little—but only a little, "what this really means is two things. One, we work to undermine the Corporations wherever possible, particularly when it comes to controlling the thoughts and desires of the average consumer. Two, we plan for the future, working out a practical alternative to offer the people when the time comes. And preparing the means to make that a reality, of course."

The words grasped the rope of the bell of frustration deep within Liam and rang it with all the vigour of a sexually frustrated French hunchback. "How? How do you do it?" the former host muttered in doe-eyed awe.

A wave of something suspiciously like embarrassment passed over the features of the four perched revolutionaries. For the first time since they'd begun this little interview, they seemed at a loss. Until now, Liam realised, everything had been going along in perfect accordance with some well rehearsed script. Uneasy, they turned to the man at the end of the line.

"Let's get one thing straight," he said at long last. "We don't want you getting the wrong idea about us. While we are, without exception, ready to lay our lives down for the cause, we are resolute pacifists. We won't take any violent action. Whatever the Corp news invents to try to twist our actions in their reports—when they bother to report them at all—we *aren't* terrorists. The real terrorists are the ones who would just as soon gun us down as look at us, if we gave them a chance to do either."

This sounded perfectly reasonable to Liam, but he couldn't shake the feeling that something wasn't right here. Then he spotted it. While the body language of the other two was still that of a stony medieval security guard, the woman on the right had somehow broken ranks. Without saying a word, her entire body language spoke of barely restrained rebellion and defiance of the bushy grey-haired man on the opposite end. Oblivious, he spoke on.

"In fact, hardly any of us have any kind of military background. I myself worked in a university before I came across a secret or two not meant for my eyes." He grinned, and Liam was heartened to see his face could look fully human. "Most of us are jurists, journalists, and actors… I guess we're just the sort of people who are drawn to action, who can bluff our way in and out of most situations." He stopped, and that calculating steel entered his gaze again. "In fact, I'd say you're exactly the right sort of person to join us, Liam Argyle. You'd get a chance to really make a difference, and I think you could bring a lot to our operation. We could really change a lot of things together."

He paused for a second, just long enough to make sure Liam was still with him, before continuing.

"But I don't want you to answer just yet. Hasty decisions are the ones we most often regret. Stay here at the Farm, think about it, and give us your answer when you feel ready. We don't want to take in anyone who isn't fully committed to joining us."

A mad, puerile impulse within Liam almost made him burst out in anger and demand they take him in right this second—but he kept the lid on it and nodded, recognising the wisdom of a waiting period before deciding anything too brash. This was potentially the whole rest of his life he was talking about, here. However long or brief.

The four intruders upon the peace of the Farm shuffled out, with the woman at the far end smirking as the main spokesperson handed Liam a piece of paper with a secure comms address. He told the former host to ask for Montague when he'd reached a decision.

As Liam followed them out into the blinding country light, he realised that, if only the man in black had demanded an answer on the spot—if he'd only been a little bit of a dick about Liam's inquiry—there might have been some way to refuse the offer to join their group.

But as it was, how could Liam possibly say no?

32

He was so fundamentally happy on the Farm, it took Liam six whole days to gather the resolve to admit to himself that he'd already made the decision, and call the comms address.

When he did eventually go ask Matt if he could use the one set of AR lenses on the Farm hooked to a cabled connection strong enough to support live comms calls, it was only under the pretext he'd go spend a few days with the other guys before coming back.

Those six days had led Liam to realise that, while he was indeed happy at the Farm—happier than he could ever remember being—he could not truly say he was content. It had never before occurred to him that there might be a difference between the two.

The move out of the Farm happened in broad daylight, a bit after lunch. Liam's dramatic instinct felt shafted and would have preferred the cover of night, but such was the way of things.

Most of the gang from the Farm assembled on the lawn to see him off. Cassie herself led that motley crew in a rousing rendition of "The Road Goes Ever On," set to Pippin's own arrangement.

It was both inspiring and haunting. Liam's QT minder shuffled about uneasily as the song went on; the final "And whither then? I cannot say" was still echoing when the QT bustled Liam through the vehicle door and slid it shut behind him.

The ride in the rattling, unmarked service van, deeper and deeper back into the Greatest London urban sprawl, was disappointingly uneventful—unless you counted the snores from Liam's hillock of an escort on the other side of the van's passenger area, which Liam would happily have done without.

And from the moment he arrived at the abandoned warehouse where these people squatted in lieu of a proper headquarters, Liam had the unmistakable feeling the whole operation reeked of bad idea.

The stench began with the living arrangements, which could scarcely be called "arranged" and definitely wasn't what Liam called "living." For starters, he hadn't thought he'd end up sleeping—or, rather, failing to sleep—atop a mouldy pile of pink fibre insulation with a bit of packing foam as a cover.

It seemed as if sleep deprivation was an essential part of the routine here. Without it, one might actually start thinking during the countless hours spent slavering away over a hot mechanical press, and who knew what kind of dissension *that* might lead to.

Indeed, whatever lofty aims they might hold, the basic, daily reality of the matter was that these people were counterfeiters.

"It's poetic justice, really," Montague explained as he showed him how to run the monstrously big chip-presses they'd crammed into the abandoned urban fringe warehouse that served as QT headquarters. "The rich don't even have to bother bossing everyone else around anymore because their money does it for them. They don't even need to think about it."

There was a heavy clunk from the elephant-sized machine, and then a blinding strobe-shimmer flashed inside it—like a discotheque for dancing silicon atoms.

"And that's when opportunity creeps in, of course," the QT leader carried on, unphased. "In this case, it started when some blessed fool of an accountant at Revenue Corp realised that paying a dime-a-billon for the quantum cryptography light-traps that protect their payment chips might be ridiculously cheap, but paying nothing at all would be even cheaper. Probably earned themselves a nice promotion for that remarkable moment of clairvoyant stupidity."

"Wait, so you're saying there's no protection at all on payment chips anymore?"

Liam had seen a lot of Corporate nonsense in his day, but this was a strain, even for him. Wasn't quantum cryptography—with little miniaturised light traps that cheated with physics to put a unique code in each chip and each device—supposed to make all payments safe?

"No, no," agreed Montague. "Every payment chip has an average of two hundred light-traps in it, just like they teach you in school. But not all of those light-traps actually have any of the rare earth ions in it that make the quantum cryptography work. The rest are duds—deliberate, cost-saving duds.

The lights flashed inside the machine again. Pensive, Liam said, "So that's what we're doing here? Testing the chips? But that doesn't make sense. Even if a few of the traps are duds, the others would still work and make the chips useless, wouldn't they?"

"Now you're thinking like a Corporate accountant!" Montague answered, giving his machine a loving pat. "But it's a slippery slope. The more duds per chip, the more savings for Revenue Corp, right? And anyway, what did it matter? It wasn't like anyone knew about the little budgetary trick, or knew enough about quantum key distribution to exploit it. Until SyneDeal bought out our university and replaced the entire Applied Physics department with a new Cosmetology Centre, that is."

The device let out a cheerful little *ding* over the local network, interrupting the conversation.

"Ah, here we go!" Montague said, cutting short his rant and rushing over to the blue packing crate set beneath a chute at the far end of the machine. A bunch of payment cards tumbled down into the crate, first in a rush, then a trickle. They had just about stopped when a little tray slid out beside the chute—holding a single little green chip on a gleaming tray.

Montague gave Liam a nudge. "Go on, pick it up."

Liam reached over and held the shiny little bit of plastic between his fingers. "Is this—"

"The statistical anomaly made possible by mad economics, yes. An active payment chip with nothing but fake, inactive light-traps, and no key distribution protection whatsoever."

It was tiny thing—a miniaturised work of art, full of potential.

"So now what?" Liam asked, his voice full of a grudging awe.

"Now, we see how many copies we can make with those machines over there," the QT leader replied, pointing at the massive printers and worktables where the rest of the on-duty crew was busy programming, soldering, and lugging around massive containers of printer plastic. "And how many fake credits we can get away with programming onto them. But the really fun part, the bit that makes it all worthwhile, is distributing these chips to those in need. They'll usually get about forty-eight hours of use out of them before the system catches on, and we need to find another safe chip to start copying."

Liam had to admit it did sound pretty awesome. Like a modern-day Robin Hood, without even having to bother with the "robbing the rich" part. Or the chaffing green tights. That was modern convenience for you, all right.

Montague took the chip back from Liam, climbed up onto a nearby storage crate, and let out a loud whistle. Everyone in the warehouse stopped what they were doing and turned to listen.

"Good news, QTs! We've got a live one!" he shouted, and his crew cheered and whistled right back. "You know what that means, folks. It's margherita time for everyone in the mess hall, last one there has to wash the glasses!"

Liam had to laugh as the QTs shoved away their interfaces and soldering irons then rushed off, as one, toward the more homey parts of their warehouse base.

But his laughter soon died when he realised he was all alone and there were bound to be a *lot* of glasses to wash, going by how much this lot could drink.

Manual labour was a staple of living among the QTs—which was mad, considering how high-tech what they did was. But their safety depended on keeping the presses and printers off-the-grid, and that meant keeping automation down to a minimum. They last thing they needed was to miss deactivating an RFID chip in some robot cargo lifter—they'd end up with the Corporate rent-a-goons crashing in on them faster than you could say "The proletarians have nothing to lose but their chains."

Liam saw the sense of it. But that didn't change how exhausted he was at the end of each day, after hours of lugging around sloshing printer stock cylinders by hand and manning the heavy presses.

There was one thing that made it better though, that made every sweat-blinded day and every disturbed night in his poor excuse for a bed worthwhile: Montague's promise that Liam could join the QT away team on their next trip out to distribute their ill-gotten riches. To live up to the "give to the poor" part of the Robin Hood equation.

In the meantime, the QTs were friendly enough when they weren't too busy to chat, and most of them didn't take themselves all that seriously.

Most, but not all.

Before the end of his first week with the QTs, Skyla, the scary blond woman from the Farm interview, came over to the dark corner where the former host was gobbling down that suppertime's offering of runny canned soup before the start of his nightshift. She sat by him with her own steaming plastic cup of nominal sustenance and glared at Liam in silence. When she did start talking, the former host wasn't sure whether it was a good or bad sign that she didn't bother with any pretence that she was interested in how he was fitting in and got straight down to what was really on her mind.

"You know, some of us aren't all that happy with the way things work around here. Doesn't feel like we're getting anywhere, you know? And who knows where all the money we make is really going. It sure isn't going into the food, eh?" She let out a chuckle as bright and cheerful as the headlights of an oncoming freight train.

"Have you tried speaking to Montague about it?" Liam asked, hoping against hope that he had succeeded in sounding noncommittal, but wincing as Skyla scoffed in response.

"Montague? The man's a math-head, for Mars's sake. He wouldn't know courage if it walked up and bashed him right on top of his fuzzy-haired noggin," she said. "We should just lay low and print chips and write bloody constitutions, he says. Need to be ready for when the time comes, he says. Hrmpf."

Liam sipped at his yeasty soup. "At least you folks are a lot more active than that lot back at the Farm. You actually do things."

"Oh, they let us out to deface some building or disrupt some public event every now and again. But it's never anything that really hurts the Corps. No. People see it and just go on with their everyday lives of petty consumption and corporate slavery. Makes you wonder, though…"

Her voice suddenly dropped half-a-dozen notches, making Liam lean closer despite himself. "Is bringing down the Corps really what our leaders have at heart?"

Liam thought about this for a while. Mostly, he desperately searched his mind for some way to avoid having to say anything committal. But she was staring at him so damned intently. He ended up saying the first thing he managed to grab out of his hurricane of thoughts.

"Say, did you know someone here called Tom?"

"Tom?" Skyla sputtered, genuinely taken aback. "Oh, Tom, sure. He came from that Farm too, didn't he?"

The grim-faced woman said "Farm" the same way a Corporate exec would say "freelance."

Liam was fascinated to realise that he officially hated this woman. He didn't normally hate people—did he?

"I heard he ran into some trouble," the fugitive host said, covering his unsettling thoughts. "What happened?"

"Well…" Skyla paused, stalling for time. "We were trying something a bit different," she said at last, begrudging every word. "And as you may already know, yes, we set out without the *official* go-ahead." She snarled a bit, as if he had been accusing her of something. "But if we're going to be ready for the Change, we're going to need weapons, right? I mean, there'll be chaos, looting, violence in the streets. How can we possibly hope to set up a new order if we don't even have the firepower to keep *ourselves* safe?"

Skyla stared at him, as if daring him to disagree, then went on. "So that's why we decided to hit the Priddy's Hard munitions depot. It was a good idea!" She snarled again, in defence against some unspoken attack. "None of it would have gone wrong if Montague had sanctioned it in the first place so we could have kitted ourselves out properly. And if Tom would have just followed orders, he would have been fine. The same goes for the others."

Others? Either Liam had spoken out loud, or Skyla could read minds, because she answered him directly.

"Tom was one of three who didn't make it out of there. Damn fool lost his nerve when the operation started going sour and ran straight in front of an automated sentry turret… How were we supposed to know there'd be alarms before we even got to the rear windows? Tom was the first to go down, but we pulled him out anyway. The guard drones got the other two on the way out. They were just too slow…"

And that was the end of that conversation, which was the last he'd had with Skyla. If he had any say in the matter, it'd be the last they'd ever have, too. In the days that followed, Liam came to recognise Skyla and her ex-military beau as leaders of a small but not inconsiderable faction within the QTs. Impatient, ambitious… and embarrassed. The QTs' petty crimes and symbolic attacks against Corporate society were nothing short of a humiliation for them. Such a mind can only take so much chip-pressing before it snaps, and before long, violence, death, and glory almost seemed like "perks" of the terrorist life—ones they were denied, yet were resolved to get their fair share of.

None of it boded well for his future here with the QTs. One way or another, it was becoming clearer and clearer this wasn't going to end well for Liam Argyle.

33

Meanwhile, back in the greater world—such as it was—the shiny git from Marketing was touting[1] *The Grass is Greener*'s Season Three finale to a severely diminished audience on AR screens around the world. The competition was down to Hattie Hughes, whose fans preferred a relatable, sympathetic hero who toiled away in Corporate indenture as she still waited for her deceased wife's pension to kick in, and Brazilian mosquito-bait disease researcher Matheus Carvalho, the runaway favourite of fans who appreciated high drama. Matheus had been lucky enough to get caught in the middle of the latest Corporate infighting over the Amazon basin and was currently being held for ransom by paramilitary forces hunkered down in the middle of the latest wildfire.

(The AIs down in Psycho-Marketing were already thinking "spinoff" and putting together focus groups to determine if the next hostage should be a world-class martial artist, an eighteen-year-old bikini model, or a Cocker Spaniel.[II])

---

[1] Originally, "to serve as a lookout for thieves," then, "to be on the lookout for customers," and now, "to pitch a product to customers." The distance between criminal theft and marketing has always been a short walk.

[II] Ultimately, they went with an eighteen-year-old world-class martial artist in a bikini, with the Cocker Spaniel leading the Special Forces rescue team.

* * *

It was nice to be outside and all, after two solid weeks stuck in the noisy, printer-stock smelling QT warehouse. But the excursion out into the wilds of the urban jungle, to strike at the foundations of the Corporate world, wasn't exactly living up to Liam's expectations.

For one, it was just as noisy, and smelled just as much of printer-stock, even if this variety had a bit more of a yeasty tang to it and was supposed to be edible.

Well, anything was edible, Liam supposed. At least once.

"I love yeast-burgers, yes I do!" sang the vending machine's stupid, upbeat jingle, as Montague handed a steaming, paper-wrapped pile of printer slop to a hungry homeless person. "Munch that one down and then I've got another for you!"

"And don't forget your side of chips," added Montague for at least the fiftieth time, pouring out a handful of their counterfeit payment chips. There was more money on each of those bits of AR-connected plastic than the folk in this long underpass queue would see in years. But how much they would get to use before the Corps caught on and the chips went dead was another question altogether.

With a sigh, Liam punched up another Release the Yeast Inside MegaBurger™. The machine gurgled, and the printer nozzle started squirting out yet another oozing bun.

"I love yeast-burgers, yes I do! Munch that one down and then I've got another for you!" If only they hadn't chosen such a fake, upbeat woman's voice for the jingle. It seemed obscene here under the rumbling overpass, amongst the sheet metal lean-tos and the barrels full of burning drone delivery boxes.

"Is the next one ready?" Montague asked, bringing Liam back to the business at hand. He wrapped up the two bun-shaped squidges with their even squidgier yeast-patty in between, then passed the scalding hot mess over to the older man.

"Here you go," he said. Then, in as low a voice he could afford against the rumble of the automated cars on the overpass above them, he added, "Is this… you know, *it*? Slinging burgers and rip-off payment chips?"

Montague's face went dark beneath his bushy grey hair. "These folks certainly think that's a lot, you know," he said, handing a burger and a handful of chips to the next person in line.

"Well, yes. I wasn't trying to say it's not important," Liam rushed to say, feeling a hot, embarrassed flush in his ears yet again. "Keeping all these people fed and alive is brilliant and all. But even if we could feed them for a year, for ten years—how much of a blow to the Corporate Council are we dealing, exactly? Aren't we actually making things easier for them? You know, dealing with the consequences of their acts so they don't have to?"

Montague paused for a moment, then replied, in a lower voice matching Liam's own. "Keep those burgers coming. But let me guess—you've been speaking with Skyla, haven't you."

"I don't agree with her, if that's what you're saying," Liam nearly growled as he stabbed at the vending printer's buttons. "But you've got to admit, we're not exactly a threat to the Corporate world-system here today, now are we?"

Liam didn't know what he expected from the old man. Orders to go back to their unmarked van, maybe. But he certainly wasn't expecting Montague to sigh and say, "You're right. And so are Skyla and her gang, in a way. The heart of the problem is they want to be doing more, but there really isn't that much more we can do right now."

"I think she's completely lost it, calling for blood and glory. Just to be clear," Liam said, bewildered at the turn the conversation had taken.

"It's not her fault, but the situation isn't healthy," the physicist went on. "I'm afraid that before long they'll do something really stupid, something that'll make our whole operation go belly-up. They're already reminiscing about the good ol' days when all they managed to do was get people killed. And for no damn reason, too… if there ever was a reason good enough to die for."

"I love yeast-burgers, yes I do! Munch that one down and then I've got another for you!" sang the vending machine, marking a pause as another nominal meal went into the next hungry homeless person's hands.

"I'm sorry to lay all this on you, Liam," Montague carried on, his voice clear and his mop of grey hair shimmering in the glare of the distant streetlights. "But I'm glad you spoke up. The tensions in our little family have been on my mind a lot lately, and to be honest, I'm glad to have someone to talk to. All too rare around here." He stopped, and Liam once again got the feeling Montague was weighing him up again, just like back at the Farm—but this time, it didn't feel all that bad.

"The fact of the matter is, I don't think this group'll hold together much longer—and that's a terrible thing to say as a leader. At this rate, they'll either find some way to get rid of me and take control, which is frankly the best solution for everyone involved, or else they'll break off and try to fend for themselves. I give both them and us a month to live if they do. And even now, I wouldn't put it past one of Skyla's malcontents to rat us all out to the Corps for a chance at getting a nice comfortable life[1] back again."

It was a horrible thought, but after so many days of rough labour followed by even rougher nights camped out in the damp abandoned warehouse somewhere around Milton Keynes, Liam knew exactly what he meant, deep down in his aching bones. He couldn't blame anyone for jumping at a chance to return to the mind-numbing comforts of Corporate society.

Montague nodded in sympathy and passed over the next lot of food and ill-gotten funds. "What we really need is something new,

---

[1] Contrary to popular belief, the fact that "life" and "lie" are so closely related in spelling actually means is that life ain't really life without a good "f" now and again.

something to shake things up a bit, to prove we're making progress… I feel like a right jackass saying this to you now, Liam, but when Cassie told me you were interested in us, I started wondering whether you might be just what we need to make that something happen."

Lost in the underpass gloom, Liam froze, unsure how to react. Nor did the QT leader seem to expect any reaction.

"We've never had anyone with your public status within the group. Or with your degree of integration into the Corporate world, for that matter. I suppose it's the nature of a group like ours to attract marginals. And a well integrated, publicly recognised marginal is a rare thing…"

Montague paused, lost in thought as the stupid, cheerful jingle played again. Liam waited in rapt silence for the vending machine to squirt out the next burger-shaped pile of slop and for the older man to continue.

"I don't want to sound dramatic, Liam, but we really do need you. I have a plan that would let us move on to bigger and greater things. I've been toying with the idea for a while now, but until you came, we had no way of pulling it off. You're the only one who could do it, Liam, but… Gods, I wish I hadn't said anything."

He turned away and rattled the printer-plastic carrier bag at his side. "Well, that's all we've got for today, folks!" he called out to the ragged people left in the seemingly endless line. "Anyone who didn't get chips today, make sure you tell the ones who did that they need to share! There's more on each of those chips than you'll ever get to use before they stop working, and anyone holding out doesn't get anything next time! Pass the word!"

The crowd muttered their thanks and started dispersing off to the far corners of the London Sprawl even before Montague had finished his little sermon. The physicist-turned-counterfeiter picked up his little bag, dusted it off, then turned back to Liam.

"It's a dangerous plan, though," the QT leader said, carrying on from where he'd left off. "Too dangerous, and I've no right to be asking anything of you at all. Listen, just forget everything I said, okay?"

Liam opened his mouth to respond, but nothing came out. He set out on this trip looking for some meaning to what he was doing and had only found vending machines and gestures that might be well meaning, but were as dangerous to Corporate society as pissing in the wind.

The last thing he expected at the end of it all was to have Montague drop the possibility of making a real difference into his lap, only to snatch it away again just as fast.

"And if you want my advice," carried on the older man, "you should get out of here while you still can. Pack your bags tonight and hitch a ride out on the morning supply run. You could be back at your Farm in time for lunch."

With those final, trembling-voiced words, Montague trundled off back to the QT van, leaving a bewildered Liam to follow behind.

Three hours later, Liam was back at the QT warehouse, thrusting the last of his meagre possessions into a worn canvas shopping bag.

He stopped, panting somewhat, and looked around at the emptied corner that had been his home for the past two weeks—you could hardly tell the difference. He'd be none the sorrier for leaving this place behind. And as for the people, well...

It wasn't like he was abandoning them or anything... was it? Not precisely, no; but the more he thought about it, the more it seemed to him like a pretty shite thing to do, whichever way you looked at it. Not up to par with the level of nobility he liked to think he upheld, that's for sure.

But then again, fuck 'em, you know? Who were these QT people to him, anyway? A bunch of strangers he'd bunked up with for a few weeks, nothing more. Nothing less either, mind you. And as far as strangers went, most of them were damned decent ones. These were, after all, people who had given up everything to fight for a better world; even for the kooky ones, that was something Liam had to respect.

Damnit all, what was he thinking? Was he really considering putting his own arse on the line for these people? No sirree Bob, not even if Montague truly did have some grand scheme that could start changing things for real and he were the only one who could it pull off. Not even if he were the only one who could make a difference.

Hmm…

Aww, Marsdamnit.

34

"It all boils down to what your friend the Professor would call the fundamental Marxist premise," Montague explained to Liam from across his chip-cluttered office desk. "The idea that nothing can change for the rest of society until control over the means of production changes. Now, sacrificing yourself to get the real horror stories of the Corporate world out in the open was a very noble thing to do, Liam. And hopefully, it will at least get a few people thinking. But when you get right down to it, it was a waste, because it just wasn't the right time for it."

They both took a swig of the aged port Montague had insisted they crack open to celebrate the occasion. After Liam's good sense had lost its battle against his mad, self-serving urge to make the world a better place, he had finally approached the erstwhile QT leader and asked just what the damn plan was, anyway.

"If you'd only tried to contact us before burning your bridges with RedCorp, this could have been so much simpler! Because that's where the means of production are today, the source of today's riches: entertainment, or rather, brain-time. Change will only be possible when people have the power to produce their own entertainment content outside of Corporate control and censorship. To free the world, we have to start by freeing the mind. And to do that, we need that *Grass is Greener* eyeNet lens technology, Liam. We need to get the printer schematics, the software, and the network protocols for them off the RedCorp servers and spread all across the Red."

"Forty-two!" Liam blurted out. "That's the password for the *Grass is Greener* servers! The one I needed when I made that broadcast. I remember it!"

"Don't be silly, Liam," Montague snapped, but not unkindly. "That's just a local server password, someone's idea of a private joke. And they will have changed all the passwords after what you did. What we need is an access point into the RedCorp network, so our people can get in there and extract all the software and specs for the eyeNet lenses. Then we just spread it all over the DarkRed, in more caches than they could possibly hope to catch up with. And all that's left is to sit back and watch the fireworks as a billion content producers set up their own distribution networks and start marketing their uncensored shows. Real life content from all over the world, and real money in individual creators' hands, instead of the Corporations' accounts. When that sort of content starts defining the culture, it's only a matter of time before people start clamouring to take political power back from the Corporations, too."

Liam shook his head and brushed back a strand of his unkempt brown mop. "Change through entertainment. Sounds like the most bloodless revolution in the history of mankind."

"Here's to that."

Both men raised their glasses and drained them in salute. Liam kept an eye out to make sure Montague was actually drinking his as well, and wasn't just trying to get him squiffy.

"So how do I fit into all this, exactly?"

"If you think it's possible, the idea would be to use your contacts to get back into your old workplace—one of the least secure points in the network structure. You demonstrated that, if there was ever any doubt. We need to get someone into the building, and onto the main system, so they can run the Trojan horse program our budding resident hacktivists have cooked up. If you can think of anyone there you can trust to let you in, then, ideally, you should be the one to go."

Liam must have visibly balked at the idea of returning to the Mews, because the man seemed to read him like a graphic novel.

"Don't be afraid of being recognised, Liam. The plan won't work unless the place is absolutely empty, anyway. The fact your face is known there is completely irrelevant. So, what do you think? Is there anyone at your old studio[1] you can trust to get us in?"

Liam gazed into his port glass. It was madness. Who could he possibly call upon at the Mews? He'd spent three years of his life there, and when it came right down to it, there wasn't a single one of them he could trust. He had definitely alienated Barry, and the techie had been the closest thing to a friend he'd had at the place.

The problem was the Corporate world. It made a bastard out of you, however legitimate your parenting. What he needed, really, was someone without any link to that diseased core, someone external…

Mary! zinged his neurons.

"Who's Mary?" Montague slurred a bit through a throatful of port. Liam decided to pretend he had intended to blurt the name out loud the entire time.

He painted Montague an impressionistic picture of the show's long-suffering outsourcing wonder, going through her trials and tribulations. He explained how the Corporate world treated her, making perhaps a bit too much of a deal of the bits and bobs of help and kindness he'd made a point of giving her over the years.

"She sounds good, Liam… yes… You know, I'm starting to think we might just pull this off!" The QT leader let out an engaging laugh. "And if we do manage to get the good stuff off the RedCorp network, Liam, the first thing we'll need is a figurehead for our movement. So we can explain what we've done and what the next steps are for anyone who wants to print their own eyeNet lenses and start making

---

[1] "Room for study," just about the worst description for Tantamount Mews.

content. And that's where the fact you are so well known comes into play. What better face for our organisation than yours, Liam? You're famous, you've got the experience, the charisma…"

"Hold on. I might have been known a few months ago, but people have the attention spans of caffeine-deprived goldfish. They'll have completely forgotten about me by now."

Montague gave Liam a wink. "You obviously haven't been keeping an eye on the viewing ratings, have you? After everything you've been through, can't say I blame you. But you might be interested to know that your show's new lad is about as popular as wet printer-toast. The viewers genuinely liked you, Liam. They miss you. There are more people binging the first two seasons than tuning in for even the biggest weekly shows, now that they're run by that slick, used-food-printer-salesman of a host."

Liam took another gulp of port, and he wasn't sure whether the tingle rushing up his spine was due to the alcohol or his burst of pride at Montague's statement.

The revolutionary physicist rose to his feet and popped a determined stopper back into the neck of the port bottle. "So… are you doing anything on Thursday?"

"I suppose I am now," Liam said, grinning through port-stained lips.

35

Damnit, in his three years of friendly socialising with Mary—determined to treat her not only as an underling but also as a fellow person—why had Liam not thought to ask for her contact details?

The fugitive former host dialled[1] up the outsourcing agency's ID in the comms suite of his new, QT-modded glasses. He typed in the QT's secure offshore bank account number when requested, for the privilege of not having to listen to advertising jingles as he fought with an AI menu for two hours before he actually got to speak directly with something more or less human. He silently blessed the fact that video calls were still a bit more expensive than plain old audio and not expected for purely business matters.

"Drones Outsourcing, by continuing this call you are accepting that it may be monitored and used against you in a court of law, Carole speaking."

"Karl Jasperson, RedCorp, Human Resources," he said in a voice he hoped wouldn't come across as too unconvincing—especially after the QTs' masking program had finished dicing, spaghettifying, shuffling, mashing, and digitally squeezing it to oblivion and back.

---

[1] An exceptionally long-lived linguistic anachronism: from the Latin word for "daily," to "daily wheel," to "sundial," to any old rotating plate, to the rotary telephone dial, to the act of entering a number into an analogue satellite-based mobile communications device.

"We're updating our files and don't seem to have any contact info for one of your people working with us. A… Mary Artworthy."

"One moment, please," chimed the voice at the far end, leaving Liam to wait in mental agony as he convinced himself the call must have triggered some security alarm. Surely, the lady on the other end was intentionally keeping him waiting while Corporate systems traced the location of this call, closing in on the warehouse, on him, *at this very moment.*

Or she might just be incompetent enough to take more than five minutes to dredge up Mary's file on her display.

When she finally came back with the requested info, it became apparent that the later scenario was, in fact, the correct one. "Will that be everything today, sir, madam, or enbie?"

"Sure is."

"Thank you for using Drones Outsourcing. All fees for this call lie solely with the user, and failure to settle will result in prosecution to the full extent of the law. We appreciate your business."

Moop, went the line as it died. A little breakdown of the extravagant cost of the call popped up in a miniscule font in a corner of Liam's display.

Well then. Nothing holding him back now. Liam could make call Mary and take Montague's plan to the next step whenever he wanted. Any time now. He could just flick open the com interface and make it a reality.

While he sat running his thoughts in self-deluding mental circles, delaying the inevitable, Liam's display got bored and decided it might as well go into power-saving mode, and at least do something useful of the evening.

Liam blinked in surprise, shaking himself back to awareness. Was that really the time? Almost suppertime, really. The call could wait until afterward. That way Mary might be at home, wherever that was. It'd be safer to call then.

* * *

Liam had almost run out of excuses to give himself by the time Montague cornered him at mealtime—a whole five days later.

"I trust everything is going well with the plan?"

"Well—yes. It's coming along well. I have all the information I need…" He faltered, bracing himself for the inevitable. "ButIhaven'tcontactedMaryyet."

Montague didn't get angry. He got quiet. "It has been days, Liam. All the support is in place for this to happen tomorrow. Is there a problem I should be aware of?" He grumbled like a straining fault line.

"No, no problem, not as such," fumbled Liam, "I'm ready to call her, I've just been waiting for the right time to do it. Don't want to get her at work and all, but you know the kind of hours these outsourcing people have to pull. And then you have to take into account that—"

"The right time is tonight, Liam."

"Yes, of course. Tonight is when I was going to call her anyway."

"Good man. Just don't make the call from around here, alright? Who knows what they might be able to trace."

36

Liam ordered the QT cargo van to park. He'd let it cruise randomly and followed the road wherever it would take him, first among the periurban sprawl of rubbish, and then into the poor excuse for a countryside which lay beyond that. This brown, grown-over field looked as likely a spot as any, and there was a solid Red connection, which was all that mattered. The van engine rumbled to a stop, and Liam decided it was time for him to stop stalling as well.

He was excited about the plan, about the possibility to make the world a better place. Wasn't he? Then why did this feel so difficult, like signing his own death warrant?

The weightless com window floating before him weighed as heavily in his mind as the core of a collapsed star. It was almost like he was a teenager again, working up the nerve to reply to a social media post from some girl from school. He gave himself a shake and thumbed in the com code.

It took a while to get an answer—just how many com-bleets, Liam couldn't have said.

"Hello?"

"Hello. Mary? It's Liam."

"Liam?"

"Liam Argyle."

"I—Liam Argyle? Oh…"

Silence ensued for at least three breaths' time. Not a good start, so Liam decided to try small talk.

"So… how have you been?"

"Oh, pretty good, all in all. You know how it is." They paused again, at an impasse, and this time the outsourcing dogsbody was the one who broke the silence. "Err… and you?"

"Oh, I've been great. It's been an interesting few months," he answered truthfully.

"I bet it has."

"Listen." Liam changed tactics, suddenly aware the call had been going on for a while already, and he still hadn't actually said anything. "I have a favour to ask you. I left some personal effects tucked away at the Mews when I left, and now I need to pick them up. If you can't help me, then just say so, and that'll be fine. But I was wondering if you could get me into the place. You know, on the sly."

Again with the silence.

"When would you want to be doing this?"

"Oh, as soon as possible, but only when it's convenient. It would only take a few minutes."

Mary fell so silent, Liam had the impression of speaking to a dead line. It took him a while to work up the nerve to check if Mary was still there.

"So… what do you think? Can you help me out?"

"Monday morning, five a.m. I'll be on clean-up duty after the big finale. The back service door will be open."

"Thank you! Thank you so m—"

MOOP

"—uch."

37

Right then, one more time.

Signal relay datakey to establish the connection for the QT hackers—check.

AR tutorsoft with guidelines as to how to use said key manually, in case "plug-and-play" doesn't live up to expectations and things get complicated—check.

Reflective anti-security camera suit and face paint—a very large check. Paramilitary-grade stuff, about the most expensive kit you could get on the black market, short of shopping for aging nuclear warheads.

Smile, for charming Mary into not triggering the alarm when she sees Liam kitted out like a commando—check.

Neurotaser, for subduing Mary, and anyone else for that matter, should the smile not work—grudgingly, check.

Complete loss of touch with reality, accompanied by a sense of swimming through mental clotted custard—

cough

Well, that was everything. Time to get this show on the road.

Liam followed his own dubious advice, and so his next fully formed thought came as he stood before the Mews, brooding in its dark dysfunctional splendour.

As promised, the converted warehouse's service door lay open a crack, and waiting.

Oh, crap.

Liam had been clinging like strangling vine onto the mad hope that Mary wouldn't have kept up her part of the bargain. There were no possible excuses left now.

The disgraced host crept along the wall, even though he knew the security cameras couldn't register his suit, and peered into the open doorway. Inside reigned the darkness of the subway tunnel[I], but after a moment Liam began to make out a swishing sort of noise, which his long-term memory eventually identified as the sound Mary made with that mop-broom thingy she used on the floors.

Encouraging enough, Liam supposed. So he gripped his AR key—the key to the downfall of the Corporate world-state, if you listened to Montague—gritted his teeth, and slid in, figuring he might as well think of England and get it over with. Caught between the feeble light dribbling in from the lampposts out in the street and the glow at the end of the corridor[II], he could just about guess the shapes of the crates and props he passed along the way.

He crossed the cavernous main room, amid the ruins of a feature show he hadn't been able to bring himself to watch. It was enough to read the news alert when Matheus Carvalho won the grand prize, a life of weightless luxury on Paradise Mars—if the SyneDeal-banked paramilitaries got him out alive from the Amazon wildfires, that was, and someone decided to pay the ransom.

The building was so alien now, so distant from him. And yet, despite himself, Liam couldn't fight off a deep sense of familiarity, of

---

[I] Nobody talked about the darkness of the tomb anymore, what with real estate prices being what they were, making the idea of owning your own home preposterous, much less owning a plot of land eternally to just lie around in.

[II] A "runner," which happens to be precisely what Liam should have pulled, had he been aware of this etymological hint.

coming home, now that he was back on the scuffed plywood boards of the *Grass is Greener* set, as they lay waiting for Mary to dismantle them and tuck them away until the next season.

The swishing grew stronger as the former host reached the far side of the central hall, and then Liam spotted Mary, hard at work at the far end of the office corridor. The sight of her hunched form brought home just how different tonight was from any other night he'd spent at the Mews. How it was the last time he'd ever see the old place.

Maybe it was just the early hour, but it didn't seem to Liam like Mary was working quite so intensely as he had always remembered. Perhaps she was anxious about whether he'd be coming or not?

In any case, the blue jumpsuit-clad agency worker stopped swooshing altogether as soon as she spotted Liam.

"So, you came." Her tone was odd, too. There was none of the surprise or panic Liam had geared himself up for, only an odd sort of guardedness which threw him off, not knowing how to reply. It was only after a tense moment's hesitation that the host realised he didn't have much choice but to get on with it. So that's just what he did.

"Hey, Mary. Aye, it's me, but don't worry." He flashed her *The Argyle Smile*™. "You don't need to get involved any further. In fact, just forget I was even here in the first place, alright?"

Now that he was closer, he could see the look of abject[1] misery distorting her face.

"I'd like nothing more, Liam. Please, believe me."

Silence flowed through the hallway like a recorded funeral procession played back on mute—broken only by the choked sobs coming from Mary, as she turned away and hid her eyes from Liam. The host's shiny reflective suit crinkled as he shuffled from foot to foot, at a loss.

---

[1] From the Latin for "to reject or throw away," which is funny since abject misery is precisely the sort that you can't simply cast off.

"Mary, it's okay," he said at last. "You don't need to worry. You won't get in trouble; they won't even know I was ever here."

The agency worker let out a half-choked chuckle. "Sure, you and your flashy camo. In and out of here, then gone forever. Just like before."

"Mary," Liam said, his suit crackling down the silent hallway as he stepped forward, "I'm sorry if you felt like—like I'd abandoned you here. On your own. It's just that there are things out there that are worth fighting for, you know?" Liam wasn't sure why he felt like he had to explain himself to Mary, who was still only an outsourced Agency worker, after all. But her choked silence was like a vacuum containment breach, sucking the words out of him. "I couldn't stay put here, not when I'd woken up to what the show, what *I* was doing to people. The lives I was helping the bosses destroy all over the world. So I had to—"

"Stop," Mary said at last, cutting him off mid-gush. "Just stop. I can't hear any more. Just go take whatever it is you came to pick up, then get out of here."

"But Mary, I'm—"

"Just go!" she grumbled through clenched teeth, the words cutting through the silence of the Mews far better than any shout.

Liam just stood in the hallway, ridiculous in his shiny camo and looking at Mary in equal parts confusion and despair. But when it became clear the long-suffering Agency worker had nothing else to say to him, he gave himself a visible shake.

He didn't have time to sort out matters with Mary. Even the most expensive camo didn't work against every alarm, and RedCorp security could be on its way right now.

The way Montague explained it, the entire future of the Corporate world-society depended on him getting his relay key into the RedCorp network. With one last glance at Mary's turned back, Liam crinkled his way over to the door to Barry Fletcher's digital domain and pushed the handle, holding his breath.

The door creaked open of its own accord, the latch mechanism completely destroyed.

Huh. Liam thought RedCorp would have repaired all traces of his little bit of rebellion by now; it had been two months, after all. But the former host decided to take it as a good omen that the Corporate world couldn't just erase acts of resistance quite so easily, and sauntered into the fusty, machine-filled den.

The bulky, archaic-looking consoles and servers hummed with dormant activity—no doubt basking in the post-finale glow and recovering from months of handling the constant live feeds from contestants around the world.

The behemoths[I] had earned their rest. But Liam needed one more task of them before they were done.

Unconsciously skirting around the patch of floor where he'd left Barry Fletcher's heaping form after knocking him out, Liam reached into a jumble of cables and started fumbling around at the back of the main uplink console. After a moment's blind panic, he finally located the connector socket.

The former host unzipped the front pocket of his shiny stealth suit and pulled out the chunky QT key—a powerful, directional signal relay, squeezed down into a plastic tab Liam could hold between his gloved fingers.

Amazing to think a small pebble like this could cause such huge ripples in the global pond.

Girding his loins[II]—and everything else —Liam moved the key into position with smooth, reverent ease, then plugged it in.

There was no mechanical whir, no flashing lights or alarms—no sound or visible change whatsoever. Only an anticlimactic little yellow light that appeared in Liam's AR overlay—the pre-arranged

---

[I] Possibly a derivation, through the Hebrew Bible, of the Egyptian *pehemau*, meaning water-ox or hippopotamus.

[II] "Side of the body of an animal used for food"

signal that connection was established, and that Liam was to remain on standby until the QT hackers could do their thing.

Back in Montague's office, waiting around had sounded like the easy bit. But now that Liam was here, standing around not doing anything while the future of humanity was at play on some inscrutable digital plane of existence was absolute torture.

Security protocol meant he couldn't even speak to anyone or get updates on how it was going. He just had to wait until that light in his overlay went green, then pull out the key and make his escape.

"Flash! A-ah... Saviour of the Universe!" came the tune and words, unbidden, to his mouth. It made Liam grin—a welcome distraction to stop himself from going completely doolally as he waited.

"Flash! A-ah... He'll save every one of us!"

Liam had just reached the bit about Flash Gordon being "Nothing but a man" when the light flickered in his display and the Queen lyrics died on his lips.

Green. There was no mistake—the light now shone a bright, uncompromising green.

He'd done it. For real this time.

Not just a symbolic rebellion, but a real change. And he'd been the one to kick it off.

Fighting back a whoop of joy, Liam crinkled his way over to the door—only to crinkle his way back to the console again to yank out the QT relay key he'd very nearly forgotten.

Still gripping that plastic implement of destiny in his gloved hand, Liam swung the door open and sauntered out into the hallway, ready to face the future and whatever it had to throw at him.

Ever ironic, what destiny had decided to throw at Liam was a welcome party.

"Oh, well done, Liam my boy!" boomed the Editor's voice from the far end of the hallway, accompanied by a slow, mocking clap. "The perfect rebel!"

With dread seeping down his spine and his legs like so much

accidental effluvium, Liam watched Ed the Editor emerge from Liam's office—his office—*the* office, Mars damnit—and eclipse the cringing form of Mary Artworthy, who was trying to fade into the background, mop and all.

"I'm sorry, Liam," she sobbed. "I told you to go. I did."

The unwitting rebel didn't have time to process Mary's words before a fresh horror washed all other thoughts away: Ms Heath also emerging from the office, towering behind the Editor's smug, bow-tied form.

It was just as well those thoughts had been washed away; they would only have gotten in the way of Liam's legs as they reacted out of pure, terrified instinct and started bolting away down the corridor, toward the main Mews hall and freedom.

Sadly, the saying that nothing was free in the Corporate-run world—especially not freedom—rang true once again. The hulking guards in their pseudo-military uniforms made the point very clear as they moved to block the end of the corridor; the crackle of the powered-up neurotasers in their beefy fists was overkill, but effective nonetheless.

For a second, Liam's traitorous survival instinct considered sliding his hand into the side pocket with his own neurotaser; then the nearest guard grinned, the harsh Mews light gleaming on their teeth and turning what might have been a nice smile under any other circumstance into a promise of gleeful violence should Liam even think about going for the taser.

Since all else had failed, Liam decided to try bluster. He spun back to face the Editor and Ms Heath.

"Ah, is this my going-away party? I did miss not having one the first time, but there was no need to come all the way back from Paradise Mars just for my sake, you know."

The Heath didn't bat an eyelid, but his lame attempt at witticism drew a nervous chuckle from the sweat-drenched Editor.

"Going away? Oh, you'll be going away, alright. We've got

everything we need to convict you for Grand Theft Data. That's six or seven life sentences right there, plus maybe another six weeks for the assault charge."

Liam glowered across the corridor at the little man. "I bet you're feeling very proud of yourself right now. Catching me must be a real feather in your cap. Think it'll be enough to get you back in the good graces of the Tulip?" he jeered, with a glance over at Ms Heath's towering and impassive form.

"You leave the Tulip to me, you dirty little rebel. Say, speaking of which," the bow-tied man added with a familiar gleam in his eye, "do you know where the word 'rebel' comes from?"

"Ed," came the warning admonition from Ms Heath. One word was all it took to make the little man blanch.

"I'll keep it short! It meant 'stubborn' in the original French. But the Latin root is *bellum*, war. And I told them—" The man grinned, positively beaming. "—I knew you'd be stubborn enough to come back here and try to broadcast another silly message, just like last time. A grand-standing, ineffectual, waffling baboon of a man like yourself just couldn't resist. Well now, for you, the war is over."

The Editor spat the last words out like a death sentence, one he'd been waiting far too long to pronounce. But his jubilant expression fell when Liam started laughing—a mad, uncontrollable laughter that welled up from someplace around his appendix and bubbled over through his vocal cords.

Liam kept on laughing, until the Editor cast a nervous look back at Ms Heath. The RedCorp big shot was not amused.

"Wait," the former host finally managed to squeeze out between gasps of laughter. "You think I came back here to—" Liam giggled, fighting for breath. "—to send another message? What, like people just didn't understand me the first time?"

He broke into laughter again, and the Editor lost it.

"You lot!" he called out to the rent-a-cops at the far end of the corridor. "Grab this fool and shake some sense into him!"

The sight of the smug little man fuming and spreading spittle in his rage made Liam laugh all the harder. It had been a long time coming.

Rough hands grabbed him from all around, but he couldn't see anything through the tears of laughter streaming down his cheeks.

"Nope, no messages today, Ed! I'm here for a withdrawal, not a deposit!"

"Search him!" shouted the Editor, his face turning into a plump tomato above his purple bowtie.

The unseen hands prodded and pried the neurotaser out of his pocket, as well as the QT dongle out of his unresisting hands.

One of the hand-people let go and did something arcane behind Liam's back; then a high-pitched voice—possibly his smiler from earlier—called out, "This is a relay. Inactivated now, but it was used recently. They burned the logs, but these can handle a lot of data."

"Shit!" swore the Editor, all notions of etymological propriety forgotten. "How the hell was I supposed to know he would somehow find someone competent who'd be willing to work with him?"

Ms Heath coughed from behind the irate little man. "This breach is on your hide, Mr Green. I doubt the Board will be impressed."

Liam was stunned into silence for a moment while he tried to figure out who Ms Heath was speaking to. Then it hit him, and the ridiculousness of it made him laugh even harder than he had so far.

Ed the Editor had a last name! And it was Green! Of course, it was Green. Fated from birth not only to be an Editor but for *The Grass is Greener* specifically.

Liam's mind reeled with the stupidity of reality; so much so that he didn't hear anything else the Editor or Ms Heath said, instead laughing his rocker off as the guards escorted him to the RedCorp security van, where they eventually decided to taser him just to shut him up.

38

Ms Heath's return to the boardroom made it painfully obvious—even to those who hadn't been privy to the supposedly confidential[I] information that had been flowing around like so many disease vectors downstream from a diarrheic buffalo—that Liam Argyle had been caught.

"Implementation of the new systems will have to wait until next year which, of course, means that redundant personnel will have to be kept on for another three quarters, at least," said the recalled[II] RedCorp chair emeritus Ms Preston in the same voice a newscaster might use to announce a deadly landslide in some overpopulated corner or another of southeast Asia.

"But in lighter news, and it's the last point on our agenda, I think we're going to hear a communication from Ms Heath, who I'm sure we're all pleased to welcome back after her leave of absence. Alyson?"

The use of the first name was noted by all, and many a suit muttered at this mark of favour. Ms Heath had been banished from the chair's chair to focus her full attention on the Argyle affair, with her predecessor once again taking up the Corporate reins in her absence. All had hoped, and many had prayed—with more than a

---

[I] "With trust." Pfft, yeah, right.

[II] Not fondly

few wagering large sums of fids—that Ms Heath's exile would be permanent. It had seemed like a safe bet until just one spoken word ago.

"Thank you, Ms Preston. Ladies, gentlemen, enbies." After just too long a pause, she also nodded at the scowling dome-headed man behind the Marketing AR plaque, silently adding a fourth, separate category to her address. "As some of you may have heard by now, we have secured Liam Argyle."

At the flick of a finger, the screen at the far end of the boardroom stopped mimicking a wall and displayed not just one picture, but four: live footage of Liam sprawled in alcoholic stupor across his hotel-prison armchair, a looping security camera replay of the events at the Mews, footage from the last weekly elimination GiG feed, and a graph showing the all-time low ratings said feed had—lower even than what they usually got during the down-season, when all they broadcast were on-demand reruns.

"We've made certain Mr Argyle understands his new position. So now, the question is: What do we do with him?"

Ms Heath naturally wasn't the sort of person to give anyone the chance to answer such a rhetorical question; not now, not ever. She allowed just enough time for them to properly react to the surprise of her having actually asked in the first place, then cut in.

"Oh, I'm sure you all have suggestions, and we'd be glad to hear them." She half-bowed to Ms Preston. "But before that, I'd like to point out there is another matter linked to this one, and it needs bearing in mind."

She turned with unabashed glee toward the fourth screen, where the crimson graph was now flatlining along, showing the feed's ratings in real-time.

"You may already have recognised the GiG ratings, here. There can be no more pretending this isn't a big deal or hoping it's just a passing slump. I don't want to be dramatic," she lied, twirling to face the attendees and somehow managing to look directly into the eyes of each and every one of them, "but the feed is dying. And if it goes, so does a good bit of our credibility on the Corporate Council."

"Now, just a minute there," the bald Head of the Marketeers barged in. "Be that as it may... Look, we all know how involved you were in the project at its beginning and how difficult it must be for you to accept the way things now are." A smug grin of condescension crossed his face. "But the feed has moved on, and I'm sorry to say I don't see how any of this is relevant to your situation with Liam Argyle."

The light caught in Ms Heath's eye like moonbeams reflected off the ice of a collision-course comet.

"Oh, but it is relevant, I do assure you," she seemed to threaten, with a grin.

"Buh... surely, you aren't proposing that we bring Argyle back as host?" squeaked and sputtered a gnome hiding behind his Accounting/Human Resources plaque. He had nothing to do with any of this, really, but he was an avid feeder, which qualified him—nay, gave him the duty—to have his say.

"Of course not. We'll deal with him later. But the present situation offers us an opportunity which I wish to put before you."

Ms Preston coughed ever so slightly. "By all means, Alyson, do not keep us in the dark any longer. We are all ears[1]."

"Thank you. Having given it much thought, I've concluded that the secret to Liam Argyle's ratings success as host was how thoroughly miserable he came across. That is, after all, the whole point of the feed, and it's the sort of thing the feeders want to see." Ms Heath took great pleasure in noting she had been correct in every single one of her predictions about how each member of the Board would react to her announcement: some squirming, some sitting to attention, some eyeing the others warily.

"Of course, this theory also explains, well, this," she added,

---

[1] A bit like most processed meats—if you're lucky.

tapping the daisy-pushing ratings graph—as if any of them could forget it.

"Now, I'm certain we could find any number of suitable candidates within our files, but I think I may already have discovered the perfect host to get the feed back on its feet. Freeze image two," she barked, turning to face the screen. "Zoom… here." She jabbed at a corner of the footage of Liam's arrest, then finished with, "Full screen."

They all stared at the high definition enlargement of a woman's face, one so thoroughly etched with despair that it formed a lunar landscape of sorrow.

"Ladies and gentlemen, this is Mary Artworthy, cleaner, caterer, secretary, hardware technician, maintenance person, contestant shepherd, and loyal promotion-hungry informant. Not only does she radiate misery so intensely that even the most down-and-out of feeders will instantly feel superior, and happier for it, but she has also proven she will go to any lengths for the Corporation and the rewards it has to offer."

She moved over to her chair as if she had never left it, sat down with a pseudo-leathery nano creak, and let them mull this over a bit. "There will be none of this conscience business with Artworthy," she cooed in tones which seemed, in comparison, so soft that they were almost a whisper. "If I may use a somewhat flowery expression, she has already sold her soul to us."

As the shocked pause dragged on, it was the stout chair emeritus Ms Preston who looked the table up and down, then prompted, "Any objections?"

The Marketing Director spluttered and scoffed. "There certainly are! Trusting our flagship feed to a—a cleaner! Someone without any show business experience whatsoever! This must be some sick sort of joke!"

The chair emeritus made a show of considering the man's words before turning back to Ms Heath. "There is a point there. After what happened with our Mr Argyle, would it be wise to put such an unexperienced face on the show?"

"I dare say Ms Artworthy knows more about the workings of that show that anyone else alive," replied Ms Heath, grinning at how Marketing had dived right into her trap. "But the question is serious, and we've given it thought ourselves. Perhaps a controllable, distinguished, and recognisable co-host would be a useful counter note to Ms Artworthy's youth and inexperience?"

Without waiting for anyone to ask if she had such a person in mind, Ms Heath waved her hand and a fresh AR screen popped up in mid-air.

On it, the smiling, weathered features of Raja Cassar beamed out their humble blessings upon the assembly.

"I presume you all remember the AI construct contestant from our latest *Grass is Greener* season?"

There was a general grumble of assent—nobody would dare confess they didn't even watch the show.

"Two humble, sympathetic co-hosts, then. Both eminently controllable, in their own way," summarised Ms Preston, with a conspicuous look at the clock read-out in her display. "Any further objections?"

There were none.

"Very well, then, it is settled. Which leaves us with the matter of what to do with our Mr Argyle."

"Umm…" came a reedy woman's voice from the far end of the table. "I have an idea about that." The speaker was little more than a girl behind her large round AR spectacles, which were thick enough to light fires. Clearly, she was taking the stereotypes associated with her "Legal Services" plaque a little too closely to, insofar as applicable, heart.

The rest of the Board simply stared. It was as if one of the uglier elements of the décor, perhaps a radiator or a stained windowsill, had suddenly spoken up after decades of uncomplaining use and abuse.

"Putting him on trial is risky. Not the trial itself, of course, it'll be a private, tightly scripted event. But there's a good chance he ends up in the custody of another Corp's prison facility, and what do you think they'll do with him then? Hide him away in an undersea labour camp scrounging copper wires from the ruins of old Key West vacation homes?"

Ms Preston pursed her lips so tightly she could see them past the tip of her nose. If she had in her possession an incarcerated celebrity whose crimes were an embarrassment to a rival Corporation, she'd make the biggest public spectacle of his captivity possible. No excuse would be too petty or trivial to trot him out in front of the cameras and remind the world of his villainy. News features, documentary exposés on life behind bars, sitcom cameos, tabloid romances, Halloween costumes, running for public office… "They'd keep on using him to whack at us, like a never-ending Corporate piñata party."

The bespectacled human radiator nodded. "So, the usual trial and guilty verdict are out of the question. But if Mr Argyle were to be declared mentally irresponsible, then he wouldn't be fit for trial… and there'd be nothing stopping the Red Corporation from stepping in as a concerned custodian—in his best interests, of course."

Ms Preston made a mental note to buy this poor fish-eyed barrister a long weekend at her favourite full-body surgical spa, because she wanted the young woman to start speaking up more often in these meetings.

"You are quite right. Mr Argyle is our burden and must remain so—poor, sad, sick fellow that he is. We must care for him in his illness, and show him pity. They last thing we want is for the world to think we fear him and his ideas," said Ms Preston. "But that still leaves the question of what we do with him afterwards."

Someone coughed in the distance, and the finely tuned air-conditioner hummed its busy hum overhead and underfoot, but no other sound broke the silence which had fallen like an ice age.

"Err…" let loose a Human Resources manager with a chin so sharp she risked impaling herself every time she sneezed.

"Yes?" Ms Preston effectively ordered her to go on, while the entire table stared her down as a single, multiocular corporate gorgon.

"Well… there's always Elysium Fields, isn't there?"

39

When Liam's mind resurfaced from the latest drug-induced haze, he realised that another handful of days had gone by. There were no after-effects, no headaches, no grogginess. There never were. They used only the finest pharmaceutical shit here, my friend.

Such was the way of things at the Fields, as they had been for so long that Liam was no longer in a position to measure the time.

"Welcome back, Mr Argyle," a white-bloused man said.

The same man had said those same words on Liam's first day here, when he'd woken up from his drunken, neurotasered stupor in this very same sterile, pastel yellow room. It had taken Liam a moment to place him; the two years since he'd visited Juliette Binns in this same facility, under the man's guidance, had been eventful.

"Dr Reiter, wasn't it?"

"Oh, well done, Mr Argyle," beamed the man, with a professional grin that put Liam's own to shame. "We'll be seeing a lot of each other in the months to come."

And so they had. Countless psychoanalysis sessions, under the effects of various medications, along with a battery of virtual reality simulations. Nothing like the terrors they'd submitted poor Juliette to, but enough to give Liam a deep sympathy for the woman, who after two years here was reduced to a speechless, blanket-wrapped huddle in a corner of the central solarium.

Time blurred into nothingness.

At least the handy display in his prescription AR lenses was still there to tell him it was Sunday. That was the only measure of time that still had any relevance to him anyway. It meant that, if he didn't misbehave and force them to put him under again too soon, he would get to watch Mary doing her bit live on the GiG's ritual weekly elimination feed; a strangely fulfilling experience, one of the few things he still had to look forward to.

What else was there to do in a medicated asylum for the rich, privileged[1], and legally insane? He hardly had any incentive to spend his precious moments of consciousness exercising a body he was feeling more and more detached from with each passing day. And everyone knew all of those grand recreation facilities, with their expensive equipment, were really just there for the benefit of the celebrity feeds which regularly filled any unfortunate gaps in their programming schedules with a "Where are they now?" piece about one or another of the Elysium Fields inmates.

Still, they must have brought him out of his medicated coma for a reason. He would have loved the excitement of a good, honest surprise, but he had the strong suspicion that this time would be just like the last however many times—and this was confirmed when the team of copy-pasted media stooges from SyneDeal showed up in his well appointed cell.

They couldn't bring any podcams, but RedCorp couldn't prevent them from coming as visitors. He was allowed visitors, after all, though no one but these leaches from SyneDeal ever came. They wanted his ideas. His scribblings. His latest, mad, drug-induced writings. And to grill him all about the references and terms used is the previous batch.

He had thought it was a pretty nifty idea when they explained it to him: To write down his memoirs, his account of life as a media

---

[1] "With their own law": Coluche's joke and Orwell's pig doctrine still apply. Some are more equal than others.

figure. He still thought it was a good one, even now, after SyneDeal had seized his approval by the throat and forced him to write it not in his brief splashes of lucidity but during his long droughts of semi-conscious delirium.

Diaries of a Media Madman, they called it.

This time, however, the pile of scribbling he had to hand over was the smallest yet, by far. Was it possible that he might have reached the end of his story? He wasn't sure what to think at the prospect.

In the mellow, detached tranquillity that was the only emotion he could ever muster here in the Fields, he was torn between relief at not having to submit to the humiliating visits anymore and anxiety at what might become of him once he wasn't even deemed interesting enough for a rival Corp to use the story of his misfortunes as a roundabout way of attacking RedCorp.

Was this what it all boiled down to? The fame, the submission, the revolt, and the fight to make the world better, at least in some small way?

The heartfelt message he'd sacrificed his wealth and safety for… it may or may not have reached the world at large, but it definitely hadn't reached the world inside the four walls of Elysium Fields.

And the only sign he'd ever seen of the stolen eyeNet technology that was supposed to free the human mind from Corporate control was the little green light on the back of the SyneDeal goons' pocket-sized transmitter.

Take all of that, add two yeast buns, and you'd get a very dry burger.

Hell, the only person he'd really managed to help was Shin Iseul, that poor orbit-born orphan, the tragic daughter of the true worst victim of the age. The story had caused enough public outcry that the local Corporate client-government in Japan had been forced into action. The latest report he'd read here at Elysium Fields said they'd bought out the toddler's Revenue Corp indenture contract and taken her in as a ward of the State, as a PR gesture.

Good for her. Knowing he had at least managed to help one person almost made the whole debacle worthwhile.

Almost.

But nonetheless, Liam thought he might enjoy reading his memoirs, once they got around to making it available on the Red. It was bound to be the sort of story that made more sense the second time around.

Liam Argyle will return in:

THIS IS THE GOOD PART

BOOK THREE OF THE GENERAL BUZZ

ACKNOWLEDGEMENTS

The Rude Eye of Rebellion has been a long, long time in the coming, and it wouldn't be here tickling your brain-fats today without the help and care of many people.

My amazing wife and three awesome children have put up with so much and offered such desperately needed support over the years it took to travel from that first draft cobbled together in between shifts rocking our newborn daughter to sleep in her pram, in a black-and-white cottage a stone's throw away from a crumbling 12th century abbey in rural England, to the here and now. My wife's hand is present on every page of this book, and I can't thank any of them enough, otherwise than through my undying devotion.

Perhaps even more so than with the first book in the General Buzz series, my editor extraordinaire Rick Lewis at Uproar Books is directly responsible for many of the bits you might have enjoyed with *Rude Eye*. This second novel would never have existed if he hadn't decided to take a chance on an unpublished author with weird ideas about etymology, humour, and political science, and if he hadn't taken the time to draw up an extensive Revise and Resubmit letter telling that author exactly what was needed to turn that first messy manuscript into two novels, the second of which is in front of your eyes today. Thank you yet again for everything, Rick.

My agent Marisa Corvisiero has been a stalwart supporter of this book and the entire series. Here's to more and more great things to come!

A huge thank you to Mary Robinette Kowal and John Scalzi for lending their platforms to spread the word about the General Buzz series (and to John especially for a memorable Nebula Conference DJ session!).

And last but not least, all my thanks to you folks out there who have read and loved *Always Greener*. *Rude Eye* is here today because of your support for *Always Greener*, so please help spread the word about *Rude Eye* as well. Come for the jokes, stay for the revolution—and just wait until all the seeds planted in *Always Greener* and *Rude Eye* start spreading their fiery blooms in the next bit!

Born in Newfoundland, Canada, raised in France, and come into his own as an author while living in rural England, J.R.H. Lawless is an attorney by day and a speculative fiction author by night, mostly adult science fiction with a sharply humorous and occasionally political edge. He now lives and writes in Atlantic Canada with his beautiful family.